BLOODED

BLADE

J.C. DANIELS

Copyright

Dedication

A special thanks to Bea, for her winning bid in Romancing the Vote. Bea's bid won her a walk-on roll in this final Kit book. Thank you, Bea, for helping to protect Democracy!

Thanks to Sara for stepping in to help with edits again! You're the best!
A special thank you to Angela Waters for her work on my covers. And thanks to all the Kit fans out there. Your support over the years, and your patience and understanding since the last book, has meant so much.

For my Patreon Supporters

Caitlin
Julie S
Suzanne R
Kayla
Dawn
Kathy D
Thaois
Kerry
Tracy
Farah
Clare
Deirdre
Larry
Margaret
Natalie
Carla

For My readers

Thank you. I know many of you have been waiting a long time for this book and I just want to tell you how much I appreciate your patience. As many of you know, I lost one of my brothers to suicide in 2017.

Following his death, I fell into the worst depression of my life. It lasted two years and writing anything was a struggle. I barely managed to keep up with my freelance work, which helped keep food on the table, but that was about it.

For a long while, I thought the creative part of me had died inside, but one day, I looked outside and realized the sun was shining, realized that it was...well, kind of beautiful. I hadn't seen beauty in a very long while.

Bit by bit, the urge to write returned, but it took longer for the drive to write Kit's books to come back. Kit's journey has always been a darker one, a harder one and until my mental health was steadier, I think my subconscious was protecting me.

Since my brother's death, there have been several other losses, including my grandmother, then my father-in-law in 2021 to COVID. Life just keeps on punching, but for the past year, it's finally gotten easier to punch back and with that, the urge to help Kit find her resolution has returned.

I *thought* this would be the final book, however...it's not.

There is one more story after this, but I promise, it won't take so long to write. And while we are coming to the end of Kit and Damon's journey, there may be more stories in this world. It's a fascinating one...and you just never know.

Thanks for hanging with me. I hope you enjoy the journey.

Forgotten Blade

Note: This short story takes place after the events of Broken Blade, when Kit & Justin went after TJ's alpha. It was meant to be part of the next book, and it wasn't included. So, here it is.

Forgotten Blade

Two years earlier
Smoky Mountain Territory

The stink was even worse than it had been when I'd ventured into this particular pack's territory months earlier while on a job for the alpha of the local wolf pack.

It had been bad then.

Now the miasma of rotting food, unwashed bodies and the decaying stink of animal entrails cloyed the air.

It was almost like these degenerate, sadistic wastes of space decided to take the remains of whatever prey they ran down, eat the meat and toss out the viscera somewhere in the sun, repeatedly, day after day, weeks on end, and then top it off with the dead bodies of whatever packmates had died—or were killed.

My eyes watered as I struggled to adapt to the stink, fighting the urge to retch.

Next to me, I felt Justin jerk, then incredibly, the air cleared. A split second later, I knew why. The air pricked with magic and I shot him a scowl.

He shrugged, then gestured back and forth between us before tapping his nose. I took that to me that whatever mojo he'd just worked would only affect the two of us.

"*Wimp,*" I mouthed to him. He responded by flipping me off just as the wind kicked up, blasting us in the face with the noxious smell again, although it was far weaker now, thanks to Justin's magic. Having a witch as one of my best friends was useful.

How did any shifter live here?

Their sense of smell was far more sensitive than mine. This should be enough to drive them insane.

Or maybe it had. That might explain that mental state of the more dominant shifters in this pathetic little pack. They were cruel, cold, and cunning, abusing the weaker members as if it was their right.

Logically, the alpha had the right to establish his own rules and do whatever the hell he wanted within his own pack. The only way to change how a pack was run would be through challenging the alpha, so if the leader was a crazy son of a bitch, then bad things could happen. Shifter rules were a far cry from the rules recognized by human society and as long as an alpha's pack didn't carry their actions out into the human world or try to tread on another dominant's territory, they could do whatever the hell they wanted.

Even if it involved the brutal amputation of a teenaged girl's legs, then cauterizing the stumps so she'd never be able to shift to heal.

Just the thought of what Dex Conrad had done to one of my closest friends when she'd been a young, vulnerable orphan in his pack made me see red.

I'd dreamt of doling out the justice he so rightly deserved for *years* but had never known who he was, because TJ refused to tell me. Months earlier, before my life went to hell in a handbasket and I'd ended up the prisoner of an arrogant, power-hungry bastard who thought he could *own* me, I'd discovered the man's identity but I hadn't been able to take care of him then...or for months after.

I could now.

We'd come loaded for bear, as the old saying went, uncertain just how many shifters would be here but their numbers had diminished even more since that first visit. The shotgun I carried was considered outdated by most people these days, but when it came to taking down shifters—fast—at a distance, the Kel-Tec KSG I'd modified did the job damn good. Its dual-tube magazine didn't carry regular ammo, but something I'd had made special. Just for this job. Each of the twenty-four shells was made from silver alloy—heavy on the silver—and designed to shatter, minimizing the risk of the injuring anybody other than the target and maximizing the damage *to* said target. When those targets were shifters, the silver ammo proved to be an effective killing machine, shredding the heart or destroying the brain as long as the shot was accurate.

There were probably some very strong alphas who could survive such a shot—I could think of one—but it would injure them badly enough that unless the shifter had protection, he or she would be easy to finish off.

Conrad was *not* that strong.

Although the hair on the back of my neck prickled from the proximity to unknown shifters, some of them dominant, none were the kind of strong that made my every instinct go on edge.

I carried several other weapons and my pockets were loaded with magazines for the Kel-Tech while my blade rode in a sheath down my spine. She was still silent. I was slowly coming to grips with the loss of her song, but I didn't need her voice to wield her. I wasn't going to give that man the dignity of cutting him down with my sword. Not unless the plan went off the rails.

Justin and I had spent the past week living on the edge of the territory owned by Conrad and his pack, some miles outside the borders of the big park. We made occasional trips inside the perimeter the first few nights, trying to get a handle on his security and the skill of his men, only to find there *was* no security and that at least a couple of his men had more fun hunting animals with a shotgun than doing it the way a normal wolf shifter would do. And they didn't shoot to kill either. They shot to wound, then feasted on the animal while it was still alive.

The sight of it had made my gorge rise and I wasn't exactly known for having a weak stomach.

3

Realizing they did nothing to protect their outer borders, we'd moved in, taking it slowly, picking a new base each night and sleeping in shifts. Now, six nights into our little camping trip, just over a week since we'd left Orlando, we finally started seeing signs of the miniscule pack, some hint that there were more than just the three random shifters we'd seen in the outer edges of the territory—and Conrad. The pack leader.

Justin and I had scaled a massive forest giant on the side of the mountain, looking down into the valley where Conrad's pack lived. It put me in the mind of a traveling caravan, one that had broken down decades ago and the owners had just abandoned everything, disappearing into the wilds around them, never to be seen again.

Through the Kel-Tech's scope, I'd studied the camp's layout and counted each building, murmuring descriptions to Justin. Thirty-eight campers, although almost a dozen were toppled and one had been completely upended and the damage to the exterior walls made it clear nothing lived inside it now.

"How do people live like this?" I muttered.

A big fire burned in the center, the wind setting the flames to flickering, spiraling higher and higher while sparks went flying on the wind. Tennessee was going through a drought and if those sparks set anything to blazing...

I shivered at the thought and started to shift my scope away to take in more of the camp when something made me pause. Two men stood by the fire, and through the high-powered scope, I could see their eyes settle on a skinny woman who was approaching. She was so thin, her cheekbones cut into her skin like knives, but her belly was fat, swollen with child. She hauled a large pot, the kind used to feed people by the masses and the weight of it threw her off-balance.

Neither of the men offered to help.

As she hefted the large pot onto a hook over the fire, one of them shifted closer.

He grabbed her and I clenched my jaw as she tried to get away—tried, and failed.

"Piece of shit," I muttered.

Magic pricked the air and I felt Justin tense next to me. I had no doubt he'd seen what was going on, too.

"We can't make our move yet," he said in an angry voice. "We don't know how many of them there are."

"We damn well better find out—*now*."

"One of them is moving up this way," Justin said, voice low.

It took more willpower than I liked to admit to drag my gaze from the woman who was now being fondled by *both* men, right there, in front of others who walked by. Some ignored it. Others leered. But nobody attempted to stop them.

And she'd stopped fighting, her shoulders slumped.

"Justin..."

"We wait, Kit. A few more minutes."

Tearing my eyes from the tableau by the fire, I focused on the man striding away from the small clearing occupied by the camp and felt another jagged bolt of rage cut into me.

He had spindly-looking legs that contrasted bizarrely with the gut that protruded over the waistband of what looked like dirty boxers in the silvered moonlight, while his barrel chest gave the indication of strength long wasted.

Even shifters could let their bodies go to shit if they tried really hard.

Dexter Conrad was proof of that.

"That's him," I told Justin.

"Stick to the plan, Kitty." He remained crouched on the branch while I stood and as he spoke, he curved his hand around my calf. After a small squeeze, he let go. "We need to know how many we're dealing with before we even think about making our first move."

"I know."

Conrad had stopped and looked back, shouting over his shoulder. The echo of his voice bounced back to us and I swore as I heard his words...*take a piss...quiet...bunch of...shit.*

"I got him. Time to make our move. You ready?"

"Do it."

As his magic rippled and pulsed in the air, I instinctively glanced back toward the camp, toward the young woman.

The man who'd originally grabbed her had been standing with his back to the fire, his friend angled toward the woman who know stood a few feet away, slowly unbuttoning her dress.

"Aw, fuh—"

The fire exploded, engulfing the man closest to the flames.

His screams shattered the night.

Like it had a life of its own, the blaze soared up and out and from my vantage point, I had a clear image when the flames *moved*, tendrils reaching out to somehow *grab* the second man. He fell face-first into the flames, screams becoming oddly muffled.

Neither one got up although their screams echoed again. And again. And again.

Staring through the scope of the Kel-tec, I saw each of them struggle to pull away, but it was like something held them glued to the blaze.

A flicker of movement caught my attention and I looked away in time to see Conrad spin on his heel, mouth open and face contorted. For a split second, his body went rigid with surprise, then he was running, bare feet pounding the earth hard. He moved fast despite his gut, despite his slovenly appearance.

But he wasn't wolf-fast. Not anymore.

I might have smiled, but the raging flames held me mesmerized.

"You can be a scary mother-fucker, Justin. But the drought..."

"I know." His voice was calm. "Be patient."

A few seconds later, the flames died down like nothing had happened. And those flames kept on dying until only a few embers glowed.

Smoke wafted from the charred bodies of the men. I saw one of them move a fraction. But still, neither rose.

The woman sat on her butt in the dirt a few feet away, horrified. "What the *fuck*!"

The exclamation came from the camp, the voice carrying easily in the quiet forest. Soon, more voices joined in.

"You counting, Kitty?"

"Stop calling me that," I said, but it was more out of habit than anything else. In my mind's eye, I still saw the fire as it all but fed on those two men.

"EIGHTEEN MEN, FIVE of them dominants. Four women. Six teenaged boys. No girls that we know of. If there are younger kids, they don't come out of the campers. And there's the alpha." Justin and I went over our plan as the camp buzzed with life.

Several of the weaker men were tasked with dealing with the two bodies. Conrad had stood over them both and when one of them had lifted a hand in silent plea, he'd smashed the fallen shifter's head in with his boot.

"Vicious," Justin had commented.

I agreed but I hadn't been surprised either. Now Conrad was close to the pregnant woman, yelling at her, his voice carrying over everything else.

Although there was nothing in his voice that reminded me of those days I'd been held captive, there was something about *her* scraped over scabs just now forming and I clenched my jaw against the memories that tried to slide past the barrier I'd slammed up.

Justin rested a hand on my shoulder, sensing the subtle shift in the air caused by my rising tension. "Not here, Kitty," he said quietly. "If you're going to freak out, we'll both be dead."

Hard words. Cold words. True words.

He squeezed lightly. "Pretend he's every mean SOB who thought he...or *she* could beat you. We're here to destroy him. Are you with me?"

"I'm with you." I covered his hand with mine and squeezed back as I met his gaze. "Crazy as you are and as much as I like you, Justin, I didn't come up here to die with you."

A fierce, wild gleam shone in his green eyes. "There's my girl."

Then he turned and leaped down from the tree, landing so lightly, he might as well be part-shifter himself.

I started monkeying my way, moving quickly although I wasn't about to jump like he had. My feet hadn't even touched the ground when I felt him gathering his magic. The ground vibrated slightly under my feet as I checked my weapons. "Don't go causing any landslides, hotshot," I told him, although it more out of nerves and adrenaline than any real fear.

"I don't have that much control over the earth, Kitty-Kitty."

"I'll hit you," I muttered. "I swear. And we're in the mountains. Don't tell me there's no iron ore or anything like that you can't pull from."

His green eyes flashed, wild and hot with excitement. "That brain of yours is so sexy. I love it. But...I think I'll use those trucks out there. Now...*go*."

I took off.

Five seconds later, there was a shriek of metal, followed by a thunderous explosion. And one more, screams painted the air.

Justin retreated farther up the mountain, laying traps the way only a witch could do.

I'd already selected my perch, another tree far enough away from him that they wouldn't be able to take us both without dividing their numbers heavily once they came for us.

And they *did* come.

Conrad might be a dense bastard, but he was alpha and he had the instincts of one, including the instincts that let him sense when a threat was on the prowl.

He sent some of the beta men first, half of them in wolf form, skulking along the ground in a way I'd never imagined a predatory shifter could do. Still, I couldn't even feel much pity as a couple of them drew closer to my scent.

We'd suspected they'd scent me faster than Justin. Shifters were very in tune with their primal instincts and when it came to males, sex was about as instinctive as it got. A smile twitching the corners of my mouth, I watched as one of those wolves started to slink in Justin's direction, nose to the ground. *Somebody likes how you smell, pretty boy,* I thought to myself.

But the wolf didn't go far. A few steps, then he dropped even lower to the ground and started to inch away meekly.

Figures, I muttered to myself.

I knew damn well that females could have alpha tendencies—or at least not give off an *I'll yield* pheromone or whatever it was that helped animals and shifters identify the leaders from the rest of the pack. I might not be alpha anything, but I wasn't one of their submissive creatures either.

But it was my scent they were tracking.

You're a woman, a voice murmured in the back of my mind. I'd grown used to hearing it—almost. I didn't want to listen to those murmurs now, yet I couldn't silence them. *They see women as prey. Even the strong ones.*

I'm not prey. I all but shouted it in the cage of my own mind as I lifted the other weapon I'd brought, this one chosen for silence. The wolf who'd caught Justin's scent was still loitering in the back, so far from the group, I had a clear shot.

I took it, the arrow flying through the air. Even before it hit home, the silver-tipped bolt burying itself in the wolf's heart, I had another wolf lined up in the sight of my crossbow. Another fell just as those leading sensed a problem. I managed to take out a third before a panicked howl tore through the night, alerting the rest of the pack.

Men came running, some bounding lithely over the undergrowth while others thrashed their way through it.

Conrad didn't run.

He prowled closer, a savage look on his face as he called out, "I smell the stink of witch and human out there, mixed with the blood of my wolves. You made a big fucking mistake." He howled then, the eerie song of the wolf ripping through the trees.

One of the more dominant wolves, still in human form, paused to throw back his head as he answered his alpha. The others followed suit.

As the unknown dominant looked backward, I noted where he stood and felt anticipation clench inside me.

Breathe, I reminded myself.

Breathe.

He took another step forward. Then another.

I felt the ground shudder and wrench. Then his body, nothing more than a silhouette in the night, disappeared. And the screaming started anew.

Score one for you, Justin.

WE HAD TO RETREAT TWICE. A wolf found my tree and Justin split the earth to keep two dominants from climbing up to get me.

The second time, somebody shot Justin.

It only grazed his thigh and he slapped a temporary bandage on it as we tore through the night to the cave we'd chosen as our bolt hole if we needed one. It was up a sheer rock face that would make an easy climb impossible.

The rope he'd rigged earlier was my focus as we raced onward, but with every passing second, Justin ran slower and the struggle to throw back magic to obscure our trail or lay some sort of small trap was wearing him down even more.

When we spilled out in front of it, I looked at him. "You first."

"Not happening, Kit."

"Yes, it is." I slid the safety off the Kel-tec and checked the ammo. "I can hold them off for a few minutes while you get up there—once you're up, it's higher ground and we've got the advantage. You can watch my back." I shot him a dark look when he hesitated. "You're wasting time. *Go.*"

He went. Injured or not, blood loss or not, he still flowed like water up the rope and I heard him hiss at me just as the first of the wolves broke through the trees.

I secured the weapon once more and started my climb, trusting the man above me to help keep watch.

The furious pack behind me raced closer, the howls and growls like something out of a nightmare. I'd just reached the top when the rope went taut.

Justin hauled me up and over the lip, then touched the rope, whispering.

Magic shimmered around us.

I smiled as somebody below started bellowing for help. The scream ended abruptly and I murmured, "Again, you're a scary motherfucker."

Conrad shouted up at me, but I ignored him and focused on Justin. "Put a real bandage on that so we can finish this."

"Your bedside manner sucks, Kitty."

I shot him a dark look, but could only hold it for a second before I started to smile, the adrenaline roaring in my veins.

"How many are left?" Justin asked, voice pitched so low, I barely heard.

Rising, I looked down and over the distance, I met Conrad's gaze.

For a long moment, we stared at each other and I saw the recognition flicker in his eyes.

Justin got to his feet and moved to stand with me. "Status?"

"One high-level dominant besides the alpha." I studied the wolves below, gauging power. It was a gift I'd always had and it came in handy. "The rest are just soldiers or weaker. Kill off the two strong ones and they're done."

"Girl," Conrad said, the growl in his voice carrying up to me in the night air. "You must have shit for brains, coming back onto my lands. And bringing just one puny witch?"

"How many dead and injured do you have, Conrad?" I asked, letting myself smile.

His eyes glowed, going wolf yellow. "You'll pay for each one. I'll take it out of your hide...in a certain kind of way. You're scrawny, but pretty enough. When I'm done, I'll turn you over to my pack."

"What's left of it, you mean?" Justin said, leaning over to smirk down at them, the casual taunt in his voice designed to elicit rage.

It worked.

Snarls filled the air and the wolves gathered around Conrad tore at the ground with their claws. Crouching low, the Kel-tec cradled in my hands, I gazed at Conrad, all the hate, ugliness and rage I felt inside flooding me and I had no doubt it showed in my sharp-edged smile. "You've lost most of your strong wolves, Conrad. If you had a lick of sense, you would have had some acting as sentries, patrolling your perimeter. Instead, you all sit around, growing lazy and fat and slow."

"You couldn't take us without that fucking gun and a witch." His gaze slid to Justin and lingered. "Just like a woman. Having a man fight her battles."

Next to me, Justin laughed. "Stupid mangy dog. She killed more of you than I did. As for that gun...it's called leveling the playing field."

But Conrad didn't look at Justin. Malevolent hate glowed hot in eyes. *Kill him,* my gut whispered. *Now. He's contained. Kill him.*

No. Not until he knew *why.*

"I've come across packs half your size that could destroy you." Canting my head to the side, I let my mouth curve in a cold smile. "I know alphas who could walk into your territory and kill every last one of you and it wouldn't be much more than an afternoon workout. You're *lazy* and *weak.*"

"You come down here, cunt, then tell me that." A hand clenched into a fist.

And his eyes flicked upward.

A few small pebbles and some dust drifted down. Savage pleasure tore through Justin—I *felt* it color the air around him. I knew why, too.

Not all witches were born with inborn gifts that connected them to the elements, but Justin had always had an affinity for earth and fire. Although his skill with metallurgy was far stronger, he could manipulate those other two elements in ways that could save lives...or end them. Like when he tore open the earth earlier and buried one of Conrad's seconds all the way to his neck, the earth clutching at him in a vice and squeezing the air from him as he slowly suffocated.

He'd taken long, long minutes to die.

Justin had set up another trap, this one in the spot above us that would have opened us up to attack.

"I think I'll stay up here," I told Conrad as the ground beneath us shuddered once more.

The wolves felt it, too and finally the alpha looked at Justin.

"I hope you're not close to the man you sent up there, asshole," Justin said in a sly voice.

"Donnie!" Conrad barked, voice echoing. "Stop! This fucker—"

It was too late.

Earth turned liquid and rocks began to slide. Through the cacophony, a man screamed. It went abruptly silent and Justin angled his head, following the sound of the noise.

More magic danced along my skin and the slide of rock and earth stopped.

"I smell dead people," I said somberly, looking down at Conrad.

A couple of the wolves gathered around his feet began to slink backward. Even the tall, strong man at his side looked wary, although rage still vibrated in the air around him.

A bare whisper of sound drifted to us. I couldn't make out the words. But I saw the movement. I had the Kel-tec up, the man in my sights before he managed to lift his own weapon, a handgun he'd had tucked into his pants at the small of his back.

A hole appeared in his forehead. A second later, a bloody stain bloomed on his chest as the second round tore through his heart, destroying it.

He toppled backward into the smaller, weaker wolves. A couple of them barely managed to evade being crushed under his weight.

"And then there was one." I swung the Kel-tech in Conrad's direction, held it there for a long moment, staring through the sight as acknowledgement bled into his eyes. "Do you want to know why?"

He spat on the ground. "Crazy fuckin' bitch like you needs a reason? I figured you came up here because that big fucker you spread your legs for wants to expand his territory."

Justin tensed next to me.

I put a hand on his arm.

"Don't," I said quietly.

Shame and humiliation had been burned out of me, it seemed—or maybe it was just apathy. If a pathetic coward like Conrad wanted to think me a whore who did somebody else's dirty work, what did I care?

"You've got shit for brains if you think Damon Lee needs anybody to do his killing for him," I said coolly. "But let me make it clear...he has nothing to do with why I'm here."

Something flickered in the back of Conrad's eyes and his gaze darted from me to Justin and back. "Then what the fuck are you doing here, killing all my men?"

"We killed your men because they got in the way—*you* are the target." Lowering the gun, I held his gaze. "You've got no idea how long I've waited for this, how many nights I stayed awake, trying to figure out just who the fuck it was, Conrad. She wouldn't tell me and wolves are notoriously tight-lipped."

A fine line appeared between his eyes and the grooves around his mouth deepened. "Why don't you drop the bullshit and just tell me why you're so pissed off? Although the way I see it, if I spilled the blood of somebody you claim as yours, I figure we're even now."

"No. No, we aren't." I looked at Justin. In a low voice, I said, "Give me the rope."

He gave me a pained look. "He's a wolf, Kit."

"He's a coward. And I want to look into his eyes when he dies, so I can tell her."

"Fine," he muttered, voice a low growl. "But you're not going alone."

I didn't attempt to argue.

We weren't even halfway down when the wolves tried to rush us. A line of fire tore up from the ground and pained yips, panicked howls rose in the night. I kicked off the sheer rock face and jumped the last fifteen feet, landing on the balls of my feet with my knees flexed and bent to absorb the impact. Justin was slower thanks to the wound in his leg, but the fire continued to burn until he was next to me, then bit by bit, he pulled it back until it was gone and the only illumination was the crescent shape of the moon overhead.

The Kel-tech hung secure and snug from the rig affixed to my chest, but I didn't pull that weapon as Conrad prowled closer. Instead, I drew the modified Desert Eagle from the drop holster on my thigh and lifted it, staring at him over the flat, matte black of the deadly weapon.

"This will blow a hole in you big enough for Justin to put a fist through," I said calmly. "I'll aim for the heart and you'll be dead before you realize it's game over."

Around him, his wolves crawled and snarled.

One rose up on her hind legs to paw at the air and Conrad responding by slamming down on her head with a closed fist, not bothering to look away from my face.

How did such a hateful man engender such loyalty? I couldn't wrap my mind around it. The wolf, struck down by Conrad but not deterred, crawled forward on its belly and settled by her alpha's feet, looking at me with malevolence.

Disregarding her, I focused back on Conrad. "I wonder if you even remember her."

"Tell me her name, girl, and you can stop wondering." He reached down and the wolf at his feet rose as if on command. He rubbed the fur between her ears, like she was a tame dog, not a member of his pack, and despite the hate in that wolf's gaze, I felt rage burn inside.

Had he treated TJ like that? Like a dog?

No, I reminded myself. He treated her worse.

"Her name's TJ."

The wolf's ears went flat and she snarled again, sinking lower to the ground.

Conrad didn't even seem to notice, his eyes narrowing on my face, full of speculation, then a slowly dawning awareness. "That weak bitch is still alive?"

I shot at the ground, the round tearing into the dirt just inches from his feet.

He heard it and reacted, but even as he fell back, I saw the knowledge in his eyes that he wouldn't be fast enough.

"I didn't miss," I told him as he sucked in a hard breath, eyes on the gouge in the earth. "Next time, I'll blow your balls off. Granted, with this gun, you'll lose a lot more than just your testicles, but I'm fine with that."

To his credit, he didn't beg, didn't demand answers. When the wolf at his feet went to lunge, he grabbed her by the scruff and threw her to the side. She flew through the air a good thirty feet and landed hard, a startled yelp escaping her. Another wolf, this one smaller, skinnier, skulked over to her side and nuzzled her.

"You mutilated her," I said in a hard voice. "Maimed her. Left her for dead. But she survived."

"Your point?" He snarled the question out, fangs flashing.

"I just wanted you to know that." I smiled and lifted the Eagle, taking aim at his heart. "I wanted you to know she's the reason you die tonight."

I fired, took aim a second time, before he'd even stumbled, fired again. A human never could have done it so fast, but the half of me that wasn't human gave me the speed and strength.

The shots found home almost simultaneously, the first destroying his heart and the second, off-center of his forehead, the adjustment I'd made for the impact of the first not one hundred percent accurate—but good enough because when he hit the earth, he was dead.

Most of the other wolves cowered, sinking to the earth as I strode forward. When I neared, two rolled to their backs and showed me their throats. I ignored them.

"Kit." Justin's low, tight voice was a warning, issued a split second before flame lit the night, separating me from the one weaker wolf who'd showed some spine.

Through the wall of flickering, dancing fire, she stared at me, eyes glowing. Shifter energy rolled, prickling my flesh and then she was in human form, crouched on the earth and staring at me through dishwasher blonde curls that mostly obscured her face.

"I'll rip your throat out," she said in a hoarse voice, the tone husky, as if she hadn't spoken in a long time. "You'll die sobbing and begging for mercy."

"Yeah? You know how many people have said that to me?"

She snarled and it was an animal sound that came from her throat.

"Get out of here," she said, slowly rising to her feet. "We have our dead to care for."

"Sure." With a brittle smile, I drew the blade from my back. "I just need to do one more thing."

Her howl, the mad, enraged song of it, made the hair on the back of my neck stand on end.

But I didn't turn from my grisly task.

And the fire between us raged higher and hotter.

WE DIDN'T STOP UNTIL we'd left the state of Tennessee long behind us and even then, we only lingered at the small, anonymous hotel long enough to shower off the dirt, dust and death from the past night.

We hadn't made it out of the mountains with our grim trophy until dawn was kissing the horizon and the painfully bright glow of the noonday sun was singeing our eyes by the time we crossed into Florida.

That was when we both breathed a sigh of relief.

"She's going to hand us our asses for this," Justin said when we were an hour away from Wolf Haven.

"I know." I'd let him take over driving nearly three hours earlier. The adrenaline had drained away at a steady flow, leaving my muscles feeling leaden and tired.

Justin, on the other hand, was revved, a nervous energy that crackled in the air around him like a trapped bird.

"Why aren't you exhausted?" I gave him a baleful look.

He laughed, the sound jagged and sharp. "I will be, once it hits. You realize how easily that could have gone south, Kitty-kitty?"

"It was a possibility." Managing a smile, I brushed my fingers over his shoulder and added, "But I had faith in my partner."

With a lopsided grin, he caught my hand and squeezed lightly, letting go before my mind processed it. "Don't know why. I'm a fuck-up of epic proportions."

That brief contact left me with a sense of loss and without any conscious decision, I reached over and took his hand in mine, squeezing. I'd missed him. Missed this. The love I'd felt for him once no longer existed, but I did still love him. He was one of my best friends, one of my dearest and I hated that he felt he could no longer touch me without it bringing up bad memories.

"You're no more a fuck-up than I am, Justin," I said softly. "And whenever I've needed you, when it counted, you were always there."

His jaw went tight and I sensed him trying to retreat. Tightening my fingers around his, I didn't let him pull away. "I'm trying to learn not to blame myself for what happened in the mountains, Justin. But it's going to be damn hard to do if the people who matter are all caught up in blaming themselves."

The air snapped tight, rigid with tension. After long, taut moments, he blew out a breath. "That's playing dirty, Kitty-kitty."

"Yeah, well. That's how you taught me to fight *and* play."

A ghost of a smile finally appeared on his hard, too-pretty face and he brought my hand to his lips, kissing the back lightly before letting go. "I'll work on it, okay, Kit?"

"Okay."

GOLIATH WAS TENSE AS we climbed out of Justin's low-slung, sleek sportscar, his nostrils flared as he scented the air. He'd already caught the stink of death. Eyes tracking from Justin to me, he held his silence until a customer pushed his way through the protective barrier TJ kept wrapped around her bar.

Once we were alone, relatively speaking, his eyes locked on mine. "Why do I smell something dead?"

In response, I went to the trunk. The hatch glided up soundlessly and I reached inside, pulling out the sealed box, the temperature within maintained at a chill forty degrees.

"I need to see her," I told him in lieu of answering.

His eyes rested on the box, a pale blue fire burning there. Goliath, always so calm, always so gentle.

After a long moment, he looked at me. "You found him."

I didn't respond but that fire blazed hotter. Goliath half-turned and pressed on the door, calling inside.

A moment later, a lean woman with a predatory prowl came outside and looked from Goliath to us. Her nostrils flared, just as Goliath's had done, but she said nothing, taking up the position where Goliath had been.

"I'm going with you," he said simply.

I didn't argue.

I adored TJ but Goliath was her rock.

She wasn't in the main area but we hadn't been inside more than a minute before she appeared in the doorway that led to the back, her eyes wide and stark, a sawed-off shotgun in her lap and her mouth pinched. She saw me, then looked to Goliath. He took a step toward her and she locked her jaw, then swiveled her chair around, maneuvering it through the door and back into the darkness.

We followed.

TJ was in her apartment, a large space that flowed from living room to kitchen to bedroom with no walls. She sat with her back to us, facing out the large, sliding glass windows that looked out over a green spread of gardens and grass that Goliath had coaxed and created into being for her over the years. It took up nearly a half block and I knew he'd bought the property with his own money so he could add some small bit of beauty to her life.

"What have you gone and done now, Kit?" she asked, her voice a rasp.

"I just kept a promise, TJ." Why did my throat feel so tight?

Look at me, I thought desperately.

It took her long, long moments but she finally did and the dark brown of her eyes glowed with a sheen of wolf-green.

"Show me." The words came out surprisingly steady and I put the box on the floor in front of her, kneeling.

Justin's magic whispered, removing the seal that had kept it secure during our travels.

Slowly, I lifted the lid.

Goliath moved in and grabbed the head by the hair, lifting it out.

TJ's eyes went pure wolf and shifter energy flooded the room, hers, Goliath's.

Then she took a deep breath and it was gone, hers sucked back inside her with phenomenal control, while Goliath's slowly ebbed away.

When she looked at me again, her eyes were human. "You're a crazy bitch, Kit."

"Yeah, well. I learned from the best."

She laughed and if it sounded a little like a sob, nobody commented on it. Rising, I inched toward her and rested a tentative hand on her shoulder.

She clamped a hand around my wrist and before I could process it, she hauled me down and wrapped strong, lean arms around me. "You crazy bitch," she whispered. "Thank you."

Blooded

"You're interrupting a formal meeting of the Assembly."

"I know." The speaker stepped into view, her voice lightly accented. She had a faint smile on her lips, but there was nothing warm about it.

Nothing warm about her gaze, either, as she scanned the room before letting her eyes settle on me.

Her smile deepened.

It didn't soften, not even a fraction.

But it spread wider until even her eyes glowed, her beauty almost incandescent.

Once, long ago, when my mother had still been alive, she'd told me that the twins had been considered the most beautiful women our people had seen in generations. *"A pity, Kitasa. The beauty goes only skin deep. Scratch the surface and all that's underneath is bile and bitterness."*

I'd been too young to understand what she meant.

I'd half expected to see madness in Reshi's eyes, but the cool emptiness was somehow worse.

Reshi had never been *cool*. In all the time I'd known her, she'd been hotheaded and quick to anger. Could grief change a person that much?

"Niece," she said.

The lack of emotion sent a shiver down my spine and my palm started to itch. Curling my hand into a fist, I held the woman's stare, too panicked to look away.

"I've come to take you home."

Those words broke the panic. I had no memory of calling my sword, but her hilt settled into my hand as I moved out from Chang's protective guard. The blade's weight in my hand a familiar one, I moved into position as I faced her, this woman whose face had haunted me for years.

She smirked at the sight of the weapon.

"Like hell." I curled my lip in disgust as I said the words, spoken softly, but they carried.

I amused her. Or maybe she had some image in mind, an image of her punching a fist through my sternum and ripping my heart out. The glint in her eyes told me that whatever she was thinking, it involved her spilling my blood—lots of it.

She smiled and the world stopped around me.

That smile—it was Rathi's smile.

It threw me back years and I was on the ground, helpless, as one of my cousins shoved a knee into my stomach as he tore at his belt, then his trousers, laughing as I tried to free myself.

My sword's grip burned hotter, almost painful now and her cry was strident and loud, no longer a gentle, soothing murmur. No, it was a battle cry: *I am HERE!*

The image of Rathias was gone and I stared past the smile so like his, forced my way through memories tearing into me like jagged teeth to focus on the present.

On Reshi.

I narrowed my eyes and stared at her amused smile, at the cold emptiness of her gaze and an expression as unforgiving as the grave. She took a step forward, her sword still in the sheath at her back, knife strapped to her thigh.

Empty-handed. She faced me empty-handed, as if I was no threat to her. It was an insult, and she'd meant it as such.

Her smug look intensified as if she could see straight through my skull to discern my thoughts. "Niece."

"I no longer call you family."

"I've come to collect you, child," she said, ignoring me. "You've run wild long enough."

Low whispers echoed around us, the tension skyrocketing. The wolves to my right had come to their feet. Behind me, the cats in attendance had spread out, their caged energy making the hair on my arms stand on end.

Damon paced, a low growl echoing out from deep in his chest as he came closer and closer.

I looked at him, saw the rage, then looked past him to Chang, Justin, and Dair.

Each of them met my gaze and though no words were said, their message was loud and clear.

It was my turn to smile as I looked at my aunt. "Are the guards the only men and women you brought? If so…it's not enough. You'll need an army to drag me back there."

She smiled.

Then two of the Royal Guards at her back stepped forward, bows drawn.

I saw the dull gleam of copper tips on the arrows, sensed movement behind me.

The rhythmic beat of drum song sounded in my ears as I called my own bow to my hands, sighting on the guard at her left, directly in front of me with no conscious thought.

"Don't," I warned him as he sighted on me.

Silver flashed. He didn't listen. As the copper-tipped projective whistled through the air, Chang grabbed me and spun around before I could move, his reflexes like lightning.

Silver flashed, once, twice, followed by the familiar *crack* as wood broke. Chang eased his protective hold as silver started to spin around us, protective, deceptively delicate-looking strands twining around and around.

Nudging free from Chang, I turned in time to see Justin hold out his arms.

Half of the narrow, thread-like silver chains folded back in on themselves, weaving back into the complicated pattern that allowed him to carry so much metal without attracting notice.

The rest of the chains contained their lazy dance in the air, spinning and twisting in a sinuous ballet, a beautiful shield between deadly silver and dangerous copper.

"Just think," Justin murmured. "Everybody thought this would be boring."

"What is the *meaning* of this?"

Wow. Somehow, I had forgotten about the Tribunal.

Damon growled as Findlay shoved past me to face off with Reshi, the vampire's slim form rigid and his voice pure ice.

Damon cupped the back of my neck, the gesture achingly familiar—possessive and protective in equal parts.

Reshi glanced past the vampire now standing before her, her eyes skipping over Damon as if he wasn't there, to lock gazes with me again. Her coolly polite smile settled back in place as she looked at Findlay. "The girl is a criminal. She has no business being here and I've come to take her back to our home and people to face a long-overdue trial. I politely request you surrender her to me."

A *criminal*?

"What's the fucking crime?" I snarled, throwing the words out in challenge, waiting for her to tell me so I could counter the charge. Fuck her if she thought she could shame me.

"We'll discuss your crimes in front of the people who will judge you," Reshi said in a cool voice, barely looking at me, as if I wasn't worth the energy to address.

"Fuck off, then," I said, my voice shaking in rage. "You'd have to drag my corpse back to get me within two thousand miles of that miserable place."

"We can arrange that."

Hundreds of eyes flew my way and somehow, despite the rage and fear pumping through my veins, I couldn't help but notice the macabre fascination directed our way. Very few knew much about me other than my name—the shortened version, and the reputation I'd built for myself here, in this place I'd finally started to call home. Having all of this play out in a very public manner was the dramatic shit some people loved.

I might have laughed at the insanity. I must have cursed. I might have screamed.

"If you aren't going to detail the crimes, then you can't claim she's a criminal," Findlay said, his annoyance giving way to anger, an icy anger that turned his voice to frost and chilled the air around us. "And the girl is her own person. She's not mine to surrender."

The vampire looked at me, a red brow cocked. "Kit, do you wish to...*surrender* your person to this woman?"

"Not a chance in hell." I gave Reshi a thin smile, even as some of the knots in my neck eased. What would she do now? Tell them I'd run away after killing a couple of monsters who would have raped me? That I'd killed a cousin who *had* raped me?

Her eyes narrowed a fraction, fine lines fanning out.

"We have several witches with empathy and truth-speaking talents in their wheelhouse," Justin said, flashing that smile that promised very bad things. "Would you like to take up this discussion of *crimes* in a more private setting and see if one of the Assembly Speakers agrees that Kit committed such offenses? Or if maybe *you* are the fucking criminal instead, hag?"

Stifled gasps echoed around us, punctuated by a couple of muffled laughs.

Reshi's cheeks flushed.

Colleen laughed and the sound was cold and hard. "She doesn't want to do that, honey. A whole lot of ugly shit about her people will come spilling out, won't it?"

"That's the plan." Justin flexed a hand and silver spiraled in a deadly circle around him, his green eyes locked on Reshi. "Say the word, bitch. Let's do that. Let's go talk about these...*crimes*."

Reshi's gaze lasered in Justin and no one else. "Should I cut your tongue out, boy?"

"Try it," he offered. Magic whispered in the air above him and several more chains separated, sliding out to dance in the air. "Let's see what you got."

"Enough," Findlay said. "Greaves, Healer Antrim, please, go join the other witches." He gestured to one of the Assembly guards and the man approached. His face was stalwart, but reluctance glinted in his eyes as he came and stood before Justin and Colleen.

Neither wanted to back down, but Colleen took Justin's hand after a moment and they both stepped back a few feet, closer to the line of witches.

"Now that you're done letting your villages idiots insult me, may I take this wayward chit and go?" Reshi demanded, her gaze boring into Findlay and demanding his submission.

"Woman." Findlay's lips twitched. "I'm tempted to let you *try*. But I've already established that the Assembly has no control over the actions of individuals, especially those who are registered under the Charter. You claim Kit Colbana has committed crimes but you refuse to detail them. To complicate matters, Greaves, the one you refer to as a *village idiot*, is a witch highly respected by the Assembly and he suggests that perhaps the *crimes* have been perpetrated by *your* people." Findlay turned his head then and gave me a long, assessing look. "I've become somewhat familiar with Ms. Colbana's history in recent days and she's been in this region for some time. She would have been quite young when she left...wherever it is you come from. I'm not inclined to turn her over to you, whoever you may be, for whatever imaginary crimes you think a child might have committed."

"She's a member of a royal family," Reshi said, the words coming out stiffly. "You wish to create an international incident, vampire?"

"First, she's a criminal and now she's a royal?" Findlay whistled. "Ms. Colbana grows more interesting by the minute. But...again, she's her own person and she's living a country that is still, more or less, a free one. She's also closely connected the shapeshifters in the area. An incident I'll happily avoid is the one that involves coming between a shapeshifter and a person they claim as one of their own—especially when there's a romantic bond with the *Alpha*. But..." He chuckled. "Perhaps you can try that *criminal* bit with the leader of the region's shapeshifters, Alpha Damon Lee. See if it works with him."

Findlay gestured to Damon and stepped aside. Then, to my surprise, the vampire winked at me.

Reshi's mouth pinched tight as she looked from Findlay to me and finally, to Damon.

"This doesn't concern you," she said in a dismissive tone. "Step aside, beast."

"I don't think so," Damon said, the words rumbling up from his deep chest to come out in a voice barely understandable.

Reshi rotated her head. Cracked her neck. "You think I'm asking permission, cat. I'm not. *Step. Aside.*"

A smile twisted Damon's lips as his people peeled away from the crowd, moving in a unit as if they'd rehearsed for this very moment a thousand times over. The air was already charged, the electric pulse of it so thick, it left the hair on my neck standing on end.

Dair glanced our way, then gave a short nod. Soon, his wolves were moving among the cats. By the time they were done, we stood surrounded by a wall of shifters.

Reshi laid a hand on the blade at her side, the look in her eyes telling me she wasn't quite ready to back down.

Damon saw it, too. He stepped forward, muscles straining, as if it was taking everything he had to hold his human form. Reshi went to speak and Damon's roar cut her off, the deep, defiant challenge of it echoing around the chamber.

Chang stepped forward to stand with me, just opposite of Damon.

In an imminently calm, polite voice, Chang said, "In case you were wondering, the Alpha's response to your...*polite* request is no."

Chapter One

Two Weeks Later

" *Scream...*"

I scrambled to tear away the claws digging into my neck, eyes locked on the horrifying visage in front of me.

Her teeth were hardly more than broken nubs, her cheeks sunken, and her eyes filmy. Her breath smelled of rotting things, so foul, I wanted to vomit.

As she leaned in closer and pressed her mouth to my cheek, I could feel my stomach turning itself inside out, knew I *would* vomit. She squeezed, as if realizing what was happening, and laughed. She'd make me choke on it, and I'd die that way—

"No," she murmured, easing her grip and backing away.

She released me and I hit the floor, curling in on myself and wrapping my arms around my knees. If I could have disappeared into the wall at my back, I would have.

"I won't kill you so easily, Kitasa," she murmured. "I've waited too long. You know that, right? You've kept me waiting for too long for me to make this *easy* on you."

She stroked my hair and I flinched away.

She seized my chin at the movement, wrenched my face and forced me to look at her.

I gaped. Sunlight fell over her perfect, cool features.

The macabre death mask from earlier was gone.

Fanis laughed, the sound girlish and tittering.

"You look like you've seen a ghost, Kitasa." She shifted her grip to my hair, slammed my head back against the concrete wall. "*Have you seen a ghost? My* ghost?"

"I..." Swallowing, I shook my head. "I don't know what you mean."

She tsked under her breath, then moved, shoving her fist forward—

No.

Not her fist—a *blade*...

I froze and looked downward. Dazed, I stared at the bronze blade connected to the ghostly being, Lemera. The boogeyman who crept out of the darkness to kill people at my grandmother's behest. The cursed blade.

"Kitasa..."

Jerking my head up, I blinked, watched Fanis's face melt into Lemera's. She smiled, reached up to cup my cheek.

"Kit."

"Kit."

She was shaking me now, shaking and talking to me in Damon's voice.

"*Kit! Damn it! Wake up!*"

With a gasp, I came awake, struggling to break free of the bonds pinning me to the wall.

"Kit?"

"...Damon?"

The bands on my wrists eased.

No. Not bands. *Hands.* Pulsing pain lingered and he swept a thumb over the tender flesh, but didn't let go. Instead, he eased up and looked at me, the faint light from the window barely casting any light on his features. It was enough for me to see his eyes, how dark and worried they were, how large the pupil was. Sweat sheened his brow and the energy of his cat loomed around him, ready to pounce and attack—not that it could kill my nightmares.

"Why are you holding me down?" I asked.

He released my hands, a weary chuckle escaping him.

As he levered away from me, I caught the hot, wild scent that was a shapeshifter's blood. "I'll show you."

Light flashed on.

"Show me...oh, *fuck*..."

I went to reach out, touch the bloody furrows in his chest, but stopped.

The bronze blade was in my hand.

I yelped at the sight of it and dropped it. It bounced off the bed to hit the floor.

I flinched at the sound. Damon didn't even glance at the old weapon, just brushed my hair back. "Are you okay?"

No.

With a smile that had to look as fake as it felt, I nudged his shoulder. "Can you go clean up? I need a minute."

I needed a minute to grab that blade, figure out how far away I could send it—

He disappeared through the door.

A shadow wavered into view in front of me.

I hissed out a breath at the sight of the ghost who'd made a spectral appearance in my dreams—but she was there, in the flesh, so to speak. She gave me a hard look as she scooped up the blade, then disappeared, as quickly as she had appeared.

"Kit?"

Whipping my head around, I stared at him.

He was in the door, chest wet, a rag in hand and a hard look in his eyes.

His nostrils flared and I didn't dare breathe as he scented the air.

"Where's the blade?"

"Away." Pulling my knees up to my chest, I curled my arms around them and buried my face in the hollow there. "I sent it away."

He didn't speak for long moments.

"I'm sorry, Damon. I don't know what in the hell I did but I'm sorry."

He still said nothing.

But a few minutes later, the light went off and he pulled me into his arms.

"It was a nightmare, Kit. That's all. It's not like I don't heal up almost right away."

He brushed a kiss against my temple, nuzzled me as he lifted me into his arms and carried me over to the couch. He tugged a blanket over us and murmured, "Sleep, baby girl. You're safe. They'll never hurt you again. I'm going to make sure of it."

I desperately wanted to believe that.

But he couldn't make that promise.

Nobody could.

"YOU CANNOT CALL THE blade like that."

I tensed at the sound of Lemera's voice, jerking my head around to search for Damon, because I knew he was in here—there. By the coffee maker. But he was...drinking coffee, and staring at his phone, like he hadn't heard her.

Slowly, I looked back at the ghost.

Yes.

She was there. Standing next to me where I still sat on the couch. I'd been trying to convince myself to get up and go apologize again, but I couldn't work up the nerve to do it. Only according to my eyes, I was laying down—*sleeping*.

"What are you doing here?" I whispered.

"Why are you whispering?"

My gaze flitted to Damon.

She glanced at him, then her gaze returned to me as a smile lit her face. "He cannot hear us. Not when we talk like this."

"Talk...how?"

"That doesn't matter." She waved a dismissive hand. "You can't call the blade again. It...the power in it. I've broken the hold between me and...its other owner, but it still *calls* things and you could cause...disturbances. Do you understand me?"

"I didn't *call* it," I said defensively. "I was having a nightmare and it was just...*there*."

"Then learn to control it." She looked exasperated. "I'm not the only thing bound to that blade, child. *Control yourself.*"

She blinked out my view as Damon looked up.

I tried to smile.

But he was staring past me, like I wasn't even there.

Slowly, I turned my head.

It was eerie, to stare at yourself in sleep. I lay there on my side, face half-under a pillow and my hand curled into a fist tucked against my breastbone.

"Well, that's weird."

My body twitched at the sound of my voice.

And behind me, the door whispered shut.

I turned, looking for Damon.

He was gone, though.

And I was falling, back into my body.

Back into sleep.

EYES FLYING OPEN, I sat bolt upright on the couch.

Then, shoving to my feet so fast I almost tripped, I spun around.

Okay, this time, I really *was* awake. Maybe. I looked around, saw the blanket Damon had pulled over us, the indentation where I'd curled up. A metallic scent hung in the air and walked over, looked down at the bed, winced at the sight of the blood staining the sheets.

"Okay," I muttered. "Awake now."

I started to shove my hair out of my face, then froze. Blood streaked my palms, stained my fingers.

"Shit, shit, shit."

Lowering my hands, I looked back at the bed and the bloody sheets, the evidence of my attacking Damon with Lemera's blade now dried a rusty brown.

Lurching forward, I grabbed the sheets, all but ripping them in my haste to get them off the bed.

I breathed a little easier when I saw the mattress, thankfully, wasn't stained. Shifters—and their lovers—sometimes played rough in bed. I knew I'd scratched Damon up plenty. Having sheets that were thicker and more resistant to stains and fluids leaking through was just common sense, right?

Still, I stripped the mattress cover off too and carried the whole bundle to the recycler, shoved it all in, then dug new linens out, selecting a deep, soft black instead of the rich burgundy in the shade I'd just ripped off.

I wanted no reminders of waking up to find Damon looming over me, chest streaked with blood because I'd cut into him while sleeping.

He could probably do without it, too, even if he had brushed it off. I needed to find him, tell him I was sorry, explain. The low-level hum of awareness under my skin told me he was still in the Lair. Since he hadn't left yet, he probably had business here for some of the morning. I could shower fast, catch him.

Nerves made me clumsy and I dropped the shampoo, the soap, got cleanser in my eyes.

Strung out and on edge when I left our quarters, I walked straight into Shanelle when I opened the door.

She caught me, eyes widening in concern when she saw me. "Kit, are you okay?"

"Crap morning," I said. "Know where Damon is?"

"Ah...no." She looked down at the laundry basket she'd dropped when she reached out to grab me. "He asked me to come by once you were up and moving."

"I already took care of it." I nudged the basket out of the way with my booted foot, face flaming hot. Closing the door behind me, I cut around her. "He doesn't need to have clanmates cleaning up behind me."

"That's not..." She gave up when I didn't stop.

I was glad because I still wasn't sure what I'd say to Damon. I sure as hell didn't want to tell anybody I'd cut into my boyfriend because I had a scary dream.

DAMON WASN'T IN THE war room. He wasn't in the gym, or the garage or in the medical area. I could still feel the prickle along my skin after checking the offices along northern arm of the Lair but unless I started knocking on individual residential units, I didn't know anywhere—

Halfway back to our quarters, I swung around.

No.

There was one other area he might be, although I hadn't heard about anybody being brought in.

The dungeon, for lack of a better word, wasn't a subterranean room. The water table in the state of Florida didn't make for the safest basements. No, the dungeon was built into reinforced section of the Lair between the garage and back wall of the lair, separated from the quarters I shared with Damon by several feet of concrete, rods of iron, and, I'd recently learned, double walls of solid plate steel. Basically, it was a bomb shelter on steroids. Damon had personally tried to break out of it and had failed.

So, it was a damn secure room.

The sight of a junior soldier on the outer door leading to the dungeon made my heart stutter.

"Hannah."

She blinked at the sight of me, her eyes going wide, the soft golden of her skin flushing a dusky pink.

"Kit!"

Glancing to the door beyond her, I asked, "Is Damon in there?"

She swallowed, jerking her gaze away. "Nobody's allowed in. Alpha's orders."

Metal creaked behind me.

"Kid, if you're fraternizing while on this rotation, your alpha is going to bust your ass."

I didn't recognize the hard voice.

Turning, I met the flat gaze of a tall, rangy man, his features unfamiliar, short black hair in a military-neat style. His eyes met mine.

"She's not fraternizing," I said. "I came in to ask a question."

He cocked his head. "You're not a shifter. You don't belong in here. Scram."

"Sir, she's—"

He cut a look at Hannah. "Be quiet, soldier."

Oh, I didn't like this guy.

"But she's—"

I touched Hannah's arm. "It's okay. I'm in a bad mood anyway."

She gulped, her eyes rounding until whites shown all around her irises.

Stepping forward, I smiled, tilting my head to the side and not flinching as his eyes slid over me.

"You want me to leave?" I asked.

"You're going to," he said. "Only chicks who should be down are the ones who can fight. That ain't you." He scraped his nails down his cheek. "But you're a cute little thing, I'll give you that. Maybe there's something else you can do—"

He'd been reaching for my arm as he spoke, but the rest of the words froze in his throat as nearly three feet of steel and silver alloy appeared between us. Pressing the tip to his neck, I smiled. "You really don't want to finish that sentence—or touch me."

The door at the end of the hall burst open.

"Gary, you *stupid* fuck!"

I heard Scott's feet pounding on the floor as he came running.

"Don't, Scott," I said, watching a flicker of awareness started to glint in the man's eyes. "Gary, is it?"

He shot a look to the door behind me, toward Hannah.

"I asked a question." Twisting the blade, I pressed, watched as a drop of blood appeared.

"Yeah. Gary." He jerked back away from the blade. "Listen, honey..."

Banishing the blade, I dropped down, swung out with my leg and took him out at the ankles.

He crashed to the floor, hard.

He was up almost as quick as I was, but the dull, ruddy flush on his cheeks made me smile.

A growl rose in his throat.

Scott grabbed him by the back of his neck and threw him. He flew across the hall to smash into the far wall.

"Kit, I'm very sorry," Scott said while the other man rolled onto his hands and knees, groaning, then cursing. "Gary's new in town, was completing a job for the Alpha."

Staring past Scott at the other man, I asked, "Is he *staying*?"

Scott went quiet.

The door behind me opened and a large shadow fell across the floor.

Shoving my hair back, I huffed out a breath and turned to meet Damon's gaze. He loomed there, arms crossed over his chest, brows drawn low over his eyes.

Those eyes were an impossibly intense shade of gray, like storm clouds right before the sky opened up. They narrowed on my face before flicking to the man at the end of the hall, then back to me.

"Who bled him?"

I grimaced. "Me."

Damon's face went tight.

"Gary. In front of me. Now."

The silence grew weighted and I cracked my knuckles, then looked at Hannah, took pity on her.

"The kid didn't do anything wrong. I was looking for you. He showed up right after I did and jumped on her. Don't take any of this out on her," I said, giving him a narrow look.

"Did she point out who you are?" Damon asked, not looking away from the man making his way toward us one slow step at a time.

"She tried. He kept cutting her off. So I told her to let it go." I looked at Gary and smiled. "That's when I decided I'd bleed him."

Damon looked at Hannah, gave her a short nod. "You're good, soldier. Step out into the other room."

She didn't wait another second, running so fast I felt the wind from her passing.

"You were *told* you'd be given a chance to plead your case *if* I was satisfied with how you handled yourself *today*, Snyder." Damon leaned in, looming over the other man although they were nearly the same height. "What makes you think you can boss *my* soldiers around or give orders to *anybody* in *my* clan? In *my* Lair?"

A bead of sweat broke out on Gary's temple, trickled down his cheek.

"I messed up, Alpha—"

"Don't call me that," Damon barked. "I haven't given you the right."

"Yes, sir. I'm sorry. I didn't know the skirt was yours—"

"The *skirt*?" I gave him a baleful look. "I should have cut you *lower. Much* lower."

"You st—"

The words ended in a gurgle as Damon grabbed him and slammed him into the wall. "Don't finish the word." He squeezed, then after several seconds, dropped him. "Don't even think about it."

Hate rolled over the man's eyes as Damon turned his back.

"Get out of Florida, Snyder. I'll have Scott cut your fee for the job on your way out, but don't ever show your face in my territory again. If you do, you're dead."

Damon had taken a step toward me when Gary lunged.

Damon spun around.

But Gary was already on his knees, staring dumbly as the silver knife punching out of his chest.

Smoky wisps curled out as I walked over, gripped the hilt. He swayed and I grabbed him by the hair to hold him still, staring into his eyes as I wrenched the knife around, once, twice.

When I let go, he collapsed.

Damon came to stand next to me, tracing his fingers over my spine.

"Now you don't have to worry about him coming back," I said.

"No." He kissed my temple, then nuzzled a path down to nip my neck. "I guess I don't."

Scott came forward and knelt by the body.

Our eyes locked.

"Was he a friend of yours?"

Scott hitched the man up on his shoulder in a fireman's hold and stood. He sighed, hard and heavy. "Once. In another life. But not for a very long time. Don't feel like you need to apologize, Kit. If you hadn't killed him for what he just tried to do, I would have." He looked at Damon. "Alpha."

Then we were left alone.

"Hi. I...ah...wanted to apologize," I said, the knife in my hand suddenly feeling heavy and awkward.

Damon took it. With his free hand, he ripped the sleeve of his shirt off, then meticulously cleaned the blade. Once he'd returned it, he cupped my face in his hands and pressed his mouth to mine.

"No apologies needed," he said after a long, slow kiss. "Although if you ever feel the need to defend my honor again..."

I stared into his gray eyes for a moment, then giggled, pressing my face into his worn shirt.

"Your *honor*?"

"My honor. My ass. Whatever it was that had you burying a blade in that shithead's chest." He cupped my head in his hand, kissed a path down my neck to lick the sensitive curve.

"He was about to attack you while you had your back turned."

"See? Defending my ass." He rubbed his lips over the bitemark on my shoulder. "Sexy as hell. Makes me want to..."

My phone rang—a strident ping I recognized all too well.

Damon gripped my hips. "Ignore it."

"I can't."

"Sure you can..." He nudged his hard erection against my belly, then boosted me up, moved to tuck me between him and the wall. "I can even make it quick."

My phone rang again. A second, a third strident beep.

Wiggling, I pushed at Damon's chest. "That's an emergency alert, Damon. Bad news."

He sighed and lowered me to the ground, but didn't release me—his mouth slammed over mine in a deep, possessive kiss. "No apologies for your nightmares, Kit. Remember that."

"Okay." My breath was ragged, thanks to the kiss and the heat in his gaze and I backed away before I could give into the temptation I saw waiting there.

"Be safe." His lids drooped low of his eyes, shielding the intensity of his emotions. "Send me a message when you can."

I jerked my head in a nod, then turned, running out of the room. Grabbing my phone on the next alert, I hit the button. "Colbana."

"Code R," the voice intoned. "Young vamps from House Whittier were being transferred to Allerton and the transport vehicle was rear-ended. Three were contained immediately, but two escaped and are at present, loose in East Orlando."

"*Shit*."

"In a word, yes. Details incoming. Apprehend if possible, but prevent loss of life to the populace, no matter what. Termination on sight if no safe means of retrieval. Acknowledge."

"Acknowledged." I swung by my room, grabbed the emergency kit I kept ready and hit the door, still running.

It would take me a long while to remember that I never did find out what—or *who*—was in the room.

By the time I thought to look again, the dungeon had been emptied.

Chapter Two

Six Weeks Later

A headache pounded behind my eyes as I dragged myself out of my car and into the Lair. My legs felt like cement blocks as I dragged myself the thirty feet or so that separated the connected parking garage from the sprawling, and ever-expanding, building that was the East Orlando Lair.

I was drained in a way I hadn't been in a long, long time.

I wasn't hungry—I was too tired for that, but I couldn't remember the last time I'd had a real meal, so I took the sandwich a juvenile shifter pushed into my hands as I passed by. I'd been tracking a runaway offshoot for the past week and had barely managed enough time to breathe, much less eat or drink.

Now that the boy was in the safe hands of his mom—human, but accepting—and his *not-human* and asshole, abusive father was locked up in a cell at the Assembly awaiting trial for abuse, trafficking and slew of other charges, I wanted to sleep for a week. Maybe a month.

The scent of roasted meat drifted up from the wrapped sandwich and my stomach grumbled, deciding that maybe I wasn't too tired to eat.

All around me, people chattered and moved about, daily life in the Lair carrying on.

Needing the fuel and rest, I kept a blank expression on my face as I strode to the quarters I shared with Damon. There were waves, smiles and greeting and I made myself respond, nodding at a couple of juveniles and waving to a little girl who often crept up to watch

Doyle as we trained together. I wasn't in the mood to socialize, but Doyle had been drumming it into my head that if I kept ignoring the Clan, they'd think they'd done something wrong.

You're part of the Clan now, Kit. Even if you're not a shifter, you're family. They don't want to crowd you, and they won't. But they're still social creatures. You're not. I get it, but they just...don't. You don't have to make eye contact, but if you walk around with your eyes on the floor, they feel like they've messed up or hurt your feelings.

I hated shifter politics and the general shifter culture. Maybe it wasn't so bad in reality, but the shifters in Florida were still coming out of the trauma of dealing with a batshit crazy Alpha who would kill somebody over the minor offense of not smiling brightly enough—or smiling over the wrong thing. I wasn't cut out for this life, but I loved the man who led these people and the clan had been willing to die for me, bleed for me. What was I supposed to do?

Fortunately, nobody tried to stop me. My stomach was making strident demands now and my mouth was watering. I dumped the plate on the counter, moving to the sink to wash up. No way was I touching food or anything else without washing up. I was filthy, stinking to high heaven.

Stripping down to my utility tank and panties, I left my filthy clothes in a tangle on the floor, stowed my gear, then did a quick wash-up in the kitchen sink. Once I climbed into the shower and the heat got to work on my sore muscles, I'd be done, so food first.

I managed to get half the sandwich down before my body decided it had had enough. My eyesight went blurry, my vision going dark—and while I was still in the middle of chewing a mouthful of roasted turkey, lettuce, and tomato, which a thick slice of smoky cheddar and creamy mayo to top it all off.

Since I didn't want to choke on the sandwich, delicious as it was, I wrapped the rest of it back up, shoved it into the fridge and went to shower.

After scrubbing off days' worth of sweat, dirty and any lingering scent of blood, I shut off the water and climbed out.

My reflection showed a woman who'd lost weight. I didn't look unhealthy, but I really needed to stop getting by on protein shakes and granola while on some of the heavier hunts I'd been doing.

I'd been called out on a *lot* of heavy hunts lately, starting with a couple of vamps who'd tried to make a break for it a little over a month earlier.

Since then, it had been one shit show after another.

Logically, I knew I wasn't the only Assembly freelancer getting slammed. We'd escaped military involvement by the skin of our teeth after an outbreak of vampiric violence, but such an outbreak almost always spiraled into more chaos.

I'd never experienced anything like what was happening in the city, but some of my colleagues and other, older full-time employees like the desk clerks and armory sergeants had been through similar cycles. *The worst of it is behind us*, I'd heard several times. I sure as hell hoped so. I was exhausted.

Findlay, a vampire who worked for the Tribunal, the highest NH authority in the country, was still stuck here in East O doing clean up after the vampiric outbreaks. Helping stabilize the vampire population wasn't a job he'd wanted but as one of the strongest vamps in the region currently, he didn't have much choice. I didn't feel sorry for him. He'd been the one to let Jude out, and Jude, as expected, had come after me almost immediately.

I'd killed him.

Findlay didn't hold that against me and I doubted he was requesting that every shit job come my way as any sort of personal vendetta.

Findlay was frozen in a body that would look forever young. His eyes blazed with intelligence and cunning, but sometimes, too, with a glint that made me think he remembered more of his human life than most vampires.

He was still an old bastard, which meant he could be an arrogant ass.

But he wasn't so arrogant that he'd put me on shit jobs just because he was pissed at being stuck here still...was he?

Brooding over it, I swiped a towel off my hair, hung it up and tugged the oversized t-shirt I'd stolen from Damon off the hook on the back of the door. It was worn and faded and smelled like my lover. Taking comfort in the scent of the forest and wild things, I pulled it on, then brushed my teeth. The fog of sleep edged closer and I trudged into the bedroom, hoping against hope to see Damon push through the door, even though I wouldn't. I'd sense him if he was anywhere close by.

And he wasn't.

Climbing into bed, I pulled the covers up, grabbed his pillow and hauled it to my chest. It felt like I'd barely closed my eyes and sleep grabbed me, pulled me under,

I rarely rested deeply when I was in this bed alone.

Tonight was no different.

The nightmare awaited—*she* awaited, lurking in this hellscape that had begun to haunt me with regularity, playing out the same way time and again almost every time I closed my eyes.

"Granddaughter." Fanis stood in front of me, her features and clothing familiar but...not. Her eyes looked hollow in her face, her cheekbones more prominent, cutting against her skin so sharply, they looked ready to slice through. Her voice was an eerie echo, as if she spoke to me from beyond the grave.

In the misty, murky space where we stood, I couldn't make out anything beyond her.

"What do you want?" I asked. Behind my back, I fisted my hands, cutting my nails into my palms in the vain hope the pain would help me wake.

Wake up, Kit...wake up. Wake up*!*

"You're weary. And weak," she said, instead of answering my question. "You shouldn't let yourself get into such a state. So much easier for the hyenas to pick you off if you let yourself grow weak, child."

"I'm so touched you care." I sneered. "What do you *want*?"

"What I want...that is my concern. Yours...well, your *concern* is to just stay alive. There is no need to divine anything in our conversations beyond what I tell you, Kitasa." She smiled as she spoke and the warmth in her expression was terrifying. "All will be revealed in time."

A stuttering fear gripped me. I fought it back.

She saw it anyway.

"You *should fear* me." She leaned closer, bringing with her the scent of spices and herbs, things I'd forgotten until now. They made my stomach clench. "I run out of time, granddaughter. I run out of patience. If you will not return, then I will come for you."

Run out of time for what? But I didn't ask.

I curled my lip at her, faking bravado. "Didn't you already try that, sending your pets out to haul me back to that hell you call home?"

"My pets." Fanis arched a brow and cocked her head, something incredibly inhuman about the movement. "You speak of Reshi."

"Sure. Yeah. Okay."

"Shhhh..." Something cold brushed against my arm, the sort of cold that sank into my bones. A ghostly whisper followed. "She doesn't know you and I are...connected, little sister."

Some strange knowledge, primal and instinctive, told me not to react to the voice, or the sudden presence of the Lemera, a chill touch along my senses. Not looking at the specter, I smirked at my grandmother. "Neither Reshi or Fenele did a very good job collecting me, Granny."

Fanis smiled. It was a lewd smile, made even worse by rich red paint she'd slicked on her lips. I'd never known my grandmother to use cosmetics—even as old as she was, she was still stunningly, staggeringly beautiful—or rather, she had *been, back when I'd still be trapped in Aneris Hall.*

The use of cosmetics would be like framing a sapphire with garishly cut glass masquerading as diamonds.

But now, the red stain on her lips was obscene, rather like decorating a days-old corpse.

"Is Reshi back, Grandmother?" I asked. From the corner of my eye, I could see Lemera. She was circling around my grandmother, head moving in strange, abrupt movements, almost batlike, a predator closing in on her quarry. "She didn't seem very happy when she left Florida. Had her tail all tucked between her legs and everything."

Fanis narrowed her eyes. "What game is this?"

"Game?"

"Both twins have been stolen away, Kitasa. I'm most displeased by this." Time seemed to blink and in a heartbeat, she was in front of me, cruel fingers squeezing my chin while nails sharpened to claws cut into my flesh.

"Reshi left weeks *ago, you old crone," I snarled, jerking free.*

"Enough of your lies. Your time is just about up, mewling whelp. I come to claim what is mine. You will take nothing more. You took Rathias. Your fool mother gave her loyalty to you rather than her queen. And you took the twins from me, stupid girl. But I'm coming for you now. And you will pay."

"Kit, wake up!"

I jerked upright, full awareness falling on me like the skies had opened to drench me in icy water.

Shivering, I sucked in a ragged breath just as Damon wrapped me in strong, warm arms and hauled me onto his chest.

"Fuck, Kit...are you okay?"

I didn't answer, burrowing into him, so desperately cold, it hurt.

"It's alright," he murmured into my ear, rolling onto his side and hauling me into the hard curve of his body. He threw one leg over mine, wrapped his arm around my waist until I was surrounded by his heat. "It's alright, baby girl. I've got you. She can't hurt you. She won't ever hurt you."

I desperately wished I could believe him.

Pressing my face into his chest, I clung to him and let the deep, rolling timbre of his voice wash over me.

WARMTH SURROUNDED ME.

I don't know how long I'd been sleeping but the solid strength of Damon's arms held me tight throughout the night and no more nightmares came. The heavy lassitude in my muscles gave me the vaguest idea—I'd finally gotten more than just two or three hours of sleep. Opening one eye, I saw light filtering in around the curtains, a soft, ethereal glow that spoke of early morning.

I might have just rolled over and burrowed deeper into Damon's warmth but my bladder demanded attention.

His arm tightened around my waist.

"Bathroom," I said, gripping his wrist and tugging until he released me.

After taking care of business, I caught sight of my reflection and cringed. Damn, I definitely needed to get a few more meals in me. My hips and collarbones were so pronounced, they looked ready to cut right through my skin. Since I'd collapsed into bed with my hair still wet, the fine, slippery strands looked like I'd decide to style them by sticking my finger in an electrical socket.

"Good thing you're not overly vain," I muttered, grabbing a brush. Once I'd smoothed my hair down, I washed my face to clear the fog from my brain then grabbed my lotion.

I almost felt normal by the time I opened the bathroom door.

Damon stood on the other side.

My heart jumped, lurching into panic mode at his sudden, completely silent appearance.

Dragging in a shaky breath, I glared at him. "I'm going to put a damn bell on you one of these days."

He didn't say anything, the intensity of his eyes slamming into me like a velvet punch. When he moved forward, crowding into my personal space, I fell back a step, then another and another, until he caught my hips to still me.

The heat of his palms on my skin was searing, almost like a brand, the barrier of my panties and sleep tank next to nothing—and then even those barriers were gone, falling away under his touch with an ease that spoke of a leopard shifter's claws.

Those claws brushed gently over my skin before he retracted them, but the eyes that held mine had gone a swirling green-gold.

"You've got to stop shredding my clothes," I said, the words ragged.

"Not if I keep buying replacements." He dipped his head, mouth going to the curve between neck and shoulder, his teeth scraping over the scar he'd left on me, a mark that told anybody who looked I was his. I'd bitten him, too, and more than once, but my normal teeth just didn't do the damage a shifter's did. Also, I healed a lot slower, giving the faint ridge of scar tissue time to form.

Although there was nothing *normal* about the scar left by Damon's bite. It seemed to get more sensitive as time went by. Now, as he scraped it with his teeth, then lingered to give it slow, teasing licks, sensation swept over me as if he was doing something much more erotic.

He turned and boosted me onto the edge of the marble counter, the cool surface a shocking contrast to skin overheating under the demanding, delicious touch of hard, hungry hands.

One of them glided up over my ribs to palm my breast and I gasped as he tugged on my nipple, shuddered as he toyed and played until it was pulsing in time with my heart.

"Damon!" I gripped his shoulders, nails digging in as he slid his free hand between my thighs, fingers seeking out the wet heat there.

He growled in rough approval before withdrawing.

Me, on the other hand? I groaned in disappointment because he'd already stopped.

Not for long, though. He shifted his grip to my knee, fingers possessive and tight.

As my center of balance changed, I sagged backward and braced my weight on my hands, eyes locked with his. The grey of his irises gave way to the swirling green-gold of his cat's and that gaze held me captive while he tucked the head of his cock against my entrance and began to push inside me.

I whimpered, head falling back and lashes fluttering down.

"Look at me."

I tried, but my lids felt weighted down, the muscles in my neck limp.

He started to withdraw and I tightened around him, curling one leg around his hip. "Don't."

"Then look at me," he said again, pushing his free hand into my hair and tugging until he had my head angled to meet his gaze.

"Bossy, grouchy cat." I smiled at him as he flexed his hips, pushing back inside me. "So pushy."

Instead of responding, he pulled out, tugged me off the counter and turned me around, the movement so quick, my head was left spinning. He kicked my legs apart then dipped his knees.

"Damon!" The strangled cry bounced off the walls of the bathroom as he drove into me, this time filling me in one hard, driving thrust.

"If you're going to call me bossy and pushy, I might as well live up to it." He adjusted his grip, dragging me up until my toes left the ground.

His length pulsed inside me and I whimpered, head falling onto his shoulder. His cock pulsed inside me. My body reacted by squeezing around him which only made him pulse again, the delicious cycle so erotic, I thought I might come even if he didn't move.

But he moved—Damon wasn't a passive lover.

He urged me forward until my weight was bent over the marble counter, the cold of it a tease against my nipples while he gripped my hips and began to ride me. Whimpering, I reached back, grabbing onto his wrist, needing something to anchor myself.

Damon only let it last a few seconds, then he caught my hand and pinned it at the small of my back. "I'm bossy and pushy, baby girl. And right now, it's all my way."

Then, almost as if to preempt the move, he took my other wrist, holding both of them pinned in one hand at the small of my back, his other hand gripping my shoulder as he thrust.

I clenched around him with a broken moan.

"Kit..." My name came out a growl on his lips, his body shuddering convulsively behind me as he swore, then began to move faster, harder, sending waves of pleasure ricocheting through me.

His need was raw and overwhelming, feeding my own until I couldn't think, see, feel anything beyond this—the hard marble supporting my body, his hands on me, restraining me, bracing me, the heat of him surrounding me as he drove into me, branding me yet again.

It was over far too soon, his name a ragged cry on my lips as I climaxed and his low, animalistic growl seemed to reach inside me, filling me up all over again.

Chapter Three

He was gone when I woke again.

That wasn't surprising. He was gone a lot these days, and usually from pretty early until pretty late. Granted, there were times he got in before I did—or times he might have beaten me home or slept in and I didn't notice because I was out on a job.

I was running my ass off. My bank account was flush, but it wasn't like I had time to enjoy it.

Rolling onto my belly, I breathed in the combined scents of our bodies, wondered if I could get another hour of sleep in, but the energized buzzing of my brain told me not to bother.

Without his body heat to warm me, the bed was too big, too empty. And even though he moved without making a sound, the air was just too...quiet.

Despite my exhaustion and the fact that I actually didn't have a job slated for the day, I was out of bed once the sleep cleared and I made the brilliant deduction that Damon was, as suspected, not around.

After an hour in my personal gym, followed by a shower and a huge meal, I ducked out through one of the side entrances. I only saw a couple of the cats around. Not all of Damon's cats lived in the Lair but there were always people coming and going, the place the business hub for the entire clan.

The skin on the back of my neck crawled as I made my way to the parking garage where I left my car. It took too much willpower not to look around, try to see who was watching me. I couldn't brush it off as a lack of sleep or my general paranoia, though. That's what I'd been doing for the past couple of days, ever since I'd thought I caught a glimpse of somebody behind me on my backtrail—far enough away I couldn't pick up their unique *'presence'* on my mental radar, but close enough they'd be able to close the distance in under a minute should they choose.

One of Damon's cats—I'd known it in my bones—so I hadn't thought much about it other than to be annoyed.

But the niggling sensation of being watched, being *followed*, had grown every day. Now it was at the point that *annoyance* no longer covered it, especially since I'd had a chance to sleep and get a decent meal in me.

Yeah, I was *pissed*, not annoyed.

"Maybe that's why he disappears so early," I muttered as I unlocked my car. Out of habit, I put my sword on the back seat before climbing into the driver's seat.

A shadow in the far corner of the garage, furtive and swift, kicked up my already low-level frustration.

With a smile, I threw the car into reverse and gunned the engine—hard.

The tires squealed as my vehicle went flying back. Spinning the wheel, I checked my mirror again, saw my would-be shadow rushing to a car at the far end of the row. Without hesitation, I put the car into drive and punched it, speeding out of the garage.

Instead of heading to my office as planned, I swung left and headed out of town. It would be a hell of a lot harder to track me without my noticing if we weren't stuck in city gridlock.

I'D ALMOST MADE IT out of the city when a call from the Assembly came in over the car's onboard computer/communications system.

Code M: All Available Suitable Personnel Respond to 10th and Spade. Be advised, NH is young and has fire capabilities, may be suffering from a psychotic break. HQ requests care be taken to avoid killing the juvenile if at all possible.

I grimaced.

A Code M *sucked*. Nobody liked dealing with rogue witches. Who would? While most rogue shifters *and* vamps could be taken down from a distance by anybody with the right weapon and half-way decent abilities, rogue witches were a different story entirely. They could take *you* out from a distance and the only weapon they needed was themselves.

With witches who could call fire, that made it even worse. And for the witch to be a *juvenile*...so much worse.

Spinning the car into a three-point turn once I'd made sure I was clear, I tried to nudge my thoughts away from one witch in particular with pyro skills. Tate was only a little younger than me and had enough power in her to terrify. She was also somebody I could see having a psychotic break, too.

If such a thing were to happen, I wouldn't want to be anywhere in the vicinity.

However, I was listed as having clearance for a Code M.

The truth was, even if the assembly hadn't cleared me, I would have gone.

A rogue pyro witch was a danger to the whole damn city and we were still cleaning up the mess from the last crazy bastard to unload on East Orlando. I couldn't sit back and do nothing.

Not with a kid in the middle of a psychotic break.

Fuck.

This already felt bad.

SHE *was* a kid, thirteen, maybe fourteen, terrified, pale and skinny, with bruises on her arms and big, dark eyes that told me she was on the edge of going into shock.

The girl was thin, the kind of thin that came from too many missed meals and growing too fast, with tangled hair hanging halfway down her back and clothes that had seen better years. The wild, panicked look in her eyes didn't quite hide the deep, wrenching well of grief.

A smaller version of her, a boy with features still soft from youth, leaned against the half-busted fence, cradling his arm and staring into nothingness with dazed eyes.

A Banner unit—the law enforcement group tasked with handling NH affairs—had a car there. One of the uniformed officers was slumped against the car. The other was standing protectively in front of him, her hand on the weapon she carried at her waist. I assumed she hadn't drawn it yet because the girl's control was shot.

If somebody fired a weapon, this entire section of the road could go up in blaze.

"Heya, Kitty."

The familiar voice and laconic drawl was so welcome, I might have turned and kissed Justin if I'd dared move my eyes from the scared teen twenty yards away.

"Fancy seeing you here, Justin. Colleen."

I hadn't seen her but her presence was as familiar to me as Justin's, and the brush of her hand against mine as she moved to my other side was a warm welcome.

"Anybody else around, sweetie?" she asked.

Colleen might be a witch—and a damn strong one—but I had a weird knack for sensing the presence of NHs, even witches, that others didn't.

"One." I angled my head to the opposite side of the street where a freelance I didn't know lurked behind the burnt out shell of a car. "Not anybody I know. Either a witch with below average abilities or an offshoot I don't know. Kind of surprised nobody else has shown up. A Code M usually brings out the greedy."

"You calling us greedy, Kit?"

Ignoring Justin's dry comment, I asked, "Either of you think we could just douse the area if she goes red hot?"

"No." This time, Justin's voice was grim. "I've only got a minor talent with earth, which won't do shit with her. Colleen's elemental abilities are still coming into focus, but the strongest seems to be air, with a weak touch of water. That won't touch anything this girl throws out. And it's not greed—nobody wants to touch a kid. The Assembly probably saved her life—and a lot of other lives—being open about her age. I don't know who made that call, but good on them."

There was a grim moment of silence as we all considered that.

"I couldn't put anything out," Colleen said in a musing voice, breaking the tension. "But if we make things a little less flammable, it could minimize the damage."

Justin considered. "Probably. But if you startle her..."

"What about trying to talk to her?" I offered. Glancing at the blackened walls and still smoking ruin of a house, I wondered about what might have happened. "It's no more dangerous than anything else we're talking about—might even be the safest option."

I could feel them both looking at me. Sighing, I glanced at Colleen, then Justin, my eyes returning almost immediately to the girl. She was pacing, a red glow encasing her hands in sputtering bursts before fading away. It returned within ten or fifteen seconds, lasted about the same period before cycling back out. "The girl's terrified. Something bad happened in that house and I don't think it's anything *she* did—or maybe what she did was in reaction to what happened."

"She *is* scared," Colleen murmured. She was quiet a moment, then sighed, the sound deep and sad. "And in shock. She...oh, poor baby." Reaching down to take my hand, Colleen squeezed. "It was her father, I think. I'm seeing..." With her free hand, she waved it vaguely in front of her face. "These flashes. The girl came in and he was hurting a woman. Her mother, maybe. And that boy over there, he was on the ground. I think..." She flinched, then, jerking her hand from mine to cradle her arm.

Justin cupped the back of her neck. "Pull back. You can't go so deep with somebody that close to the edge."

Colleen was primarily a Healer—she always had been. She'd been brutalized and forced to remake herself, but the healing abilities had always been there, coupled with an empathy that let her see deep inside others. And sometimes, she did go too deep.

With a shudder, she blew out a hard breath. "Yeah. Thanks, baby. There's just so much hurt there."

"I'll try to talk to her," I said. I took a deliberate step forward, then another, slowly closing the distance between us and making no attempt to be stealthy or subtle about it. She was so focused on the Banner unit and the boy who had to be her brother, she didn't notice me, though, until I was roughly twenty feet away.

The girl's eyes locked with mine and I froze.

"Easy, sweetheart," I said. Holding her gaze, I knelt and put my blade on the ground. She wasn't likely to notice any of my other weapons, I figured, and if I started stripping them all off, that probably wouldn't help put her at ease. As her hazel eyes met mine, I lifted my now-empty hands. "I want to come and talk. Just talk."

She jerked her head back and forth.

"We kind of have to," I told her, angling my head toward the Banner unit. "The folks at Banner don't like taking in kids, but they can't have you burning houses down, either." I paused a second. "Might be a good idea to talk about what's going on so they understand why the house went up in flames. I mean, I doubt you did it on purpose, right?"

She bit her lip, then slowly shook her head.

"So...can we talk?"

A long taut moment passed before she nodded. I could hear a collective sigh of relief from the others, including the Banner unit, but I didn't look away from her until I was about five feet away. Nodding to the boy, I asked, "Is he your brother?"

"Yes," she said, her voice a bare whisper, gaze darting from mine to linger on the boy.

"Can I see his arm? I won't hurt him." I waited until she looked back at me. "I promise."

"O-okay. I think it's broken." She sniffed, then blinked back tears. "He broke his arm!"

Under the fear and shock, there was a low, *powerful* thread of fury and it made the red haze around her hands deepen and spread.

She kept staring at me, the intensity in her gaze growing. "He *hurt* him."

Each word shook. Each word *vibrated* with her rage and pain. I didn't even have to ask.

"Your father," I said softly. "He's the one who broke your brother's arm."

Her eyes widened slightly, but she nodded. "Yes. He hurt my brother, and...my mom..." A sob escaped and she clamped a hand over her mouth, the way a child would when they'd learned the hard way not to make a sound as they cried.

"I'm sorry, honey," I said, daring another step forward. "I'm so sorry. Let me help. Let me help you and your brother, okay?"

She gave another jerky nod before wheeling away to stare at the Banner cops, the hand on her mouth falling away.

Crouching by the boy, I smiled. He gave me a couple of slow sleepy blinks. He was definitely in shock—and the arm was definitely broken, but I doubted that was the only cause of his pain.

Up until I'd started living at the Lair with Damon, I'd only had limited interactions with kids, especially the younger versions, like this one. I couldn't begin to guess at his age and figured his head might reach my breastbone standing up, but that wasn't a good way to estimate.

"What's your name?" I asked.

"Ben." He swallowed and looked past me to his sister. "Dina isn't s'posed to let her fire out. He'll hurt her if he sees."

"Don't you worry about that." I wasn't going to tell the kid that their dad was probably past hurting people now. It wouldn't do him or Dina any good at this point. Instead, I smiled at him. "I brought friends with me. They won't let him hurt you or Dina."

Hope shone out at me from his eyes, eyes so big they dominated his young face. "Really?"

"Yeah, really." Angling my head toward Colleen and Justin, I asked, "You see that pretty lady with red hair?"

"By the guy with the shiny jacket?"

I swallowed a chuckle. "Yeah. That's a *special* shiny jacket, Ben. Those two are both witches, like your sister."

His cheeks went red, shame, probably fear, too.

"What's wrong, kiddo?" I asked as his gaze slid away.

"We weren't s'posed to let anybody know she's a witch. It's bad."

"No." Shaking my head, I stroked his soft, downy hair back from his eyes. "It's not bad. It's just what some people are. You're bad if you do bad things on purpose. Just being a witch doesn't make anybody *bad*. It's like saying somebody is bad because they were born with red hair or left-handed. How silly would that be?"

He swallowed, those big eyes so full of fear.

"You don't really think your sister is bad, do you? Seems to me she's trying to protect you."

"She was." His gaze moved toward her before coming back to me again. "She's always trying to protect me."

"Okay, then. So she's not bad. It doesn't matter if she's a witch. It matters what she does." I stroked his hair once more. "You know what the Assembly is?"

"Yes." He nodded jerkily. "We had to come live here b'cuz 'Sembly people said so. Dad has..." His brow furrowed as he tried to remember. "He said his mom was a double... the *b* word and that made her a monster, so we're all monsters, but Dina was the biggest monster of all."

His eyes filled with tears. "But if being a witch doesn't mean you're bad, does that mean we're not monsters?"

"You're absolutely not monsters." Brushing his hair back, I said, "Sounds like your dad might be one, but you're not. And I know all about monsters... the scary, bad kind and the not-so-bad but scary kind *and* the not-so-bad and not-so-scary kind."

"You know monsters who aren't scary?" His eyes almost popped out of his head.

The shock in his voice and on his young face gave me some hope. He was still a child, had pieces in him that weren't broken.

"I do. Maybe we can talk about that sometime. But first..." Nodding to Colleen again, I said, "That pretty red-haired witch? She heals people. Can she come look at your arm if your sister is okay with it?"

He bit his lip, looking at Dina.

"Will she take him away?" Dina asked, resigned fear in her voice.

"No." I didn't look at her but had sensed her moving closer while Ben and I talked. Tossing Colleen a look, I thought of Mandy, the daughter Colleen had lost. "Colleen loves kids. She won't let anybody hurt either of you."

"She can come help him."

Dina didn't say it, but I heard the doubt and fear—she didn't think she deserved love, didn't see herself as worthy of help. My heart broke a little. Waiting until Colleen was by my side before rising, I mentally braced myself.

Turning to face Dina again, I tried a small smile this time. "Dina's a pretty name."

She flinched. "It's awful. It was my grandma's name and she's the reason we had to come here. She's why my dad hates—*hated* us." She met my gaze, then, and I saw the truth there.

She'd killed him. She knew she had and she both hated the knowledge and reveled in it.

"Your dad probably hated something in himself, Dina, and he took it out on you." It was a good thing he was dead, too, because I didn't have to fight the urge to hurt him. "That just makes him a coward, and an asshole."

Her eyes widened. A second later, her mouth fell open.

"I guess that's not how I'm supposed to respond." From behind me, I heard Justin's soft chuckle. I reached up to scratch my neck and with my hand obscured, I flipped the amused guy behind me off. "Dina, what happened in there? The fire...was that you?"

She flexed her hands, bringing them up between us to stare at the flickering red glow. She almost looked confused when she lifted her head up. "He didn't know I could do witch stuff. Like fire. Mama said it came from her family and I had to hide it until she could figure out what to do—but...Dad's mama was a witch. We weren't supposed to know that. She was a witch and she could do fire. It was getting harder and harder to hide it and if I'm mad or scared..."

A sob tore out of her and again she clapped her hands over her mouth, but it did little to muffle the keening sound.

I touched her arm.

She flinched, but when she didn't tear away, I reached up and curled my hand over her shoulder.

"It will be okay, Dina," I told her. "You're a witch. That's just who you are. That doesn't make you evil or bad or wrong."

She took a hesitant step toward me.

"They'll..." Her voice broke.

The red haze sparked and the temperature around us swelled, sweat breaking out across my brow and neck almost instantly as my heart started racing in panic.

"Easy." Colleen's soothing voice came like a whisper of cool air.

She'd joined us, subtly nudging me out of the way so she could face Dina. Her hands gripped the girl's forearms, just above the wrist, where that swirl of deadly heat twisted.

"You don't have to be afraid, Dina." Colleen did more than just *speak* with the words. I could feel the power in them, but beyond that, I didn't understand.

"But I—" Dina's voice broke.

"I know. *I know.*" Power, magic, compassion, everything that was Colleen twined around them and somehow penetrated the girl's fear and shock.

Tension melted away and Dina's lids drooped.

The red haze of a pyro's uncontrolled fire magic started to fade.

Relief crashed into me as I realized the crisis was over.

But then, at the very edge of my awareness, I felt something—no. *Somebody.*

Hot, raw energy danced up my spine and I stiffened.

Colleen's eyes flew to mine.

Shit, shit, shit, shit!

One of Damon's cats, a big, brawny bastard by the name of Blue, bounded onto the scene, moving heavier than most cats usually do—he was the one I'd seen trailing me a few days back.

His eyes connected with mine, then dropped to the girl's hands and the fading telltale glow, a sign of a pyromancer with poor control.

He lunged.

Dina saw him and backed away with a startled cry. She flung one hand up as I turned, hoping to grab Blue.

It all happened way too fast.

Pain shot through me.

Silver flashed.

Blue's throaty snarl drowned out the warnings from Banner as they went to flank him.

The shifter moved too fast for the uniformed officers but he couldn't stop the silver now spinning around him in a dizzying cage of ever-shrinking circles.

That silver wouldn't help me, though.

Pain chewed through my thigh, so intense, even adrenaline couldn't counter it. I'd been burned before. Had even been burned bad. But not like this—*never* like this. I was going to puke—or pass out—or worse. My leg threatened to buckle and I locked my opposite knee, balanced all my weight on it. *Stay upright. Stay upright—*

Dina was panting, her brother crying.

"It's okay," Colleen said, talking to the girl.

"Put her under," I said to my friend while the heat around us rose and spiraled.

Colleen swore, but a second later, Dina cried out, a thin, strident sound—and then the heat was gone and Colleen caught Dina, lowered her to the ground.

It was over.

Fuck. It was over.

My blood roared in my ears, darkness crowding in my vision. *Not yet. Don't pass out. Not yet.* Calling my blade, I snapped my arm out, the tip less than six inches from Blue's nose.

He was trapped, held immobile by a cage of silver chains, forged by Justin only a split second after Dina's control over her fire slipped.

"What the fuck, Kit?" Justin said, anger scoring his words.

Blue didn't even acknowledge my blade, his eyes flashing gold as he glared at Justin. "You wanna die, boy?"

"Big and stupid, huh?" Justin's brows shot up and he glanced at me. "Can I kill him?"

"No." Voice shaking and my leg screaming in pain, I said, "I'm about two seconds from doing that myself."

Justin's sharp grin faded and he looked from Blue to me, eyes widening, then narrowing as he looked me up and down. "Shit. Colleen!"

She was on her feet in a second.

I was hot, cold all over, my heart beating so hard and fast, I thought it might explode.

"Lower the blade, Kit," Justin said while Colleen moved in from my side.

"No." Glaring into Blue's eyes, I said, "You just terrified a broken, abused, scared girl. Why the *fuck* shouldn't I make you bleed?"

Blue went to respond, then frowned and looked past me.

The gold faded, replaced by the bland hazel of his human eyes, and he swallowed hard before looking at me. "Kit, I—"

"Shut up," I said, only barely managing to my voice quiet. "Get the fuck out of here. I don't care where you go—the Lair, the beach, or straight to hell. But if I see you anywhere *near* me, I'll start stabbing."

"The Alpha—"

Justin looked at him and clenched his fist. The wires went taut and Blue was jerked into the air, then flung away—hard.

Blue's pained roar faded, a reverse sort of echo that scraped on my nerves.

"Guess somebody's going to be in the dog house..." Justin's attempt to defuse the tension with humor fell flat as he looked me over, his eyes going sharp with anger. "Fuck, Kit. Your leg."

He stepped toward me just as my strength gave out and I pitched to the side.

Chapter Four

"**D**amn, Kit. I don't know how you're not screaming right now."

Wincing as Colleen gently probed the flesh around the burn that ran from hip almost to knee, I focused on Justin's too-pretty face and his bright green eyes.

"The girl?"

"She came around a few minutes ago. Serene and Tate are talking to her."

"Why the fuck couldn't they have arrived on scene two minutes sooner?" I muttered, my hands clenched into bloodless fists as agony splintered through me, like burning shards of glass racing through my veins. I'd *never* hurt like this.

"Bad fucking luck," Justin muttered. "Tate's actually talking to the girl. Serene is handling the Banner cops. She asked me to do it, then stopped when she saw my face. Guess she didn't want to risk me getting into a fight with anybody."

Justin wasn't on good terms with some of the folks at Banner—which was understandable considering their history. They were trying to clean their house, but it would be a long time before some of us trusted them. I was thinking about considering the day after the world ended myself.

"Those kids have been traumatized." Focusing on that wasn't helping much but it was a distraction from the horrible pain in my leg. "Is Tate handling them okay?"

Colleen glanced at me with a half-smile. "Actually, yeah. She's settled quite a bit recently. And these two...well, she'll understand them on the same level you do."

"Yeah, maybe. I've got an idea what her dad was like." I hissed out a breath as she put her hands directly on my flesh this time, just outside the raw, ugly burn running along the outside of my thigh. "Crazy asshole. Oh, *fuck*, that hurts."

"I know." Colleen gave me a swift look, winced. "I'm sorry, Justin."

I tensed but still wasn't prepared for the hard strength of his hands tightening on my shoulders, or for the sudden, agonizing blast of pain that lanced outward from my thigh to tunnel through every vein, every nerve cell. Only sheer instinct, born from too many years of brutal beatings that worsened the more I screamed, kept me quiet.

Blood filled my mouth as I bit my tongue, tears burned my eyes and the world turned into nothing but endless pain.

It dragged on forever, ended in a flash and when Colleen said my name, it took a couple of tries to focus on her. A cold, thick sweat coated my entire body and my bones felt like sludge.

"Don't let go, Justin," Colleen snapped just as he started to do that.

Hurriedly, he steadied me again, lower legs on either side of my hips as an extra support. Colleen leaned in and stroked my cheek. "You with us, honey?"

"Dunno," I said, trying to breathe past the constriction in my throat.

"You're teetering on the edge of shock. Just breathe, okay? If you're still this unsteady when we're done here, one of us will drive you to the Lair. You look like a kitten could knock you over," she said. Through the tears blurring my vision, I saw her frown and she reached up, touched my lips. "You almost bit your tongue in half, Kit...shit."

A faint warmth tingled in my mouth, and a pain I'd barely registered disappeared. "There. That's easily handled, at least. Give us a few minutes to wrangle the lunatics here while you get steadier. They're bitching about a report, but it can wait."

"Their report?" I asked, my voice cracking. Some of the fog was starting to drift away so I chanced to look at my leg. A faint pink scar lingered and I touched it gingerly.

"They can fuck themselves," Justin said in a sour voice, smoothing my hair back from my face with a gentle hand. "Breathe, Kit. Just breathe."

I was trying to remember how. I didn't tell him that, just stared at the mark on my leg with a strange, detached horror.

"It went deep." Colleen brushed her hand over mine. "That idiot cat could have gotten somebody killed. If you'd been human...hell, I don't know how you stayed upright."

Her words broke through that sense of detachment and anger hit hard and fast.

Closing one hand into a fist, I met her eyes.

"I'll deal with it," I said grimly, glancing in the direction I'd last glimpsed Blue, hurtling through the air in a cage of silver.

"Just what is *it* you're going to deal with?" Justin asked, the chilly tone of his voice conveying just how furious he was.

"That's the first thing I'm going to find out." I touched his arm, wasn't surprised when he took my hand. "Damon's down south dealing with another one of the subpacks but I'm going to tear into him about this. I'm done with the babysitters he keeps trying to stick on me."

"Down south?" The ice was gone from his voice, replaced by a tone I hadn't ever heard from him.

I looked at him, but he was staring at Colleen.

So I shifted my gaze to her as well, but she had her gaze on her hands.

"What?" I asked tightly.

She shook her head. "Nothing."

"Bullshit. That's not a *nothing* wince," I said.

"I..." She hesitated. "Why do you think he's down south?"

"Because he's had to do that a lot lately. All the upheaval, ever since Puck..." My words trailed off as Colleen's gaze flicked away. Adrenaline kicked in, chasing away any lingering fog and the fatigue that followed major healings. Surging to my feet, I shifted to stand between the two so I could look at them both.

"What gives?"

Colleen gave Justin a hard look.

"Talk, Justin," I said, ignoring one friend to demand truth from another.

"If he's got her thinking he's running around doing shit in the opposite part of the state, she deserves to know that's not the case." He scowled at Colleen before looking at me. "We were up about an hour north of here checking on a mom Colleen helped last week—baby delivery, almost went to hell. On the way back, we stopped for some food at a truck stop. Damon was there, coming out just as we'd parked."

North. Frowning, I looked at Colleen, then back at Justin.

The only shifter group worth mentioning north of East Orlando was a small fox den. Dair dealt with them for the most part. Damon had met with the alpha of that pack, but only as a formality.

"Did he see you?"

Justin shrugged. "Of course. It was obvious he wasn't in a mood to chat, so as much as it broke my heart, we just nodded at him and he went on his merry way."

The dry sarcasm was probably an attempt to lighten the mood. It didn't work.

Silver caught the sunlight, the chains back in place on Justin's jacket. Staring hard at those potentially deadly delicate links, I thought about Blue's stupid blunder earlier, and all the times I'd sensed somebody trailing me over the past few weeks.

"Don't tell Damon you mentioned any of this," I said, keeping my voice low.

Colleen took my hand. "What's wrong, Kit?"

"I don't know." I met her gaze. "But my gut's gone ice cold."

I PARKED MY CAR IN front of the Lair in the same fashion I'd used early on in my relationship with Damon, fast, hard and loud. As I slammed the door shut with more fury than needed, several gazes flew my way.

Smiles fell, friendly looks turned nervous and by the time I reached the pathway leading to the main entrance, nobody was looking at me and there wasn't so much as a whisper.

One of Damon's younger soldiers cut in front of me, opened the doors but when I looked at him, he had his eyes on his feet.

It made my skin crawl even more.

"Has Blue returned?" I asked.

The kid glanced at me, then away. He was probably about Doyle's age, although you couldn't tell by looking at him. He didn't have that hardened set to his eyes, to his jawline that said he'd been through some shit.

But then again, maybe I was just too damn jaded because of all the shit I'd been through.

"Yes, ma'am," he said, eyes still not meeting mine. "He's...ah, he's with Chang. Here. He's with Chang, in the war room."

His disjointed response and that skittering gaze made more sense now. Chang was typically a laidback type of guy. Not much got under his skin. When you were one of the most dangerous people in the country, there was no reason for things to get under your skin, was there?

But when he was pissed, it wasn't a pretty sight.

It didn't do me any good to hear he was with Blue, though.

I was planning on dealing with that asshole. Striding past the kid and ignoring everybody around me, I took the long main hall that led to the aptly-named war room, used by Damon and his top people for their frequent meetings and the less-frequent meetings with other faction leaders, like Dair or the heads of nearby houses of witches.

The hall was eerily quiet—and empty. It wasn't an easy silence and the emptiness put my back up, because there should have been activity going on. The clan members who handled the group's finances worked out of the office I'd just passed.

Opposite that one sat another room, one usually occupied by Shantelle. I didn't *entirely* understand her job, but it had something to do with PR and monitoring the 'public façade' of the shifters in the region. She'd been busting her ass ever since the debacle with Puck and the rather bloody killings that had rocked the region's vamp population weeks earlier.

Shantelle had a firm open-door policy. Not because the job had a lot of people coming to her, but because she was just that nosy and talkative.

The door was now closed and I had no doubt she was in there hoping to ride out the coming storm without being noticed.

A tension headache pounded behind my eyes, lingering exhaustion from the healing Colleen had done adding to my overall lousy mood. When the door to the war room swung open to reveal Blue, battered, bruised and bloody, I stopped in my tracks.

He had his shoulders hunched and was staring hard at the ground. Either the job done to his nose had seriously screwed with his sense of smell, or he was too worried about whoever was at his back, because he didn't notice me until he was only an arm's length away.

He jerked to a stop, eyes widening as they landed on my face.

"Kit. I wasn't expecting you to return so soon." Chang came around Blue and the bigger, taller shifter fell several steps back, giving way to the older male. Not that Chang *looked* old. Slim, with skin of a light gold and ebony hair, he could easily pass for a man in his late twenties or early thirties—until you looked in his eyes.

Those deep brown eyes were ageless.

In all the time I'd known him, I had rarely seen anything but a hint of humor.

I'd known him for years before I ever saw an emotion stronger than irritation.

Beings that were thousands of years old had plenty of time to learn self control.

I was only making a wild guess at his age, but the beast I'd seen him shift into was nothing even remotely modern, so I had to assume he measured his years in millennia rather than centuries.

As I glared, he tugged a snowy white handkerchief from within his suit jacket and wiped his knuckles off. They were bloody. Bruised, too, but the mottled discolorations faded as I watched.

"If I'd known you were coming, I would have left him alone and watched as you tore a few strips off his hide," Chang said when I didn't respond. "How is the girl and her brother?"

"Colleen convinced Banner to let her take them to the Road." I'd been clenching my teeth so tightly together, my jaw hurt. Looking away from Chang to glare at Blue, I added, "It took a lot more convincing than it should have and it didn't help that they'd watched her lose control of her pyro abilities and burn an Assembly freelancer clear down to the *bone*. If I'd been human, I'd be dead—all because *you* scared the shit out of a thirteen-year-old victim of child abuse."

Blue looked away, a vein throbbing near his temple.

"What, aren't you going to bitch about whatever it was your alpha told you to do?" I said with false sweetness.

Blue didn't respond.

"He fucked up in a very big way, Kit." Chang folded the handkerchief, tucked it away. "But either kill him, bleed him or step aside. He's already in deep shit once Damon returns."

Blue flinched.

But I locked on that last couple of words. "You know what...I think that's something I'd rather talk about. Blue, get away from me so I'm not tempted to turn you into a pin cushion."

Blue hesitated, eyes flicking to Chang.

The older shifter's eyes went cold. "You heard her. *Go.*"

Pissed off all over again, I cut around both of them and exited the hall, heading for the door at the end of the hall. The room reeked of violence—the wet-iron stink of blood and fear putting me on edge.

I opened the window that faced out over the inner courtyard, grateful the skies were clouding over, the promise of rain lingering in the air. Hearing the door click quietly behind me, I clenched my fists on the window sill and forced myself to breathe.

"Blue is an idiot, but he didn't mean any harm, Kit. He's terribly sorry he scared a child."

Closing my eyes, I bit back my instinctive response. As pissed as I was at Blue, he wasn't the main target of my fury. Turning, I braced my hips against the window sill and folded my arms over my chest.

"Why is he having me followed, Chang? Don't you jackasses know by now I can take care of myself?"

There—that flicker of aggravation. He blinked and it was so quick I could have imagined it. Except I hadn't.

"I'm sorry, am I annoying you here? Putting you out?" I asked, my voice dripping saccharine.

"Trust me, Kit. You're not the target of my annoyance." Chang sighed as he moved to the small kitchenette. After putting water on to boil, he looked at me. "I know all too well that you're quite capable. Damon does, too. That's not what this is about—and for the record, I told him it was a bad idea. But...well, in the end, you know how he is. Once he makes up his mind, very few things can get him off the path he has set for himself."

His lips tugged up in a smile, real amusement in his eyes now. "In fact, the few times he *has* deviated, it's almost always been because of you."

"That's nice, but you didn't answer my question."

"You're right, I didn't." Chang angled his head to the side, eyes narrowing slightly. One brow rose, then he smiled. It wasn't a smile of pleasure, though. "I disagreed with Damon's decision, Kit. That doesn't mean I'm going to violate his trust. Besides, he's here now. I hear him near the entrance. Why ask me when all I can do is speculate? Damon can tell you exactly what he was thinking. Would you like a cup of tea?"

"Sure." I flung myself down into one of the chairs at the table, staring at the closed door. I could feel him now, too. Agitated, I picked up one of palm-sized crystal globes somebody had placed on the table. The round, perfectly polished crystals sat in a bowl, the lights from overhead reflecting off them and bouncing rainbows onto the walls. "Why the hell not? I'll drink some tea and pretend to feel civilized."

Chang put a cup and saucer in front of me. He eyed me with a touch of wary speculation, gaze shifting from my face to the crystal sphere I smoothly passed from one hand to the other.

"Shall I leave or am I invited to watch the fireworks?"

Heat rolled down my spine, my low level awareness of Damon pulsing through me. The sensation buzzed and vibrated, prickling against my skin like angry hornets.

"Oh, now, then. Isn't *he* in a mood?" I murmured, shifting the pale lavender globe to my left hand and picking up my tea with my right. I took a sip and leaned back in the chair. Just as I kicked my feet up to rest on the polished wood of the table, the door opened.

Damon filled the frame, the barely caged energy of his beast vibrating around him, somehow making him look even bigger. His gaze unerringly found mine, roaming over every inch, scanning for any visible injuries—and hesitating on my leg, locking on the scorched, gaping hole, no doubt searching for any sign of the burn barely healed.

As much as I wanted a shower, I'd been focused on answers and now I was acutely aware of my own smell.

His nostrils flared and he inhaled slowly. He could scent the damage, even though it was healed—he could smell the burnt flesh, the sweat that had coated every inch of me, exposed tissue and charred muscle, blood...tears.

The skin over his high cheekbones drew even tighter, a vein ticking in his temple, while his leopard's eyes of green-gold swirled with stormy gray.

"Hello, Damon." Chang took a seat in the chair opposite mine, apparently deciding he was going to stay for the show.

"Why in the hell don't you pop some popcorn?" I muttered.

Damon's gaze cut toward Chang, lingered. "Blue?"

"Dealt with, although he's still walking." Chang took a drink of his tea. "As far as issues that might fall into...other, more personal areas, I'll leave that to others to handle. However, I addressed his lack of control that led to his terrorizing of a child. I believe he'll show more caution in the future."

"If the prick has a future." Damon jerked his head to the door, a clear dismissal of the other man.

Chang didn't rise, eyes narrowing in consideration.

Damon turned his head and their gazes locked. It hit like a sonic boom, a violent clash of wills, two dominant shifters who normally walked in step, their relationship allowing them not to just coexist together, but to live as friends—as *family*.

I'd never realized, until that moment, just how much of *himself* Chang kept leashed.

But as the walls of Chang's control came crashing down, I felt the punch of his power like a blow to my psyche and it knocked the breath from my lungs.

My heart jumped into my throat, my mouth going dry as Chang's eyes bled to a yellow so pale, the color didn't seem real.

I don't know when I'd done it, but I was on my feet, heart knocking against my ribs at a speed that left me breathless.

The cool crystal globe warmed in my hand as I clenched my fingers tight, willed the instinctive fear clouding my head to settle. No matter how angry these two were—or whatever the cause—they had a bond that went deeper than heart or soul. They might bitch, piss or moan—or at least Damon might, if you subbed out pissing and moaning for snarling and growling—but they'd never truly harm each other.

So this power display, even if unintentional, was just that.

I hoped.

Those tense moments dragged on forever, but in reality, barely a minute passed. I used every one of those sixty seconds to drag my instinctive fear under control before stepping between them, focusing on Chang.

By putting my body between theirs, I broke their prolonged stare and caught Chang's gaze.

"As fascinating as this testosterone overload is, Chang, I'd rather have my personal relationship matters kept just that—personal."

Damon's gaze bore into the back of my head, his heat crowding closer as he closed in on me, crowding into my space.

"Since whatever has Damon treating me like I'm a child incapable of taking care of myself is clearly *personal*..." I paused and shot him a dark look over my shoulder before directing my attention back to Chang. "Then it's best the two of us discuss this in private. You'll have to get your jollies somewhere else."

Chang cocked his head. After a moment, he dipped his chin, a gracious acknowledgement from the ages-old shifter. "Of course, Kit."

He came toward me, though, instead of circling the table to leave.

"Even after all this time, you never act the way I expect." He rested his hands on my shoulders, then leaned in, placed a kiss that felt almost...paternal on my brow. "I'll speak with the soldiers and other dominants, Kit. What happened today will never happen again."

Then he cut around me.

It seemed that he was going to leave without addressing Damon at all.

But he stopped only a few feet from the other man—one who stood easily a half foot taller and outweighed him by a good hundred pounds, minimum.

That ancient, endless power wound around Chang again as he looked at Damon, and the expression in his eyes was something vast, older than time. It made the hair on the back of my neck stand on end.

"You're not doing her any favors. Or yourself."

"Get the fuck out," Damon said, his voice barely more than a snarl.

Chang sighed, then cut his gaze back to mine. "After I speak with the dominants and soldiers currently on duty, I'd like to check in on the girl and boy. That wouldn't be a problem with Colleen, would it?"

"Doubt it." I lifted a shoulder. "Just call her first."

He inclined his head then left without saying another word to Damon.

The door had barely closed before Damon started toward me.

I backed up a few feet, my hand up in warning. "Don't. I'm so furious with you, I can't think straight."

Chapter Five

Damon narrowed his eyes, the swirling gold narrowed down to mere slits.

"I'm in quite a mood myself, baby girl. So if you feel like fighting?" He bared his teeth at me. "Let's go."

The noise that escaped me was closer to a growl than anything remotely human and it deepened as he took another step in my direction.

"Keep back," I said. "I don't want you so much as breathing on me right now."

"And of course, what Kit wants, Kit gets." He went hunting still, the vivid flags of color on his cheeks deepening. "Shall I sit down so you don't have to crane your head while you read me the riot act over whatever has you so pissed?"

I threw the crystal globe in my hand.

There was no conscious decision to do it, but that snarled sneer on his face and the...*meanness* of it pushed me over the edge. I flung the weighted glass, both of us watching as it arrowed in on him.

He barely reacted in time, ducking down to let it go sailing over his head. It hit the far wall with a crash that shattered the crystal and turned it into a million glittering shards.

"Fuck you," I said, breathing raggedly.

Damon straightened and he was breathing just as hard but I couldn't even look at him anymore. Cutting around him, I headed for the door.

He caught my arm a second before I turned the knob.

"Wait," he said, voice low.

"Why?" I shrugged him off violently and shoved away from between him and the door when he didn't back off. Stalking deeper into the room, I flung a furious look at him over my shoulder. "So you can insult and belittle me again? So you can treat me like some fragile bit of fluff who needs a big, strong shapeshifter around so I don't fall and scrape my knee?"

He didn't respond, eyes averted.

"Why in the hell do you have your men trailing me?" I demanded.

He didn't answer. I almost grabbed something else to throw at him. Instead, I just yelled, "Why the fuck have you decided I need babysitters?"

"They aren't babysitters." A muscle ticked in his jaw and he finally swung his gaze back to mine, let it trip down along my body to linger on my thigh. "How badly were you hurt?"

"No." I folded my arms over my chest, my heart a strange, hollow ache inside. What was going on? Why was he acting like this...and why wasn't he talking to me? "No. You don't get the courtesy of a reply on that until you explain the reason for Blue's presence today, since *he's the fucking reason it happened*."

"I'll make sure—"

He dodged to the side but even as fast as he was, he only barely missed the projectile I hurled at him. This time, it was a heavy bronze statuette of an Amazon warrior Shanelle had given me. It made a huge hole and was trapped, the base securing it in plaster and drywall.

"Decided to have a tantrum, huh?" He gave me an arrogant smile. "Going to pick up something else to throw? Great way to handle this, Kit."

"*You* are the reason that mess happened today—the reason a *child* got terrified—the reason *I* got burned to the fucking *bone*, Damon!" It hurt to just force those words out through my tight throat. I was so furious I could barely breathe. And under the fury, there was hurt. For a second, I felt the prick of tears and the thought that I might actually *cry* left me paralyzed.

Damon saw something in my expression and he sucked in a breath, swore quietly.

But when he started toward me again, I backed up.

"No," I said, shaking my head. "No."

This time, he listened.

"Blue was there, following his fucking Alpha's orders. He makes a great little soldier, Damon, but he's not too great at thinking on his own." I was cold now, so cold I had chills and I had to fight the urge to cross my arms over myself and huddle in for warmth. "Whatever *reasons* you have for putting your toy soldiers on my ass, *you* were the reason I ended up with burns all the way from my hip down to my knee, burns that went down to my fucking *femur* in some places. If I had been just a *little* more human, I'd have died from shock alone—even Colleen being *right there* wouldn't have been able to save me."

Damon's jaw went tight.

"Tell me why I'm being followed!"

He spun away, prowling the floor like the leopard that lived just under his skin was trying to claw free. "It's only been a few weeks since one of your grandmother's psycho spawn came looking to drag you back to her, Kit. Have you forgotten?"

The viscous ache inside deepened, went cold. He was lying—or twisting the truth to suit him. I wasn't sure which, but he wasn't being honest. I felt it in my bones and the knowledge cut deep, slashed through my anger and fear to draw blood straight from my heart.

Talk to me, I thought. *Give me something.*

Some bit of truth.

When he didn't, I cut around the table and headed for the door.

"What, no smart-ass remark?"

I looked at him, that cold inside now spreading through every limb, every cell, leaving me numb.

"There's no point in continuing this conversation, Damon. You'll only keep lying and it's not like I can stop you." My throat hurt, the knot there so huge, it pained me to speak. Something here was wrong—*very* wrong and the words Chang had uttered to Damon earlier only made my gut tighten even more. "But don't expect me to stand around and pretend I don't know you're lying, either."

He reached me before I had the door open.

"I'm not lying," he said, the words so deep and rough, they were barely intelligible. He slammed a broad hand against the door, my strength no match for his. "You know damn well it's not over."

"Move your hand, Damon."

"No. You were about ready to tear my head off a minute ago—spoiling for a fight, so let's have it out. Throw something else. Hit me."

I looked up into his eyes, saw the flicker of worry, maybe even panic, but it was gone almost as soon as it had appeared.

"Why? All you'll do is lie or sidestep when I ask you the same question." The lines around his eyes deepened and he flinched, although whether it was because of the truth I'd flung at him or the weird, flat tone in my voice.

Backing away from him, I shook my head.

How many mornings had I woken up to reach for him, only to find he was already gone? How many nights had he come in after I was already asleep?

Too many to count. It would be easy to brush it off due to the chaos in the city, but my gut told me not to. I thought of the morning just a few days earlier when he'd touched me, all greed and need. But had he been there when I woke later? Now that I thought of it, he hadn't been there when I woke for *weeks*.

We hadn't had a real conversation in weeks.

"This isn't even the first lie you've told lately, is it?"

He didn't deny it.

"That's what I thought." The misery inside was almost too big, too intense and I thought it would crush me. Pushing through it, I gave a short nod. "Since you're not ready to be honest with me, there's no point in fighting. Not over lies and half-truths."

His hand fell away.

I slipped out of the room, the long corridor in front of me no longer empty as it had been earlier. I ignored them all, save for the tall, lean man at the very end who stood talking to Chang.

"Why are you here?" I stopped a few feet from Justin, acutely aware of Damon standing in the open door behind me, watching all three of us.

"Colleen sent me. The two rug rats sort of bonded with her—like instantaneously." He reached up, brushed my hair back from my face, tucked it behind my ear. "General consensus was that you probably didn't have any of the tonics she'd want you to drink after that healing earlier."

He held out a small cloth bag.

I took it. "Thanks."

Vivid green eyes, bright as new spring grass, narrowed slightly as he studied me. "One of the brews is a newer blend," he said. "She wants you to try that one first, told me how to prepare it, but wants me to hang for a little bit, see if it's doing the trick—might be too strong, or not strong enough. She healed you up all the way, but there might be some muscle aches or cramps—it was a bad injury and she doesn't want you hurting once the adrenaline wears off. She wasn't sure, so she wanted to be on hand, but...well, rug rats."

He was lying—or, rather, twisting the truth to suit his needs. Justin had been the one to teach me that little trick. But he'd rarely used it *on* me and despite being weary of lies and twisted truths, I could have kissed my friend for the easy out he'd offered, for knowing I needed it without me saying a word.

I didn't want to give Damon a reason to pick a fight with my best friend—or *another* reason. Damon and Justin got along better than they used to, but it wasn't always an easy fit, and it sure as hell wasn't friendship.

I definitely didn't want to talk to Damon anymore so I stepped back and nodded at Justin. "I'm still not feeling altogether right, so it might be a good idea to just have her check me out again. Can you run me over in a bit?"

"Do you even have to ask, Kitty-kitty?" Justin gave me a charming smile.

Behind me, Damon's breath came out in a low, raspy snarl.

I caught Chang looking at us but before I could jerk my gaze away, he gave me a sad smile. "Perhaps I'll visit the children another day, Kit. Get some rest. You need it."

Rest...fuck. How could I *rest* here?

"Won't be able to do that yet," I said, sidestepping the truth without lying, well aware of a pair grey eyes boring into me from several yards away. Two could play at this 'lie-without-lying' game of his. "That poor girl isn't out of the woods yet. Reports have to be filed and a bunch of other shit any time something like this happens. Justin, you good with running me around, then driving me out to see Colleen? *Somebody* thinks I need a babysitter and I'm fucking exhausted anyway."

I heard a growl behind me, felt Damon's hot glare on the back of my neck.

But he said nothing.

What was there to say at this point?

Chang's brows came together slightly, his eyes intent on my face and I knew he was picking up on far more than I'd like. But he didn't out me.

"You bet, Kit. Let's get to HQ and make sure we've got the kids squared away." Justin nodded at Chang as he spoke, then led me to outside to where his bike waited.

WE LEFT THE LAIR, DRIVING in the direction of HQ, but once we were a mile away, he pulled over and stopped, then, without looking at me, he said, "You do know I took care of that report, right?"

I just nodded. "Get me out of here, okay?"

"Where to?"

"Colleen's." I could have some quiet there, think. That was all that mattered right now. "But be careful. We might have a tail."

"Give me some credit, Kitty-kitty." Then, in a dazzling display of speed, he pulled away from the curb and hit the ground-to-air controls, leaving East O. behind while I clung to his waist and buried my face against the leather of his jacket.

The next half hour sped by in a blur of wind and power and speed and I pretended nothing existed but my friend, his bike and the miles speeding by.

But too soon, he was putting down in front of Colleen's house.

Now, powering down the sport craft, Justin waited for me to climb off before slanting a look at me. His big, vivid green eyes were full of concern. "You want to talk about any of that?"

After turning over the helmet, I considered the question. It didn't take long to decide I most definitely did *not* want to talk about 'that,' so I started to shake my head, then swallowed. "I don't know. He's lying to me about something. And it's more than just him being in another part of the state earlier today. Whatever it is he's hiding, Justin, it's...big. It's bad. He's been... on edge for weeks but with everything going on, I brushed it off. Now...I just can't.."

"We're all on edge, honey." Justin sighed, averting his head to stare off into the distance. "I don't like the dick, but he's the leader of several thousand shifters and they're under a shitload of pressure right now after everything that's happened the last few months. Maybe—"

"No." I closed my arms over my mid-section, an attempt to comfort myself against something I couldn't begin to name. "Whatever this is, it has something to do with me, Justin. I can feel it."

You're not doing her or you any favors.

Chang's words circled through my mind again, the way he'd looked at Damon. What he'd said to me only minutes earlier.

And...

Shifting my attention to Justin, I said, "You ran into him earlier. North of the city."

"Yeah." He shrugged, moving his shoulders restlessly, as if the leather jacket and his muscles didn't settle quite right on his frame. "Look, Kit, he's got..."

The words trailed off as he caught sight of my face, his jaw going tight.

"Something wrong," he said, giving up on whatever comfort he'd been ready to offer.

He didn't particularly like Damon, probably never would, but he knew I loved the big bastard, knew Damon would go to the ends of the earth to protect me, care for me. He also had a fair amount of respect for the other man, much as Damon had for him.

But Justin knew me well, recognizing the signs of uneasiness I couldn't set aside.

"Wrong?" I laughed weakly and shoved shaking hands through my hair. My fingers caught on snags and snarls, the sweat from the day's events still clinging to me. I wanted a bath—*craved* it, but I was so damn tired, I'd probably fall asleep if I tried to soak in a tub. "I don't know if something is *wrong* now or if something's going to *be* wrong. I just know things aren't...right."

"Is there a difference?"

I glanced at him. "You know there is. Whatever this is, it's *bad*, Justin, and it's going to get worse."

His scowl deepened, then smoothed, jaw going tight as he considered what I said. "Kit, I don't like that prick but he loves you. He'd slaughter whatever came between the two of you."

Thinking of Dina now, I shook my head. "After everything that's happened today, I don't think that's as comforting as you want it to be."

Justin grimaced.

A door slammed before either of us found more words to fill the silence. I looked over at the sound of small feet hitting the paved stones between us and Colleen's house.

The small tow-headed boy I'd met earlier came to a stop in front of me, small chest heaving as he tipped his head back to stare at me.

"You're alright."

No, I wasn't. But I wouldn't tell a small boy that.

"Hello, Master Ben."

He blinked, thick lashes shielding big blue eyes. "Me and Dina didn't know if you were...Dina, she burned you bad. We both knew it. Are you here to take her away?"

"Ben..." Justin sighed.

I lifted a hand to Justin, letting him know I'd handle it. Then, hunkering down in front of the boy, I smiled. "I don't *take away* girls *or* boys just because they get scared, Ben."

"But she hurt you. When a witch hurts a human, she's gotta be punished."

"Well, I suppose it's a good thing I'm not human." The surprised expression on his face tugged a thread of amusement from me and I scrunched my face at him. "What, did you think I was human?"

"You don't feel like a shapeshifter," he said, darting a look from my face to Justin's. "And you're not a witch—you would have been able to do something to stop Dina if you were. And I hear your heart so you're not a vampire, either."

Rocking back on my heels, I appraised the boy. "You can hear my heart?"

His face paled and he stumbled back a few steps.

"Easy, Ben." Hands up, I said, "I'm not going to hurt you. Nobody here wants to hurt you *or* your sister. I was just asking because...well, that's pretty cool. I don't know anybody other than shifters or vamps who can hear that good."

Too sore and tired to remain in the position I was in, I rose. Ben didn't come any closer but the tension eased and he gave me a tentative smile. The lingering fear in his eyes gutted me.

"Listen...the laws about humans and non-humans are fu...messed up. But nobody is going to do anything to Dina about what happened earlier, okay?" Desperate to do *one* thing right today, one thing good, I brushed his hair back from his face and some of the tension in my chest eased when he slowly nodded. I caught sight of that hope in his eyes, the barest flicker. Ruffling his blond hair, I offered my hand. "Think Dina would be okay if I checked in on her?"

He accepted it, tucking his much smaller hand into mine. Justin fell into step next to us as we started up the smooth river stones that made up the path to Colleen's front door.

She waited for us there, opening it wide as we came in and once she shooed Justin and Ben off, she pulled me into a hug. "What in the hell, Kit? You're so raw inside, it's like somebody's been playing kickball with your heart."

"Excellent analogy." I wasn't familiar with kickball, but if it was anything like what it sounded like? Then, yeah. I sure as hell felt like somebody had been kicking my heart around—somebody with big-ass size 14 boots at that. Darting a look toward the sound of muffled laughter, I said, "We'll talk outside, but I want to see the girl first. Let her know I'm okay."

Colleen studied me, then gave a slow nod. "Alright. Do that. But then we talk...and you're drinking some tea." I made a face and she smiled. "I'll be nice and spike it with some honey and whiskey, though."

Chapter Six

The smell of bacon, eggs, coffee and fresh bread greeted me when I left the bedroom the next morning and made my way to Colleen's big, airy kitchen. Justin had his hips resting against the island, both hands on Colleen's waist and they were locked in a kiss that left me wondering if they'd notice me.

Since I wanted caffeine like I wanted air, I decided to risk it.

"I told you we shouldn't start breakfast," Justin said as I reached into the cupboard for a mug. "She's got a nose for bacon and coffee."

"Ignore me." I grabbed a big blue mug and closed the cabinet, my back to my friends. "I just want caffeine so if you two want to keep playing tonsil hockey, have at it."

There were a few quiet sounds, then a grunt from Justin before Colleen announced, "*I* was all for staying in bed, thank you very much. But this mama hen over here figured you'd be up and moving around early and he wanted to cluck over you for a few minutes."

She joined me at the counter and when I looked at her, she studied my face. After heaving out a weary sigh, she said, "Well, at least you slept. That's something, I guess."

"I drank that damn tea—sleeping wasn't a choice. I don't remember much of anything after you decided we should finish up the discussion in my room." I flexed my right thigh, wary of the injury from the day before, relieved to find there wasn't even a lingering ache. The dull throbbing that had started on the ride over was gone, too. "Leg feels good as new, though, so I guess the tea did the trick."

"Nah. The tea was to help you sleep. It was the tonic I gave you while we were outside that helped with the leg." She arched a brow when I shot her a hard look. "What? You needed some rest. All I did was give you some tea with belladonna and valerian."

"Belladonna...*nightshade*?" I gaped at her. "You gave me *poison*?"

Justin choked on the drink of coffee he'd just taken, while Colleen snorted. "If you were fully human and I gave you a high enough dose? Sure. It would be poison, Kit. As it was, it was enough to just help you *sleep*." She huffed out a breath. "After all these years, you're suddenly questioning my skills with herbal healing remedies?"

"Yeah, because you just told me you gave me *nightshade*!"

"Please." She came closer to lean over the counter and smirk, the deep, forest-green of her eyes glinting with mirth. "You're still breathing, aren't you?"

Justin moved in on her while she was distracted with me and boxed her in against the island.

"Hey!" Laughing, she spun around to push him away, but he just pinned her again, and Colleen didn't try very hard to evade him. After a moment, she reached up to cup his face in her hands, his warm brown skin a stunning contrast against her paler hands. The look on his face was one of sheer, utter adoration and it made me smile.

But the sight filled me with a strange ache, too. Now, feeling more lonely than ever *and* irritated by the idea of my friend using nightshade on me so I'd sleep, I spun away from them both and came to an abrupt stop, reaching out to steady the woman who'd just come around the corner into the kitchen.

She was older, standing roughly my height. Heavier, with a face gone soft with age, the typical eye might have glanced past her. Mine didn't. I held her gaze for several moments, because her direct, frank inspection made it clear *soft* wasn't the right word for her.

Belatedly, I realized I recognized her. We'd seen each other a few times, but only in passing, and most of the few occasions had been either here or at the local Green Road House in East O. She was one of the witches there, which gave me *something* of an excuse for not picking up more readily on her presence. But only a little.

Fuck, my head was a mess.

"Ah...hi," I said, heat creeping up my neck as I backed up a couple of steps. I'd been about ready to smash right into her when I spun around, throwing her off balance. She was still gripping the wall in an attempt to steady herself, her knuckles gone white with the effort. "Sorry about that."

She gave me a polite nod, her gaze drifting past me to seek out Colleen. "Colleen, how are the children?"

The children—

Fuck. I'd totally forgotten about the boy and his sister. Shifting, I watched the unknown witch move around me toward Colleen.

"Still sleeping, Bea." Colleen glanced past Bea to give me a reassuring smile. "Bea, this is my friend, Kit. Kit, Bea helped me settle the children yesterday. She had to leave for a while and by the time she came back, you were already in bed."

"Okay." I glanced at the woman again.

Bea offered a short nod, her eyes moving away again.

"Oh, the two of you will get along *splendidly*," Colleen muttered with a roll of her eyes.

Bea snorted and eased around me, moving with the care of somebody who lived with pain. I saw Colleen's eyes darken with worry as she watched Bea.

The other woman made her way to the teapot on the stove, not paying me any mind.

Colleen noticed my attention and gave me a speaking look: *Be nice.*

This time, I was the one who rolled her eyes.

"Bea's a talker, Kit, which you probably noticed," she said to me. "I asked her to come meet the kids. She's already spoken to them a little, will spend more time with them today."

"Why?"

It was the older woman who answered, not looking away from her ministrations with the tea kettle as she did so. "The girl needs training. They both need love, and a home. Colleen thought I might be useful."

This woman seemed about a cheerful and loving as a porcupine at the moment.

Then she glanced at me, the look lasting a little longer this time. "I'm not really awake yet and unless you're a child, it's in my nature to *not* like you. If you want to subject me to an inquisition right now, do it at your own peril, or wait until I wake up and get some coffee in me."

That startled a laugh out of me. "Okay, I can relate to that. I'm a bitch in the morning, too."

There was a flickering glint of humor in the other woman's gaze as well, but then she turned away and went back to preparing tea, putting bread in the toaster and generally ignoring me.

"Bea's one of the few witches with the Road who has a gift over fire," Colleen said, bringing me a cup of coffee and a plate of eggs and bacon. "Plus, she's spent a lot of time working with...damaged children. There's nobody I'd trust with Ben and Dina more right now. They need her."

"Okay." I didn't even have to consider it. Colleen was one of a very few who had earned my unquestioned trust. A stab of hurt deep inside made me realize that list was smaller than I'd realized.

Yes, I trusted Damon with a lot of things. My life. My love. But it had just been driven home that I couldn't trust him to be honest with me. I couldn't trust *him* to trust *me*. And fuck if that didn't feel like somebody had ripped a massive hole in my chest.

"You're still hurting," Colleen murmured.

"My leg's fine," I said absently. I poked at the food she'd put in front of me, leaning against the island once more, too on edge to sit, my skin tight and itchy and my heart aching.

"Not what I meant." She held something to me and I reached out, took it reflexively.

My phone. Turning it over, I stared at the blank screen.

"I turned it off last night," she said. "Asshole kept calling and I got tired of hearing it."

My thoughts turned to the tension that had been growing between me and Damon. I hadn't realized just *how* tense things had gotten until it had all nearly boiled over and burned us both last night.

He'd called four times since I'd left the Lair, sent a half-dozen messages, the texts ranging from his typical brooding self to apologetic and back to asshole.

A knot settled in my throat and I put down the coffee without taking a drink. As I reached up to rub at my temples, I blew out a breath.

A shadow fell over me.

"You okay, sweetheart?"

Meeting Justin's eyes, I gave a half-hearted shrug. "I don't know. The mess with Damon yesterday, then finding out he's been lying about where he's going when he leaves..." The ache in my chest grew and I rubbed my fist over it. It didn't do anything to ease the clenching pain. Unable to stay still, I paced over to the window. "Something's going on with him."

"He's scared." Justin hooked his arm around my neck and pulled me in for a hug. "Damon Lee is a big, mean, mouthy bastard who can pretty much just snarl at anybody who gets in his way and they back down. The few who don't? Well, if they are stupid enough to go toe to toe with him, he shreds them. But now he's facing this threat he can't terrify into submission—and it's not him that's in danger, Kit. It's you. Guys like him don't do fear well."

"You think I *like* fear?" I muttered. I knew Justin was right. Well, maybe not *right*, but nothing he'd said was wrong. But I don't know if fear was driving Damon right now. I'd seen him in the driver's seat when fear was the force behind his actions. This was...different.

He was in a place where I couldn't reach him.

He'd been cold—*hard*. Practically a stranger, and icy in a way he'd never been, even when we'd first met. And *mean*.

"Talk to him."

"Yeah, I tried that. Didn't go over well." Nudging him back, I pressed my fingers to my temples, the headache there edging in and demanding attention.

Justin saw and turned away, then came back, pushing my coffee into my hands. "Get some caffeine in you, then sit down. You need a meal."

Nodding, I took a sip, then trudged back to the table and my waiting food. I'd managed two drinks and got down three pieces of bacon before a familiar metallic *ping* chimed in the air, two long notes followed by two shorter notes.

"Great," I muttered with a dark look at the phone. One text dispatch from the Assembly lit up my screen. I didn't have a chance to read through before it was followed by a second.

My phone rang thirty seconds later and I answered, the familiar voice of an Assembly dispatch officer barking out my name, "Colbana?"

"Yeah?"

"You're being called to the field. General alert will follow shortly, going out to every available asset, but everybody with silver clearance gets the initial notice. Details being sent in five." The man's gruff voice went silent for a brief pause, then he said, "Heard you took an injury yesterday. You mobile?"

Rubbing the back of my neck, I responded, "I'm good. A healer was on hand, so I was only down a night."

"Good. Target is a rogue shifter, last seen in the area of the Everglades. Wanted DOA. He's already killed a couple of humans, so we need him taken down fast."

"Got it." But he'd already hung up. Without looking at Justin or Colleen, I said, "Guess I'm skipping the rest of breakfast. Got a rogue shifter and I've been specifically called to join the hunt. Lucky me."

"You want company?" Justin asked.

I looked back over my shoulder at him, smiled. "No. Right now, finding and killing something will probably be therapeutic."

"Killing?"

I glanced at Colleen. "Wanted DOA—dead or alive. Apparently, he's already killed several humans, so they want him found fast. Since he's DOA, taking him down and bringing him in dead will be the easiest."

"Why DOA?" she asked, the healer in her clearly uneasy.

Justin stroked a soothing hand down her back. "Whoever it is has gone rogue, baby, so there's no choice. It's either the shifter, or a bunch of other people."

Over her head, he met my gaze. "Be careful—and if you get in a bad place, call me."

"Yeah, yeah." I crooked a smile at him, then gulped another swallow of coffee. I wasn't about to tell him that I really needed a hunt like this—a bloody, brutal hunt might be the only way to clear some of the shit out of my head. And wasn't that just a sign of how fucked up I was?

I looked over to say goodbye to Bea. But she'd already left.

Damn. She was quiet.

I went to hug Colleen instead.

"You good to give me a ride back?" I asked Justin.

"Sure thing." He looked me over one more time, his gaze direct. "You've got from here to East O. to convince me you're fit to go on your own."

Narrowing my eyes, I said, "Don't you start."

"Shut it," he advised. "We used to be partners. I know you better than just about anybody else, so that gives me the right to ask if you're in the right head space for a hunt that could turn fatal. And you'd do the same for me."

His hard green gaze killed any anger I might have felt, because he was right.

"Fuck, you really are a mama hen. Fine. Let me grab my stuff." Over my shoulder, I flipped him off.

DAMON WAS GONE BY THE time Justin dropped me off at the Lair.

He'd sent a text not long after Justin and I had left Colleen's place for East Orlando and I'd responded, keeping it short and not particularly sweet.

> *Heading out on a hunt soon. DOA down south so I'll have my hands full for a while. Not feeling particularly chatty right now, either, so stop bothering me.*

I'd debated on whether to tell him anything else and decided against it. I didn't need my head any more messed up than it already was.

Ten minutes before we got to the Lair, he sent back a terse response.

> *Fine. Stay safe. We'll talk when you're back. ILY.*

The shorthand for *I love you* had my throat going tight *and* left me wanting to call him just to yell. I shoved both urges aside, locked them down to deal with later.

Once I hit the long hallway that led to our quarters, I made a beeline straight for the door, grateful the place was quiet, doubly grateful I didn't sense him anywhere near the area.

Now, as I finished strapping a drop-leg holster into place, I stubbornly pushed out all thoughts of our fight out of my mind. Hunting a rogue shifter while worrying about my love life might actually be a cure to those problems, but I'd prefer a less lethal solution than ending up dead because I got distracted on the job.

"Kit?"

I studiously didn't look at the tall, broad-shouldered young man standing in the door, focusing instead on collecting the proper ammo for the weapon I'd be carrying.

"What is it, Doyle?" Collecting several boxes of custom-made silver alloy ammo, I added them to my pack. Feeling his gaze on me, I turned and met my cousin's blue eyes. Cousin. It was weird thinking of him like that, even now. Looking at him with the knowledge I had, it was so obvious, I couldn't believe I'd ever missed it.

Doyle's eyes slid away from mine and he shifted uncomfortably. "I can't stay long."

The tension in his voice had me looking at him. "You still avoiding Scott?"

"Avoiding? No. Just don't particularly want to be around him for the time being—my tiger still wants to peel his skin off." Doyle grimaced. "Since I can't take him yet, it's best to keep my distance until the anger levels off."

A few weeks earlier, Scott and Doyle had been in a very bloody fight. I'd learned some of the details from Doyle after the fact—and Doyle had learned the truth about our relationship, that his mother and mine were sisters.

For a brief period of time, I'd worried the secret I'd been forced to keep would damage the bonds we'd formed, but he'd forgiven me.

Whether he'd forgive his mother, Rana, I had no idea, but I could understand his anger. I had plenty of my own I was still dealing with.

"I still feel like shooting Scott through with another barbed arrow," I offered. "So, there's that."

He smirked. "That remains one of my favorite memories, Kit, truly." His smile faded a moment later and he looked away. "Ah, hey, listen...I heard about yesterday. And Blue. I'm sorry."

"It's not your fault."

"In a way, yeah, maybe it is." He blew out a breath. "See, the thing is...that's why Scott kept trying to run me down. He was going to put me on Kit watch. I refused to do it—that's why I've been taking assignments from Chang for the past month. Maybe if I'd ..."

His words trailed off as he caught sight of my face. "Look, I'm not saying I wish I'd agreed, but I would have known better than to rush in on a scared kid."

"I'm not mad at you, Doyle." Sucking in air, I fought the urge to scream. "I'm not, okay? And I understand how Clan hierarchy works. You have to follow orders."

"I'm not going to be used to spy on my cousin," he bit off, the words coming out in a rough growl. "Scott's let the issue go because I've been reassigned to work under Chang. And he knows I won't be used against you. But...Damon's mentioned it a couple of times. I've told him I won't do it but he keeps asking—right now, it's *just* asking, too. But I don't know if that will change. He's got some idea in his head you won't argue with me which makes me wonder if he's lost his fucking mind."

"That's entirely possible." I offered him a tired smile. "I argue with *everybody*."

Doyle didn't smile back. He came a few steps closer, his normally too-mature expression looking far too vulnerable. "I...look, I asked Chang for something that would get me out of the city for a while and he gave it to me. I'm heading out of the state here once I'm done talking to you. I just had to make sure you were okay and..." He stopped, looking uncertain.

"I'm alright, Doyle. Really." Not comfortable with the easy touch that so many shifters gave, I moved in and gave him a quick hug.

His arms came around me before I could back away, squeezing tight.

"Hey...hey, I'm okay," I told him, hugging him back. Several seconds passed and I realized it wasn't really that awkward. Not with him. He was...family. No. It was more than that. Family had never been a good thing for me. Doyle was *more* than family. He loved me. I loved him. And he was safe.

"My head's buzzing lately," he said, finally breaking away. "You know how you've been helping me with...everything. And there's something going on with Damon. Whenever I'm around him, I'm on edge, like I'm going to come out of my skin and my tiger's too unsettled right now anyway. So I've got to get away for a bit."

He glanced away as he said it, and I realized he felt guilty. "It's okay. I understand. Get out of here. Damon and I had it out last night over that very thing—I *know* he's hiding something and I've had it. This babysitting shit just put me over the top. I'm heading out myself here in a few—HQ sent out an alert and I was requested. There's a DOA hunt and I'm actually looking forward to it."

His eyes narrowed. "DOA...you got a handle on it?"

"I'll be fine." I gestured to the door. "Go. Get out while the getting is good. And...thanks for...everything."

He came back to me, crushed me close in another tight hug. "Don't say thanks. If I'd been with you yesterday, you wouldn't have gotten hurt. I know better than to scare a little witch."

"Not your fault." I hugged him back, then nudged him toward the door. "Go. Get out of my hair so I can gather up my kit and get out of here myself."

He was gone before I finished speaking.

Not five minutes passed before I felt the prickle of one of the stronger shifters ripple over my field of awareness—faint, then growing stronger. The longer I was with Damon, the more acutely aware I became of his top soldiers, including the lieutenants who helped run the far-reaching pack. Scott made an appearance another minute or two later, knocking on the door Doyle hadn't shut, probably because he'd expected the older shifter to show before I cleared out.

"I'm on my way out, Scott. I've got an assignment in the 'Glades." Leveling a look on him, I added, "Just an FYI, I've got silver-spiked ammo in the .45 I'm carrying and if I see even *one* shifter on my tail, I'll shoot—and I won't miss."

A muscle pulsed in his cheek as he inclined his head. "How's the leg?"

"Fuck you," I said succinctly. "Make sure you advise Damon of the warning about the silver ammo, because I'm not kidding and I will not miss. You assholes could have gotten me killed once already this week—don't add to it."

He stood in stiff silence, not replying as I stormed past him. I wasn't sure if it was because he didn't want to lie—or because he had nothing to say.

Since I didn't trust him to pass on my message, once I got to the car, I called Chang.

His smile faded as his eyes connected with mine on the monitor. "You don't look like you slept well, Kit."

"I slept well enough. I'm heading south on a DOA hunt."

Chang inclined his head. "Riordan."

"Yeah. You know much about the case?" I hadn't called for any insights, but I'd be a fool not to take any advice Chang offered.

"Precious little. He can't be saved, though. He took human lives, brutalized people while his own children were within hearing range. Regardless of the provocation, he's stepped over the line." Chang delivered the words in a cool voice, gaze void of pity.

He had no sympathy for somebody who'd do anything that harmed a child.

"That was my take. I'm not really calling for insight on him, though. I need you to leash Damon while I'm gone."

Chang's brows rose. "Leash the Alpha."

"Don't use that tone," I said, anger scoring each word. "You can pull him back. I've seen you do it. If he sends somebody to tail me while I'm on a DOA, it's as likely to get me killed as anything else. You know it as well as I do."

Chang looked away but after a few seconds, he gave a short nod. "Try to avoid complicating my life by getting hurt, Kit. Damon's already a rather large pain in my ass at the moment. He'll become unbearable if you get hurt." He looked back at me, smiling finally. "And I rather like you in one piece myself."

Chapter Seven

Crouched in a hide, I swiped my forearm over my brow. Who in the hell would choose to live on the edge of a Louisiana bayou?

I'd been tracking the wolf from the emergency alert for two days now, first discovering the lead about the 'Glades sighting had been bogus, then tracking my target to this hot, miserable spit of land in the bayou.

All but two other teams had been recalled.

I was also *sans* chaperone. Chang had taken me at my word. I'd received a text from him a day into the hunt, after several more bodies had been left in Riordan's wake.

> *No local shifters will interfere with your hunt for L. Riordan. But please endeavor to avoid making my life difficult by not getting hurt too badly.*
>
> *Damon is troublesome enough to deal with as it is. If he gets any worse, I might strangle him.*
>
> *I've already had to interfere with an offer from a small pack of black bears in Louisiana.*
>
> *They heard you were on the DOA and made the offer and I told them to stay out of the way but the Alpha wasn't happy. She only stepped down after I told her that I'd take any interference personally.*

L. Riordan—aka Liam Riordan—wasn't an unknown name, not in this region, and not in general. Born human but changed over in a violent attack three years earlier, Liam Riordan had been a popular rising music star living on the outskirts of Nashville, Tennessee before his attack.

After the attack, he'd disappeared from public life. A lot of people assumed he'd died. Dair had filled me in as I made my drive down. The wolf Alpha had all kinds of information about Riordan, and he'd relayed all of it with a grim tone in his voice.

Riordan had been living in the region of a sub-pack under Dair's control, watched over by an alpha who had, at one point, been one of Dair's top people.

Natalie Winslow was tall, willowy and model-beautiful—and according to the reports I'd heard, her dominance was enough to make you want to shrink back, just being in the same room with her.

She was just a step or two lower on the power scale than Damon and Alisdair, the two Alphas who reigned supreme in the more southern regions of the country.

According to Natalie, Liam had apparently been looking to get back into music, hoping to reestablish some semblance of his old life.

He'd managed to get control over his beast and the raging wildness of the power within, so Natalie hadn't seen any reason to keep a constant watch over him when he left the pack lands that dominated much of western Tennessee.

Her territory now encompassed the land of the Smoky Mountains, too. Her people had established a smaller satellite den in the general region where Justin and I had once hunted a vicious alpha who thought nothing of mutilating his own kind.

It had been one of Natalie's pack members who'd reported Liam's kill, after Natalie sensed something *off* in whatever connection alphas had with their packs and clans.

That had been five days ago.

His fiancée and his former manager had been found dead in the cabin Riordan had designed and had custom built on the outskirts of Nashville, identified only through DNA—numerous body parts were missing.

Two children had been found, unhurt, locked in a bedroom, a large, bloody pawprint on the door, along with the words:

The son of a bitch stole my fiancé, my life and my boys.

On the counter in the kitchen near the cooling bodies had been a telephone, an email app left open.

"The attack was premeditated, Kit," Dair had told me. *"I've had people looking into it and I'll find the wolf who was hired, assuming he isn't already dead. If he's alive, he won't be much longer. The manager and Riordan's wife were having an affair and they wanted to get Riordan out of the way in a fashion that couldn't be tracked back to either of them. I have no idea how he found out, but he did and...well, I can't say I blame him for killing the manager, even the ex. This was straight-up attempted murder by bite. If it was just those two, I might have tried to intervene with the Assembly, although I doubt I'd succeed. But he killed others who had nothing to do with the attack and he traumatized his children, forced them to listen as he murdered his ex and his former manager."*

"He wants to die."

Alisdair's long, lingering silence had told me the answer before he even spoke. *"Yes."*

Now, as the sun sank closer and closer to the horizon, I watched the little shack where Riordan had holed up. He knew I was out there. Twice, he'd passed in front of the small, grimy window and peered in my direction. I couldn't make out his face, not at this distance in this low light, but I'd felt the intensity of his gaze and knew he sensed me. Considering the sauna-like heat around me, he could certainly *smell* me.

I could smell me.

I was tired of jobs that required me to end up sticky, sweaty and smelly.

I was getting tired of waiting, too.

The thick growth of the bayou provided excellent coverage and if it wasn't a shifter in the little structure roughly a thousand yards away, I wouldn't even worry about being spotted. Hell, I would have moved closer, taken my shot and called in for reinforcements—Liam Riordan was a big bastard. DOA or not, I might need a hand to haul his ass out of here, but if there was a chance I could plug him with a couple of tranqs and take him in alive? I'd do it. Not out of consideration for him, because he'd left hurting people behind who deserved to face him.

But the rage beating at my skin, boiling out of that little shack wasn't giving me a good feeling about my odds of making that happen.

He passed by the window again, the gloom of the coming night making it harder for me to pierce the shadows cast by numerous trees. Tree trunks, cypress and tupelo, ranged from spindly to massive and the canopy overhead created a false twilight that made it clear I'd have to make a decision sooner rather than later.

Night was coming and the aggression beating at my skin warned me that Riordan was still out for blood—even if he was chasing his own death, he wouldn't mind spilling more on his way to meet his own end.

He wasn't going to add mine to the mix.

Going head to head with a predator blessed with night vision in a swamp seemed like a *supremely* bad idea.

No, I needed to get this done, and now, before it got any darker.

"Well, let's do it then," I muttered. Readjusting the close-fitting skullcap I wore to hide my pale hair, I eased out of the tree, moving quietly and taking care to watch the front of the cabin.

I'd just let go so I could drop to the earth when the door opened—slowly, so slowly, I could hear the ominous creaking of hinges desperately in need of repair.

Landing in a crouch, I moved to put the tree's bulk between me and the shack, eyes trained on the building as Riordan emerged.

I'd looked him up while doing my preliminary work on the job. There had been nothing of use online to help in my hunt, but the pictures of him in his former life—before the attack—had shown a man who'd been almost ridiculously good-looking, with an easy smile and bright, friendly blue eyes, a tousled mane of blond-streaked brown hair that likely required regular salon treatments.

There was nothing of that person in the enraged man staring out into the night at me from the ramshackle stoop barely attached to the shack.

His blue eyes swirled between their natural shade and the amber-gold of a wolf's. Dried blood streaked his face, bare chest and forearms. I couldn't see his hands well, but had no doubt that they'd show the evidence of his murderous rampage, too.

The thick, matted strands of his hair were dark, likely with blood and other things. Although the swamp carried a number of scents, I caught the stink of decay and blood wafting in the air. My sense of smell was nowhere as near as sensitive as a shifter's, but he reeked so badly, it stained the air. He hadn't washed any of the blood off—at all. He'd been wearing the blood of his former fiancée and her lover all this time.

"Who did they send for me to kill this time?" Riordan called out.

Despite the madness, I could hear the golden tones, the lyrical cadence that had launched him into stardom. I'd never been a fan of country music, but this guy's voice was something else.

I didn't answer or move.

When he spoke again, the lyrical tones deepened, made less beautiful as a primitive growl took hold. "Come out, girlie. Don't make me hunt you. You won't like it."

"Why is it guys always think shit like that is going to work?" I'd held off answering as I readied my weapons. Task done, I came around the tree, the modified firearm in my hand lifted and aimed before I'd even finished speaking.

He'd been smiling but at the sight of me, the smile faded. "You think that little toy is going to do the trick?"

"It's done well enough in the past. I don't suppose I can convince you to make things easy on us both and just come along quietly?"

Something flashed in his eyes. A flicker of grief, regret...then rage.

"Come along quietly." He spat on the ground. "Assembly fucks sent you after me, didn't they?"

"You killed your ex, her lover, and three innocent bystanders on your way out of Tennessee and two more on the way down here. What did you think would happen?"

Instead of answering, he threw back his head, an enraged howl tearing from his throat. His body started to change, clothes ripping and muscles swelling while bones broke and reformed. His upright form was almost perfect and when he lowered his head to stare at me, the cutting intellect in his piercing gaze struck hard.

This was a tragedy.

"You didn't have to do this," I said softly. "You got dealt a shitty hand, but why turn around and murder innocent people because two people you cared about fucked you over?"

He snarled, powerful body dropping into a crouch.

"Don't." Some stupid part of me felt pity. I saw the hurt and anguish in his gaze and felt *pity*. "You don't want to take this route, Riordan. It won't end well."

"You should be running, girlie. That gun won't stop me."

"Yeah. It will."

He lunged.

I fired, hit center mass, exactly where I'd aimed. The iron-rich scent of blood filled the air.

He kept coming.

I fired again.

Then again.

By the fourth squeeze, he was on top of me, his lips back in a grotesque approximation of a smile just before that ugly maw, a meld of lupine and man, lowered to my neck. I dropped the gun, struck out with a fist and hit him in the throat.

He started to choke, surprise filling his eyes. His movements had finally started to slow and his gaze began to cloud. Thank God.

"Yeah, I'm stronger and faster than I look." Shoving and pulling, I started to wiggle out from under him.

The sounds of the swamp resumed around us, birds calling out, insects chittering and farther out, gators with their sonorous bellows.

Claws tore into one bicep as I finally wrenched free of his weight and I couldn't bite back a yelp of pain. It ended in a screech that was half-rage, half-agony as monstrous teeth closed around my left forearm. Instinct and training took over, my sword coming to my free hand as Riordan jerked at my limb in a frenzy, his hindbrain finally clicked to what was happening.

I thrust the blade into his gut.

He tightened his grip and grabbed for my throat.

Too close for the sword—

Another weapon came to my hand, one with a ghostly whisper, like wind through a bone yard.

I struck, another gut wound.

The world turned sideways, pain at my trapped hand still tearing through me, then I was free.

"Move, little sister."

The voice. "Aw, shit...not you again. Not *now*."

Even as that thought circled through my head, my body took over and I rolled over the ground until I hit my knees. The shifter thrashed next to me, still fighting although the powerful sedative was at work in his system and blood loss from the wounds in his gut would further weaken him. I hurtled to my feet, blood pounding like a scream in my ears—

No. That *was* screaming.

Actual screaming.

Cradling my wounded forearm to my abdomen, I staggered up the small stoop before turning.

In the final, dying light of day, I stared down at Liam Riordan as he beat sluggishly at a monstrous alligator. The prehistoric creature had massive jaws locked around Riordan's thigh. In his half form, Riordan's thighs were thicker than my waist and he was likely close to seven feet. But he was no match for the gator. Maybe if he hadn't had four doses of Night in him...

His gaze locked with mine, agony in them.

No. He definitely wasn't getting the easy way.

Drawing the firearm I carried in a drop holster at my thigh, I sighted on Riordan. It took a few seconds—the gator's thrashing and Riordan's own desperate struggles redefined *moving target*.

The blast seemed far louder than normal. The sight of the wound on his forehead, a bloody circle, was immediately followed by the silence of his screams and the end of his struggles—all his struggles. Keeping an eye on the gator and trying to ignore the nauseating pain in my left forearm, I ran to grab my dart gun.

If Night, a powerful sedative, could take down raging shifters, it could put a big-ass gator to sleep, right?

The alligator spied me, but with the carcass of Riordan between us, he probably decided he had enough food.

"Good boy," I told him, retreating to the questionable safety of the shack. Once on the stoop, I sited on the gator, grimacing at the thick, scaled hide. I plugged him twice.

"I only need a little bit of him, you big lizard. Then you can have the rest."

It took several minutes for the sedative to work its way through the gator's system. While I waited, I bandaged my injured arm with some of the supplies in the small kit I'd zipped into one of the numerous pockets on my vest. I had a larger kit in my pack that I'd left secured in my car and another one in the smaller pack still stowed in the tree, but neither did me any good here.

Mind flashing back to another time I'd had to hide in a forested, swampy wetland, I paused.

The sound of bone crunching stirred me and I shook the memories off.

This definitely wasn't the time to get distracted.

The gator's heavy lids drooped slowly, then lifted and he moved with his prey toward in the direction of the water.

"Fuck," I muttered soundlessly.

But the gator only moved a few more feet before it stopped. Riordan's body hung from its jaws at an odd angle and even in the weak light, I could see the ever-growing wet pool spreading from the mouth.

If the leg wasn't severed, it was close to it.

As I neared, I could see the gator's eyes had finally closed. I didn't immediately approach, though. I'd had enough of being bitten today and until my arm healed, I was well and truly handicapped. There was no way I could win against an alligator—especially not one that size.

Tossing a sturdy, short stick at it from several feet away, I waited. He didn't move.

Riordan's head was turned in my direction, dead eyes staring at me in accusation, as if he knew what I planned.

Not my fault, you prick. You didn't have to go stark-raving mad and kill people.

After a few more seconds of watching the gator, I approached. The big lizard didn't move and although the hair on the back of my neck stood on end, my gut told me it was out for the next little while.

Keeping the corpse between us, I caught Riordan's outstretched hand in my good one. Slowly, I started to drag.

There was no movement from the reptile.

Gristle, muscle and sinew kept me from separating Riordan from the gator, especially one-handed. I used my sword to make short work of that before hauling my grisly prize farther away.

I let the bigger predator keep the leg. He'd earned it.

Then, I went about the second part of the job.

Since there was no way I could walk Riordan himself out of here to prove the job had been completed, I had to provide other proof.

It was hard work, one-handed, and by the time I finished, it was completely dark. Dragging the head into the shack with me, I dumped it by the door and fumbled a small flashlight from my pocket. After making sure there were no surprises waiting inside, I turned the thin beam of light on the sightless eyes of Liam Riordan.

"You stupid asshole. I should have put a bullet in you the second you walked in front of the window the first time."

But I hadn't and now I was stuck in the small, smelly, shack until morning. Even worse? I got to do it with minimal supplies, while dealing with the coming fever.

The chills were already started and my skin felt hot.

The virus in Riordan's saliva had been in my system long enough for my body to start fighting it. It wasn't possible for me to change into a shifter and I'd been bitten often enough that my body recognized the invasive virus quickly—and fought back aggressively.

Riordan had been fighting to kill, too, sinking his fangs deep and holding tight, sending that toxic poison deep, deep inside.

Stumbling toward the small bed I'd spied, I grabbed the blanket and yanked it off. It was stained with blood and smelled.

The sheets looked almost clean, though. With a weak laugh, I collapsed, still clutching the small flashlight in my hand.

"This is going to be so, so much fun..."

Chapter Eight

W*ake, little sister.*
   I did just that, the nasty, bitter taste of fear and the acrid taint of nightmares coating my tongue.

Worse, I was sweaty, stinking to high heaven and aching from long hours spent gripped with fever as the damn virus fought my immune system and lost.

Light fell in through grimy windows, my surroundings unfamiliar. The scent in the air was rank, choked with old blood, death and fetid water.

My memories were a hazy mess—alligators and wolf eyes...?

And none of that bothered me as much as the voice whispering in my mind.

Wake, little sister. People come.

It was a familiar voice, one filled with echoes and the chill of death.

"Okay. Hearing the boogeyman. Not good," I mumbled, my tongue all but sticking to the roof of my mouth. "Not good at all."

Dragging myself upright, I looked around. With each passing second, the sticky cobwebs cleared from my head. My gaze landed on something by the door.

In a blink, the events of the past night were instantly clear.

I went to drag a hand down my face, but yelped at the sight of the knife in my grasp.

The blade was old, beyond ancient, but if one went by looks alone, one might think she was newly made, fashioned to resemble a weapon from antiquity. But I could *feel* the age in her; it was a weight that made my teeth ache and left my hand almost numb at first touch, although that faded within moments.

Like almost every weapon I'd ever touched, the blade *spoke*. But unlike most of the tools of my trade, this weapon's 'voice' wasn't very clear.

Unless Lemera chose to whisper to me from it, it wasn't just one voice I heard, but a meld of them, so many, I couldn't pick them apart.

And sometimes...I heard *screams*.

I couldn't identify just when I'd started to hear those. The music of my weapons existed in the back of my head all the time, a quiet hum I'd grown used to, first from my sword, then slowly growing with each new weapon I acquired.

This blade's eerie whisper could have started the moment I'd picked her up, but been lost in the chaos.

But it had never been this clear.

Never.

I could pick apart individual voices as I sat there. And some spoke in a language I recognized...the language from my nightmares.

Throwing the blade down on the bed, I shoved upright and paced a few feet away.

"Stop," I said softly. Sweat beaded on my brow. Swiping my forehead with my arm, I stared out the filthy window and made my breathing slow, willed my racing heart to calm.

The blade didn't *want* me to calm down, those erratic whispers rising in a deafening roar.

Spinning around, I shouted, "Shut up!"

And there stood Lemera.

The other voices faded as the ghoulish being cocked her head. "You must *leave*. Do you not hear them warning you?"

"Is that what that was? A *warning*?" Flinging a hand toward the knife, I said, "Since when did that thing speak in tongues?"

She blinked slowly, an eerie as fuck action, since her lids were rotting away. "The blood know many languages, little sister. But that is not important. People come. People who hunt—"

I wanted to scream. Talking to a being who had been dead for centuries was a pain in the ass. The deadly specter who was, in effect, my grandmother's pet killer, wasn't exactly obtuse, but she sure as hell wasn't easy to have a casual conversation with.

And I'd been having a number of conversations with her. For some reason, Lemera liked talking to me.

This wasn't the first time she'd warned me of danger, either.

If she said people were coming, she was probably right.

"Do you hear me?" she demanded, her words now filled with an ominous echo that told me she was either getting pissed or impatient.

Probably both, and I hated that I could read this spooky bitch well enough to know that.

"I hear you," I said wearily. Grabbing the knife, I checked to make sure it was clean, then jammed it into the sheath in my boot. My head spun a bit as I straightened and I flung out a hand to steady myself, but there was nothing to grab onto.

My knees started to wobble.

"Easy, little sister."

Her cold hands touched my arms. They were solid and scary strong and I instinctively jerked away, memories of blood and meat and gobbets of tissue that should never see the light of day flickering through my mind.

Gorge rose up the black of my throat and I swallowed it down.

"Sit," she ordered and her strong, dead hands made sure I did just that.

A wave of nauseating pain rolled through me as my butt hit the thin, dirty mattress. I would have kept on going backward if she hadn't stopped me.

Icy fingers touched my brow as I sat there, sweating and panting.

"What are you doing here? I didn't call you. I left your blade at home," I said weakly.

"No, little sister." Those fingers, as cold as the waters of the North Atlantic that had surrounded the home of my childhood, traced my brow, then withdrew.

Instinct forced my eyes open and I looked up, watching her study my arm as the thin, scraggly strands of hair that might have once been the same gleaming blonde as my own fell into her face. That hair was dull and large patches were missing, showing the scalp, and in some places, the skull.

A shitty night besieged by fever and pain from a shifter's bite had slowed my reaction time—a *lot*.

Maybe if my reserves hadn't been completely drained during the healing Colleen had done after I'd been burned, I wouldn't be running on empty now, but I was.

I hadn't had anything to eat or drink all night, my body burning through fuel as I fought the fever from the bite. My food and water was still stowed, secure up in the tree to keep it safe from creepy-crawlies while I dealt with Riordan. After he bit me, I'd been hurting too much to try and get it. Now I was paying the price.

A pallid, powerful hand clamped around my arm.

Pain tore through me with jagged, razored claws.

The agony was even worse than it had been when Riordan had bitten me.

So, *so* much worse. I screamed, spine arching as I jerked to tear away from her. Adrenaline did nothing to numb the impact, either.

I felt her nails, the jagged, sharp stubs digging into flesh.

I felt the freezing kiss of her proximity as she bent closer, catching my right wrist as I swung out in delayed reaction, squeezing, squeezing, squeezing until I dropped my sword. It fell onto my lap, then clattered to the floor.

I heard her voice even above the roar of blood in my ears and the thin sound of my scream.

"Be still, little sister," she said, her voice was hollow as always, and flat. "Too many others are tracking the one you killed and you cannot fight them with this wound. You will die. I have seen enough of the blood die. I will not see it happen to you. Not today."

Sweat broke out over my skin, clammy and thick, so viscous, it might have been blood.

The pain in my arm started to pulse and under it, cold spread.

"Let me go," I said as my teeth began to chatter. "Let...muh-me...guh-go..."

Ice spread up my arm to my shoulder and neck, up and down, until I felt it in my brain and chest. And on and on...it closed around my heart in a brutal fist.

"Try not to fight it, little sister. It will not kill you."

"Luh...luh...let..." I could barely move my lips. They were so stiff.

I'd never been this cold. Not even when I dragged myself out of the water all those years ago.

"Luh..."

Darkness crowded in on my vision.

Pain exploded through my chest as she slammed a fist onto it.

"You will breathe," she ordered. "Breathe *now*."

The adrenaline rush I'd been denied finally hit. With a ragged, hoarse scream, I tore from her and lurched upright. Everything whirled around me and my limbs resisted each movement, but I stumbled across the small cabin, eyes locked on the muted sunlight coming in through the filthy panes of glass.

I heard no movement but I sensed her behind me.

Spinning, I turned and reacted, the music in my head drowning out the rush of blood and dulling the pain, panic. My sword hadn't been in my hand when I turned, but by the time I lifted my arm, she was there.

I pointed it at the specter made flesh.

"What in the *fuck* was that?"

Lemera smiled, the gaping maw of her lipless mouth oddly...different. Her eyes were clearer—fuller. Something that might have been amusement glinted there.

"You needed full use of your arms," she said.

There was nothing threatening in her words.

In fact, her voice sounded more corporeal than it ever had.

And that absolutely terrified me.

As if she sensed what I was thinking, her smile widened. "Does it not feel better?"

"Does..." Swallowing, I tore my gaze from her and looked down at my left arm. The bloodied bandages were still in place. Slowly, I made a fist.

There was no pain—*none*.

Sucking in a breath, I stumbled and only barely managed to steady myself before I fell backward. Tearing the bandages away, I looked at my forearm. There was a scar, the skin pink and new and beneath it, I felt the deep ache of an injury still healing, of muscles needing rest and time to recover.

But my arm was *whole*.

Curling my hand into a fist, then releasing it, I watched as the muscles flexed smoothly under my skin. That bite had been *bad*—very bad. If I hadn't been so sick last night, I probably wouldn't have slept worth a shit as I'd worried about possible nerve or tissue damage.

Stunned amazement tore at me and I slowly looked at the being in front of me. "What did you do?"

"I take in much power when I collect the souls of the blood," she said, her voice pulsating with a terrible, awful knowledge. "And much power when I reap vengeance. But I cannot use it. It is the power of the living. It sits within me, a useless thing in a dead vessel. It has been collecting for...a very long time. I gave some of it to you."

Mind racing with those words, I tried to understand what she meant. A thousand questions formed.

I had no time to ask a single one.

"They come from the east," she murmured. "You must go. Your injury is healed but the fever drained you. You do not need to fight if it can be avoided."

THE PROBLEM WITH DOA tags is that they bring out some of the worst sort of people.

The sanctioned teams had been recalled once Riordan was pinned down—a trapped animal will lash out, bite and kill and too many in one spot doesn't necessarily improve the odds.

But with a DOA tag, there's nothing you can do about the *unsanctioned* teams. They'll hunt until the person is dead and the bounty is collected.

A lot of bounty hunters will stay away from the typical Assembly DOA contract. There are always crazy, desperate or just plain stupid fools out there who will risk it, though, and those people have a way of picking up chatter when it comes to shit that will get them money.

Most of them were little more than scum, some even worse than the killers they hunted, because they weren't operating on instinct or driven mad by blood hunger or a shifter bite.

They were just greedy and didn't care who got hurt, as long as they got their money.

The only good news was that most of them stayed cleared of NH hunts, DOA or otherwise.

But the bounty on Riordan was massive, the concern for public safety rampant after his attacks through Tennessee and the other lives he'd taken as he headed south. It had called the greedy out in droves and my already shitty hunt had just gotten worse.

Eying the nasty metal trap in front of me, I rubbed the back of my neck, then shoved upright.

"You are being too slow," Lemera said, talking to me as if I were a child.

I didn't respond, looking around for something heavy enough to set it off. I couldn't leave it here like this. It didn't matter if the men I heard were drawing closer. This trap would kill just about any human unlucky enough to get caught in it. I wasn't having that on my conscience.

I adjusted the quick-release band at my chest that held my gear secure, taking a wide berth around the trap.

Lemera appeared in front of me, blocking my way.

"You need to *run*," she said, voice urgent. "You retrieved your weapons and the dead wolf's head, but now you are wasting time. Run."

Getting pissed, I pointed at the trap. "Do you not see that?"

"As you have been staring at it since we stopped, yes, I have seen it." Her eyes glowed, eerie and bright. "It's a trap. Are you going to die over it?"

"I'm going to disarm it," I said, the words coming out through clenched teeth.

There had been a case about five years back. A wolf shifter kid, not even ten years old, had been roaming in the back country out west and came across a trap not too dissimilar from this—it had severed his right leg.

He hadn't yet hit his spike, either. The spike, the period of puberty for shifter youth that kicks off the change in their bodies that allows for greater speed, increased healing, strength *and* the ability to shapeshift, usually doesn't hit until fourteen or fifteen at least. He'd been far too young.

Even though one of his friends had been close and heard him scream, help hadn't arrived in time.

He'd died of blood loss before his father arrived.

They'd been able to locate the fucker who put the trap down and even though the piece of shit was arrested for reckless homicide, he was found *not guilty*.

If the kid had been human, the man would have gone to jail.

But shifter kids aren't worth such consideration in the eyes of too many.

I went to cut around Lemera again, the memory of the boy's face haunting me.

"You do not have time for this. You can't fight all of them."

I looked away from her to the trap. It was big enough to bring down a bear—or a full-grown shapeshifter. "If I don't disarm it, it could kill somebody, because they won't come back to take care of it—they never do."

It had been well-hidden. Only a faint glint of light reflecting on metal at *just* the right moment and a prickle of awareness on the back of my neck had alerted me to it.

The thing *definitely* would have brought me down.

"Traps like these kill people—they've killed children."

Lemera blinked, head canting to the side as if she were considering, then her expression cleared, as if she understood a puzzle I'd placed before her. "Yes. We shouldn't leave it." Then, slowly, a smile curved her lips. "It could also kill the men who placed such traps, yes?"

Eerie power emanated from her and her visage rippled. She smiled again while the whispers in my mind grew louder and I fought to block them out.

I was almost grateful when I heard leaves rustling behind me—still some distance away, but enough to warn me I needed to get moving.

"You do not have time to disarm this." She frowned.

Rising, I glared at her. "I'm not leaving this here where it could kill some unsuspecting hiker. A human, a shifter kid? They'd stand no chance."

"I know. I understand now. You can go, Kitasa," she urged. "I will make sure it harms no child. I will deal with the trap."

Indecision warred inside as I studied her, gripping the sack that now held Riordan's severed head.

"You cannot wait. They hunt *you* now—they know you killed the prey they sought. That makes you their target." Her head canted to the side and she tipped her face back, drew in a breath slowly, scenting it, tasting it. "They lust for blood and gold and pain."

There probably wasn't any reason to tell her people didn't get paid in gold these days. Her point was clear.

And it made my decision rather obvious.

I'd been hunted in a wetland like this before.

I had no desire to do it again.

I also didn't have any problem with people dying if they had intentions to harm me.

If I let creepy ghost girl handle things, I didn't have to worry about shit coming back on me, either.

At least, I *hoped* that was the case.

I HEARD THE SCREAM less than ten minutes later.

It was a sound so full of pain, it raised the hairs on the back of my neck. I froze, the urge to go help so strong, I spun around and was twenty feet back down the path before I realized what I was doing.

The second I stopped, the cacophony of whispers rose in my head. *Run, run, run...they're coming, girl! Run!*

The rush of noise, a flurry of whispers that roared in my ears like blood chased me as I spun back around and retraced my steps, continuing out of the wetlands. The screaming continued, too, but after a couple of minutes, it became fainter, then, faded altogether.

He would die. We were too isolated and I'd gotten no sense he was anything but human. They wouldn't have a chance to get a medical team out here in time, so he would die. It was a weight I had to carry, but better him than some innocent person. They had set the traps, after all.

No! Not that way! An overwhelming rush of panic grabbed hold of me just as my own instincts whispered a warning, urging me away from the trail I'd been about to take—the one that led out of this hot, miserable hellhole

Hissing out a breath, I looked around and tried to think.

There. That way, one of the voices in my head whispered.

"I'm going crazy," I muttered. But I listened, and took off down what couldn't even be called a game trail.

The whispers in my head fell to a faint murmur, the words less distinct now. I couldn't hear any noise on my backtrail. I heard voices behind shortly after, realized there was more than one group out here.

Fuck.

The flurry of whispers rose, but ebbed, something about the cadence soothing this time. Twice more, an almost overwhelming rush of fear sent me heading in a different direction than I'd planned, a primal fear that made me certain some nightmare creature was about to emerge from the shadows and devour me.

Of course, there *was* a nightmare creature in the area. She'd healed my arm.

Then she'd knelt in front of a massive metal trap meant to capture bears and the like.

After giving me another one of those strange smiles, she'd touched the trap, then both she and the metal contraption had disappeared.

I had no doubt she'd gone to place it in the path of the men tracking me and one of them was probably dead now, the others furious over what had happened.

A brush of cold against my skin was the only warning I had before Lemera appeared next to me.

The noise in my head went silent, or maybe it was drowned out by *her*. There was no room for anything in my head when she was near. Even the music of my blade was muffled, dulled by a thunderous, crashing white noise that made simple *thought* difficult.

"Hurry," she said. "There are more. Two more groups. Three men stayed with the dying one, but they won't be long now. They'll hunt you. They are angry." She gave me that unsettling smile once more. "I showed myself to them—only a glimpse. They do not realize what they saw. If they come for you again, I will show them what happens when they seek to harm one of the blood."

Uneasy, I looked back in the direction of the shack.

"If you make a mess like last time..." Back in Orlando, her kills had been...well, disturbing wasn't quite right, but I couldn't think of a word gross enough to do her work justice.

Brow furrowing, she studied me. Her stare pierced, as though she could see straight into my skull and divine every thought circulating through my head. Her smile returned, even wider than before and she gestured again.

"Go, little sister. I will run them into their own traps, or into the waters where other predators will make a meal of them. They will not know who hunts them. Be swift. I am weary and must rest."

She was gone in a blink, far too fast to tell her I didn't need her help.

And how in the hell could she be *weary*? Ghosts didn't get tired, did they? They were already dead. It wasn't like flitting back and forth was some sort of cardio exercise.

I went to shift the pack on my back and my left forearm twinged, that lingering ache reminding me of what she'd done. I shivered and got back on the move. Creepy ghost girl could handle the humans out there.

The more distance I got between me and this mess, and soon, the better.

Glancing down at my arm, I brushed my fingers over the pink scar.

Run, run, run...you have to run.

The storm of whispers and screams returned, slamming into me with a force that almost knocked me to my knees.

"Fuck," I muttered, driving the heel of my right hand against my eye socket, trying to push those memories out of my head.

I take in much power when I collect the souls of the blood.

A shudder raced through me as I considered just what that might mean.

"Fuck. Fuck. Fuckity fuck..." With a groan and more effort than I liked, I shoved those thoughts aside, and then, using training I'd learned from Colleen, I erected a mental barrier against those ghostly screams and whispers. "Hope that doesn't affect my weapons."

As if she knew I needed the reassurance, my sword's song rose in the back of my mind for a single moment before falling silent. My palm heated and I called her to my hand, the well-worn leather of her grip familiar.

Chapter Nine

Hours later, after driving non-stop save for a break to refuel and empty my bladder, I arrived at HQ and dumped Liam Riordan's head on the desk.

It was still in the cooler from my trunk and as the uniformed guard studied it, I nudged it closer.

"I want my fee deposited. Now."

The older HQ task manager pushed a pair of eyeglasses up his nose, then gave up after they slid back down, taking them off and settling them on top of a thatch of thick, curly gray hair.

"Our Mr. Riordan, I assume?" he asked, sounding bored as he came off his stool and sniffed the cooler before unsealing it.

"No. It's Tinker Bell. She's on the top of the DOA list last I heard."

The task manager barely blinked. "You're in a foul mood, aren't you?"

I didn't answer. I'd been feeling miserable for days and today hadn't helped at all. I was still filthy, stinking to high heaven and sticky with sweat and blood, but I hadn't wanted to stop to deal with any of that. Those voices, endless whispers in the back of my head, hadn't silenced more than a few minutes here and there until I'd crossed into East Orlando.

I desperately wanted to crawl someplace quiet and hide so I could figure out what was going on.

But the one place that had felt safe didn't feel so safe anymore and fuck Damon for doing that to me.

If the old guy across the collections' desk counters from me was put out by my silence, he didn't show it.

"Alpha Lee's looking for you," he said as he hefted the pressure-locked lid off the bio-hazard cooler. "Just in case you're wondering."

"Peachy." That was the last thing I needed to hear. "Can you confirm identity?"

"Hold your horses." He sighed, clearly unconcerned about my impatience, and pulled on gloves to reach into the cooler. "Where's the rest of him?"

"In the gullet of a big, hungry gator."

That caught his attention. "A gator."

"He holed up in a shack in some Louisiana bayou and put up a fight, tried to take my throat out. I loaded him up with Night and an alligator decided he wanted to take him off my hands." Hitching up a shoulder, I offered a bland smile. "Since he was a DOA tag, I figured I only needed the head, so why fight the gator?"

The desk clerk grunted. "Guess the head shot was to put him out of his misery?"

"Yeah." I made the mistake of looking down in Riordan's wide, filmy eyes. "Poor, dumb bastard."

"He chose to go on a killing spree, Colbana. You did what you had to." The clerk used some blood from the neck stump, dabbed it on a slide. While the DNA scan hummed away, he tried to get a retinal scan but grunted and gave up after a minute. "Too dead for it. Better scanners in the morgue, but as long as the blood trace checks out, you'll be fine."

In under five minutes, he'd confirmed the kill, gotten my signature for delivery and payment processing and finished all needed paperwork.

"Is there a solo bunk handy?" I asked as I did a status check on the payment for the finished job.

The old man eyed me over the table, eyes squinted, but when I offered nothing, he shrugged. "Matters have slowed down a mite. Nobody taking up any of the bunks here in HQ—even the infirmary's cleaned out. You did hear me when I told you Alpha Lee's been checking in on you, right?"

"I'm not deaf." Holding out a hand, I said, "Solo bunk? Preferably in a quiet hall."

He sighed and reached under the desk, pulled out a key. "North hall. Last room on the end. Dunno why you'd stay here in a coffin when you got the Alpha—"

Turning away, I strode toward the door without waiting for him to finish.

No less than five cats from Damon's clan had seen me come into East Orlando and I had no doubt each one had contacted the Lair to pass on an update on my location.

Damon would know I was fine.

Tomorrow, we could duke this out. Tonight, I needed a shower and sleep.

ASSEMBLY HQ HAD FACILITIES onsite for contract employees. There was nothing fancy about them, but they were clean and had plenty of hot water. I kept a locker there with clean clothes and a small stash of toiletries so I wasn't forced to use the industrial-strength quality of the soap they kept on hand. The heat of the water revived me at first but by the time I'd washed my hair a third time, my arms were so heavy it was a struggle to lift them and I rushed through the rest of the shower.

Clean but exhausted to the bone, I shoved my dirty clothes into my pack and rummaged around until I found a protein bar I hadn't eaten. After shoving my boots on and swiping a towel over my wet hair, I hefted my pack onto my shoulder and headed out.

I'd already emptied the canteen I'd refilled upon hitting HQ and stopped to refill the insulated container a second time. I devoured the rest of the energy bar as I made my way to the small, private bunk I'd been assigned.

Cold chills raced up my spine as the whispers in the back of my mind started up once more and the now-healed wound pulsed with a dull ache. Fuck, I was tired.

Pushing the door at the end of the hall open, I stepped in, kicked the door closed and fell against the wall, shrugging out of my pack and letting it fall with a hard thud to the floor.

The whispers grew louder, rising to a crescendo.

I was two seconds away from clapping my hands over my ears and begging for silence when the strange, eerie echoes went quiet.

Jaw clenched, I held still, almost afraid to move for fear they'd start again.

After ten seconds of silence, I breathed out a sigh of relief. *Lemera, you scary bitch, what did you do?*

I almost expected her to pop into view in front of me.

Whether I was too exhausted from the events over the past few days or if the number Lemera had done on me had fried my instincts, I was utterly unaware that I wasn't alone in the room.

When the light clicked on, I shoved off the wall, going for the gun at my hip.

I never pulled it, my gaze landing on the big, heavily muscled shifter as he uncurled from the chair.

"Kit." Damon's low, growling voice filled the room, even though he'd been quiet.

The cold chills were gone, my skin now hot and tight, a sensation that grew under the intensity of his gaze. Some of my lethargy faded and if I hadn't still been so angry, I might have flown at him.

133

Instead, I took another drink of water from my canteen, then capped it and threw it on the narrow bunk.

"I see my babysitters checked in accordingly," I said in a mocking, sugar-sweet tone. "Give them a tip before you send them home, Daddy. They do such good work."

"Nobody was following you, baby girl." He paused a moment, then added, "But you already know. You made sure of it by telling Chang how if I tried to have you watched it would probably just end up getting you killed."

"Well, you don't listen to me." I shrugged, not feeling even a little guilty for throwing Chang in Damon's way.

He opened his mouth, then snapped it shut. Eyes narrowed on me, he gave me a look from head to toe, scrutinizing me. "You're not hurt."

Not now. My chest tightened, heat, hunger, need flaring to life inside.

"Your powers of observation are amazing." I bared my teeth in a sharp smile.

He blew out a slow, controlled breath.

The sound of it pleased me. I was pissing him off and I was petty enough to take pleasure in it. Dropping on the bunk, I bent down and unlaced my boots. "Whatever you want to say, say it, then go away. I'm tired."

When he didn't say anything, I looked up. My damp hair fell into my eyes but I was too tired to push it back so I stared at him through a fringe of the pale, damp strands.

His eyes burned gold in the dim room. Now, gazes locked, he came over to me.

My breath hitched as he knelt in front of me.

But he stayed silent and reached for the boot, brushing my hands aside to take over the task.

I straightened, hands curling into fists, skin tingling where he'd touched me.

He had his head bent low, the short, wavy strands of his hair gleaming in the dim light. I started to lift a hand to stroke, stopped myself. Tangling my fingers in the thin blanket beneath me, I fell back on sarcasm, needing distance. "You planning on leaving the Alpha industry behind, Damon? Looking for a long, rewarding career as a valet?"

He tugged the second boot off, hands warm against my skin. "Getting mouthy and prickly isn't going to work, baby girl."

My brain short-circuited as he gripped my ankles, then slid them up my lower legs to my knees. Muscles clenched, trembling, I tightened my hold on the blanket as he lifted his head to meet my gaze.

Maybe if I'd been able to look into his gaze—*glare* at him, *maybe* I could have held him off.

But my gaze fell to his lips and his breath shuddered out of him, an echoing breath tripped out of my lungs, forcing my breasts to rise against the thin material of the support tank I'd pulled out of my bag.

His eyes dropped, slid down the column of my neck, lower. Under the weight of his gaze, my nipples tightened, stabbing into the thin, form-fitting material of the black tank.

He reached up, hooked a hand around the back of my neck and yanked me to him and our mouths came together in a clash of lips, teeth and tongue. Breathless, I broke the kiss and tore free. "We shouldn't do this here."

Damon tugged at my nipple, pulling a cry from my lips as he lowered his head to my neck. "You chose the location, baby girl. Fuck, your scent...you're already wet. I can smell it..."

Danger and something I couldn't quite name emanated from him, surrounding me in a pulsating, seductive cloak. My blood felt too hot, too thick and my heart raced in an effort to keep it pumping.

"Just about anybody who walks by will hear us," I said. "It's not like the Assembly bothers to soundproof these rooms."

"Fuck the Assembly." He flexed his hand, fingers spreading wide. Two of them lay along my lower jaw now and he grasped it, angling my face up toward his. At the same time, he slid his free hand down to cup me between the thighs.

Pleasure jolted through me.

Need tightened in my belly like a fist as he stroked me through my pants, the thin, breathable material no barrier to a determined, hungry Alpha cat.

My anger at him wasn't much of one, either. At least not right then.

He pressed against me as his mouth captured mine, stealing my surprised gasp with his lips.

Tongue licking into my mouth, Damon made a growling sound low in his chest and it vibrated into me, flooding me with raw, naked need.

My pulse beat frantically, blood roaring in my veins. Releasing the blanket, I grabbed at his arms and sank my nails into his biceps, the taut muscle firm under my touch.

He grunted and slid his hand from between my thighs. I didn't have time to feel disappointed, though, because he gripped my hips and hauled me to the edge of the bunk, flush against his pelvis. I shuddered at the feel of his hard, heavy length, now pulsing against me.

Rubbing against him, I broke the kiss and gasped for air.

As my head fell back, he bit my neck.

"I want you naked—now," he whispered against my skin. "Say yes."

The small part of my brain that was still somewhat grounded in logic tried to step in. *No. You've got way too much unresolved shit between you two. Say no.*

The bigger part of my brain was more interested in lust, and the close call I'd had the night before, combined with my own need for Damon, the love, fury and fear, it all combined into a volatile mixture.

"Stop talking," I said. Tangling my fingers in his short hair, I yanked, hard, and he arched his neck to the side, giving me access to the sensitive spot on his neck—the vulnerable area he allowed nobody to access...save for me. I bit him.

A hard shudder racked him. Damon caught me against him and rose, hauling me close. I fumbled with his shirt, struggling to push it up until he dealt with it by simply shredding it.

I went to pull at my support tank. He took over, grabbing the hem and stripping upward. I lifted my arms to help him, but once he had them tangled in the material over my head while half the tank still covered my face, he fisted my wrists in his hand.

I moaned as he dipped his head and took my nipple into his mouth. Heat exploded between my thighs and I rocked against him, desperate to have him inside me, desperate for him to fill the emptiness.

He painted a trail up my collarbone with his mouth and the fabric covering my mouth was nudged out of the way, although only just, leaving me effectively blindfolded as he slanted his lips over mine.

His tongue stabbed into my mouth, stroked over mine, exploring me as if it had been a lifetime since we'd kissed...as if committing the feel and taste to memory.

The thought pricked at me, unsettling.

As if he'd sensed the slight withdrawal, Damon broke the kiss. But he wasn't done—he was *far* from done. Spinning me around, he

137

pulled at the tank again, finally freeing my head—and my arms—but when I went to reach back for him, I found my wrists and forearms bound up in the stretchy confines of the material again, his strong hand holding me in place while the other came around to yank at the button of my trousers, then the zipper. He worked the material half-way down my thighs, then bent me over the bed, one hand in the material of the tank, keeping my hands and arms pinned, the other at my hip.

I gasped at the feel of his cock pressing against my sensitive folds, then pushing inside, stretching me as he filled me in one strong, deep stroke.

He grunted as he seated himself inside me, his body hot where we touched. He pulled out and when I tried to follow, the hand on my hip tightened, holding me in place. "Be still, baby girl."

The sheer dominance in his voice wrapped around me, compelling me to do just as he'd ordered. I didn't take commands from him but right now, my body seemed happy to do just that—*more* than happy. As he started to withdraw the second time, I clenched down around him, a keening, desperate noise tearing free from my throat.

The whimper turned into a cry that bounced around the small room, but I was too far gone to notice and if he noticed, he didn't care.

Trying again to push back onto him, I groaned in frustration as he resisted, his body controlling mine completely.

"Damon, *please!*"

He released the grip on my tank, freeing my arms. Before I could react, he caught me around the waist and pulled me back against him, his chest to my naked back. I reached backward and cupped his neck, spine arching as I twisted against him, impaled on him, so full I ached but still needing more.

"Please," I whispered mindlessly.

"Please what?" He bit my earlobe. "What do you need?"

"You." I shuddered as his cock pulsed inside me. "I need you."

He moved with the mind-blurring speed again and soon I was propped on the edge of the bed with him kneeling before me. He stripped my trousers all the way off and pushed my thighs wide apart. Holding my gaze, he hooked his arms under my knees and hauled me closer, half my body on the bed, the other half supported by his strength.

Naked and vulnerable, I watched his dark head bow, his hands stroking over me.

His mouth brushed over my core and I gasped as the heated caress turned my bones molten and my blood to lava.

With a moan, I curled my hands in the blanket and shuddered. His tongue flicked, lashed, teased and stroked, working me to the edge as I thrashed and arched under his touch.

"Damon!" I cried out, not caring if the entire Assembly was gathered outside the door as he gave me a long, slow lick.

"Moan for me, baby girl," he growled.

Like I could control it. I cupped my hands over his head, nails scraping over his skin as I arched closer.

He growled, the vibration jolting through me, an erotic thrill I couldn't define. The air around us grew heavy and damp, filled with the scent of the arousal he'd pulled from me. His tongue stabbed against me, again and again, and then I was twisting against his hands, shuddering, shaking with climax. He lowered me, then pulled me onto him, filling me hard and fast while I convulsed in orgasmic delight.

"*Fuck*," he grunted. "You're like a fist... give it to me, kitten...give it to me..."

I whimpered, all but impaled on him, stretched tight, my inner muscles gripping and squeezing at him as he worked himself deeper.

Then he was buried inside me, one hand tangled in my hair, his face buried against my neck. I felt the edge of his teeth as he grazed the skin.

"Baby girl…" he rasped.

"Damon." I clung to him, nails digging into his skin and he grunted, thrusting his hips, then flexing to as if he couldn't sink deep enough inside me. He shoved upright, then turned and spun, taking two steps before pressing my back to the door.

His lips trailed down my neck, leaving a burning path to my shoulder.

One arm braced at my hips, he caught my other leg in his hand and pushed it up and out, opening me wide.

"Look at me," he said, voice rough and deep, barely above a growl.

His eyes glowed green-gold in the dim room, casting light on both of us, highlighting the stark, ravaging hunger on his features.

Slowly, he pulled out, then surged back inside, just as slow.

I grabbed his shoulders, sinking my short nails in.

He grunted in approval, still riding me with those slow, lazy strokes.

"Damon…please…" Desperate, I tightened my grip on him, not realizing I'd broken the skin until the sharp, metallic bite of shifter blood filled the air. But I couldn't stop. "*Please!*"

He dipped his head to rub his mouth over mine. "There's no hurry."

I bit his lip. Hard. He stiffened.

Tangling my fingers in the short strands of his hair, I tugged at his head. He didn't yield…but I didn't need him to. I pressed my mouth to his neck, to that one sensitive vulnerable area and bit. This time, *he* was the one who shuddered and the hand in my hair tightened almost to the point of pain as he tried to pull me back.

I didn't let go, arching and rubbing against him.

He swore raggedly, muscles taut, body tense. I eased up the grip with my teeth, then sucked, tasting the salt of his skin, the wildness of the forest, and clan and cat that was my lover. "Damon..."

He slammed into me.

Again.

Again.

Again.

I cried out as the orgasm hit, feeling his cock swell just as overwhelming pleasure erupted.

And he shuddered, shivering in my arms as the pleasure swept out to overwhelm him, too.

Chapter Ten

It could have been ten minutes that passed. It could have been an hour. Longer.

I had no way to tell, the only measure of time the thudding of my heart and his as he leaned into me, pinning me between him and the door, forearm bracing my weight at my hips, the other stroking the curve of my hip as he nuzzled at my neck.

I think I'd started to doze by the time he pulled out and swung me into his arms. Grumbling at the loss of his heat, I curled into his chest immediately. Damon rubbed his cheek against my hair but didn't speak.

Neither did I.

Even as he carried me over to the bed and lay down, stretching out with me tucked between him and the wall, I stayed quiet.

He shifted around, then the thin blanket covered us.

When he kissed my shoulder, I closed my eyes.

Long moments passed before he finally spoke. "You were on the Riordan job. How did it go?"

"He's dead. I'm not." Beyond that, I didn't want to talk about it. Even thinking about the events after Riordan's death were enough to make my arm ache, enough to make my brain freeze, as if preparing for an onslaught of alien whispers.

He turned his face into my hair and breathed in.

It took everything I had not to tense.

"I smell her, Kit."

"I'm too tired to talk about this, Damon." I burrowed deeper into the miserably thin mattress. "And considering how you're holding back on me, it's got you in a bad place to insist that we be open with each other, doesn't it?"

The hand on my hip tightened and his body tensed.

But he didn't get up, didn't pull back.

Instead, he kissed my shoulder. "I love you. I'd die to protect you."

I didn't respond to that. I just said, "Don't ask for my secrets until you're ready to share yours. Now, I'm tired."

He said nothing else, pulling me into the hard curve of his body.

And as angry as I still was, as hurt, tucked against him still felt like the safest place in the world.

I was asleep in moments.

SOMETHING NUZZLED MY nape.

Grumpy and tired, I shoved my head under my pillow. The soft brush against my neck came again, then stopped. Too sleepy to care, I shivered, then snuggled deeper into the pillow, pulling the arm around my waist more completely around me.

It didn't help. I was still chilled.

Long moments passed as I burrowed closer and closer to Damon. "Little sister."

Eyes flying open, I jacked upright and spun around, one hand automatically flying up to press to Damon's chest.

He wasn't there.

I shot a look around the room, spotted the shadowy corner where Lemera was shimmering into view, then turned my head around to focus on Damon.

My jaw fell open, because it wasn't just Damon lying there—*I* was curled up right next to him, his hand snug on my hip. As I shivered and squirmed closer, he reached out, apparently still asleep and pulled on one of the thin blankets, flipping it higher up over my body.

I felt the scratchy brush of the fabric echo over my skin.

"What did you do?" I demanded, looking at the specter crouching in the corner.

"We need to speak," she said, her voice a hollow echo—one that came from the grave. "He...intrudes. Gets in the way."

"How rude."

She didn't hear the scathing mockery in my voice. Rising from the crouch where she'd been perched in wait, she lifted a shoulder. "He serves his purpose. Clearly, he loves you. He protects you. But I wish to speak to you, not your lover. Especially as he reeks with lies."

The words turned my stomach. "Do you know anything about those? The lies, I mean?"

She angled her head to the side, eyes narrowed. Those eyes were more...real than normal. More human. *She* looked more human, even more alive than she had earlier. It was eerie as hell. No. It was fucking *scary*.

"I have...suspicions," she said slowly, clearly taking her time to answer, although I wasn't sure if it was because she didn't understand how to respond or if she was reluctant to offer much detail.

Frustrated, I pushed off the bed and glanced back at him—us. "And is that why you've got me walking around in...what, am I dreaming?"

"In a fashion."

"You've done this before," I said, mind spiraling back to a dream weeks earlier, when I'd come awake to find that I'd cut into Damon with that bronze blade bound to Lemera. She'd pulled me into a dream—or something. "Haven't you?"

Her brows came together. "The dream paths have always been open to us. It's easier to reach you this way. I've never had much luck reaching others of the blood like this. Not since..." She looked away. "Not for a very long time. But you are easy. It's as if I reach out and you are there. The old ways are all but lost to the others. This displeases me."

"What are these *dream paths*?"

The scowl deepened. "Did they teach you nothing?"

"No. They didn't." Hands on my hips, I scowled back. "I'm a half-breed disgrace or haven't you figured that part out? The *blood*, as you call my so-called people, want nothing to do with me. My grandmother, her staunchest supporters, they all want me *dead*. I'm a mongrel—*unclean blood*—human blood."

"You are not unclean." Lemera sniffed derisively. "The queen has kept the bloodline...limited. It weakens us. But not you. Your human blood makes you strong."

I gaped at her. Then I started to laugh. Falling back against the wall, I laughed and laughed, unable to stop, even as her disproving glare cut into me. "My human blood is the reason I was kicked around like a dog."

"No." She came closer, her steps liquid and graceful, like her bones were made of something altogether new. "Your human blood gave you unique strength, but it also made you...stubborn, child. The queen, the one you call grandmother, wanted you broken before you grew into an adult." Now she smiled and the teeth that were once broken and rotten were full, the right front one slightly crooked, while the bottom left showed a slight chip. Those two imperfections made her seem so...*human*. "She failed. She wanted nothing more than to move on, but she cannot and now she hunts you with desperation."

Something about that statement struck a chord. I had no time to probe for more because Lemera took my hand and pulled. "Come. We must talk."

The world spun away and reformed. My head whirled crazily when it was done and we stood on a narrow, two-lane country road, the kind that had been neglected by the local and federal government for so long, it was in a state of disrepair that left it almost unusable.

Trees thick with Spanish moss dripped over the stretch of busted pavement, deepening the darkness and giving it an eerie feel.

"Where are we?" I asked.

The sound of my own voice made me jump. I sounded like I was speaking from the depths of a well.

Lemera didn't notice.

She turned around and began to walk. "Presently, we are still in your room at the place where you let people pay you poorly for jobs that nearly kill you. This is a dream path—an echo, I believe you might call it. I found it while searching for the one they sent to take you back to the fouled queen."

"You've said dream path twice, like I'm supposed to know what that is." I wrapped my arms around my mid-section, hugging myself. It didn't do anything to ease the chills. "I don't."

"You're a smart child." Her perfectly imperfect teeth flashed in another of her disturbing smiles. "You can work it out. This isn't...real. It's an echo—a thought that's no more."

"You mean a memory?"

"Yes." She turned the word over, then nodded. "A memory. I found this while searching for Reshi. She has hidden herself from me."

The cold uneasiness in me grew. "Why are you looking for her? Didn't she return to the Hall when she left Florida?"

"She never left." Lemera's eyes met mine. "And...something in her isn't wholly Reshi."

"What does that mean?"

Instead of answering, she said, "The queen, the one you call Fanis, she is...not as she should be. It has taken me many years, lifetimes, perhaps, to fully remember all I know of her. I lay in the earth for so long and when she pulled me out, it was with such haste and for so short a time, my thoughts were...muddled. It took time to...remember." Lemera's eyes narrowed and she passed a hand over her head. "The thoughts in her mind are not as they should be."

"You mean she's crazy?"

Lemera cocked her head. "I mean she is *unnatural*. Her thoughts, her mind—they are...they don't *fit* her body, child. She's *unnatural*. Like Reshi now. Reshi's thoughts are too often those of the queen, instead of her own."

I come to claim what is mine.

A shiver raced down my spine as that echo from a dream came whispering to me from the back of my mind.

You took the twins from me.

"You're certain Reshi never returned to the Hall?" I asked, uneasiness spreading through me in a cold wave, numbing everything.

"Yes." Lemera's head tilted to the side. "You're starting to see the picture."

Something warm brushed my arm and my skin prickled, the way it did when Damon was near. I felt the brush of his lips against my cheek and I hissed out a breath.

"You said we were still in a room at the Assembly. So...I'm still in bed with Damon?"

"You are still in bed," she said.

I didn't like the way she said those words. "I have to get back."

She breathed out, slow and careful, before inclining her head. "Your cat lies to you, Kitasa. He thinks he protects you but he doesn't. Be wary."

A moment later, she was gone and I was back in bed.

Alone.

Chapter Eleven

There was far too much energy buzzing through the halls as I made my way toward one of the side exits of HQ. I'd already had to bypass two of Damon's lieutenants and after the first, I'd faded out of sight, going invisible because the man watching that door had been Scott.

I didn't know where Damon was, but he was definitely still in the building. I felt him, a whisper against my skin, an awareness humming in my blood.

He thinks he protects you but he doesn't. Be wary.

I clenched my jaw against the headache pounding at the base of my skull, anger a pulse at the back of my mouth.

I'd spied three of Damon's top lieutenants in the time since I'd slipped out, and several higher ranking Assembly officials. I had a bad feeling about why I'd woken to find myself alone, and why they were now searching for me. I was furious, but it wasn't the ideal time to focus on the fury.

I needed to get out of there.

When I passed a hall that led to one of the side exits, I went to turn, but stopped, instincts flashing a warning.

A moment later, I felt the familiar hot prickle on my nape that told me he was close.

Squaring my shoulders, I made a decision.

Since it was obvious Damon and his toy soldiers were looking for me and expected me to go out the side doors, I'd go out the front.

I passed by several Assembly guards and a fellow contract merc but none of them noticed.

A witch coming out of one of the private libraries stilled, head cocked, but if she picked up on my presence, she didn't make any other sign.

The front doors were closed and I hesitated only a second before starting toward them.

I was still five feet away when one near the end abruptly opened. Justin strode inside, Colleen at his back, although she stopped halfway inside and leaned against the door, her head averted.

I froze as Justin's gaze came toward me and unerringly landed on the exact space where I stood. His head cocked, then his brows came together slightly.

After a second, his mouth quirked up and his lips formed a single word: *Go.*

Then, not waiting for Colleen, he strode to the sign-in desk and planted his hands on the surface. "Exactly *why* have I been called in to assist the *fucking cats*?"

The cold anger in his voice conveyed just enough *Don't fuck with me* that the HQ employee sitting behind the desk immediately jerked to attention. "Mr. Greaves. Sir, I'm unaware of any assignments requesting—"

"Then find somebody who *is*," Justin barked.

I chose that moment to walk past him, still cloaked in invisibility. As I passed through the door still held open by Colleen, she said to somebody outside, "No. We're not moving the car because we're not staying."

I slipped past her.

Something brushed my hip.

"Take these," she said, pitching her voice so low, I barely heard it. "You'll have to hitch or hoof it to get there, but watch your back. Damon's claiming *imminent threat* so he's calling all his people in—and he says that includes you. Keys are to Justin's bike. Parked behind an old church an hour north of the city—Justin said you'd know the place. You worked a job there with him. Phone's in the saddle bag. We'll call."

I didn't dare speak.

"Antrim, move the fucking car *now!*" The guard at the base of the stairs shouted at us, clearly not aware Colleen had been quietly passing on a message.

Behind us, Justin was still raising hell—his voice carrying.

Colleen's phone chose that moment to start ringing. Loudly.

Somebody came around the corner, moving in a long-legged stride, moving with the easy grace of a shifter. As he mounted the steps, he glanced toward Colleen. I focused on him, saw how his nostrils flared.

I recognized him. One of Dair's wolves.

He cocked his head, scenting the air.

A breeze picked up, one that tasted spring and green...and of a friend's unique magic, breaking up the scents.

Whispering a silent prayer of thanks to Colleen and Justin, I took off running, securing my pack as I moved. I didn't go for my car. I headed straight for the road. If Damon was making some noise about an imminent threat and trying to call all his people in—claiming it *included me*—then the Assembly would be scouring HQ top to bottom to comply, as well as putting eyes on my vehicle and surveillance on my phone.

The bastard.

I had no idea what *imminent threat* bullshit he'd dreamed up to try to pin me into place—and I didn't care. I was so furious, I practically tasted blood on my tongue. The adrenaline pumping through my veins was enough that I just might be able to run the distance to where Justin had left his bike and still be fuming when I got there.

I ran until I was maybe five miles from HQ, but I'd taken care not to head straight north. I'd gone west, moving toward Orlando proper, and the Abyss. Wild, weird magic flowed thick there, as did a general mistrust of any and all authority, including the local alphas.

When I neared a barbecue joint I liked on the edge of the Abyss, one owned by a witch who was *very* unfriendly to shifters and prone to spiking the sauce with spices that affected their sense of smell, I pulled out my phone and disabled all tracking capabilities, then turned it off. I started to slide it back into the zippered pocket on my hip, then stopped, swearing. With a growl, I pulled out one of the needle thin knives from an inner pocket on my vest and used it to separate the thin metal frame from the back of the phone. Taking out the small chip that did all the gadget's computing, I put it into yet another pocket. That done, I stowed the phone, the knife, then readjusted my pack.

Now I had to move.

Once I was far enough from East O and Damon's reach, I'd see about finding a quicker mode of transportation so I could get to Justin's bike—and the phone. I needed to call them, see what the fuck was going on, although I was starting to piece it all together.

I found it while searching for the one they sent to take you back to the undeserving queen.

He thinks he protects you but he doesn't. Be wary.

Whatever was going on had to do with Reshi. I was now sure of that.

And if Damon was tied up in it...

That all added up to bad news.

AFTER NEARLY NINETY minutes at a quick jog, keeping at a pace that put distance between me and the Assembly without me running outright, I stopped at a fueling station. I'd only had a few basic staples in my pack and I'd already drained one bottle of water.

I wasn't going to hold out on catching a ride but if the opportunity came along, I'd damn well take it.

I told myself I'd give it twenty minutes, long enough for me to rest a bit and plow through the ham and cheese sandwich I'd bought from the small deli at the back of the store. As cars and trucks came and went, I discarded one alternative after another.

Finally, just as I was finishing my sandwich, a busted-up old pick-up truck with a hard-sided, high-rising cap pulled into the fueling station. Eying it, I watched as a handful of tired, grubby men eased from the back of the covered truck bed and two more from the truck's cab.

Migrants, and all of them human.

It only took seconds to peg them, a few more to look over their vehicle. The truck bed's cap was in decent shape, if you didn't mind that the windows were all gone, busted or knocked out at some point. Since the bed had no fewer than six migrant workers crammed together in the back, the missing windows was likely a blessing.

And the missing windows didn't bother me at all.

I wasn't going to fit in the back nor would I ask about riding in the front, but I'd seen trucks like this, hard-working human folks, roaming from one job to the next, usually taking on the grueling manual labor offered at farms and such as they tried to stay out of the public eye as much as possible. I'd seen them turn in off the road heading north and decided this would do just fine.

Once everybody had made their way from the truck to the fueling station, I grabbed my bag, sword and bottle of water and headed to the road, moving at an angle that would take me directly in front of the truck where it sat parked up against the curb, separated from overgrown, brown grasses by the pitted and broken pavement.

I took another quick look around, saw nobody. Kneeling, I hitched my backpack into place, stowed my water in my hip pocket and gripped my sword in my left hand. Then, with a deep, calming breath, I faded from sight.

The truck barely swayed under my weight as I climbed on top of the truck bed's cap, then slid off my pack, securing it to my belt so I didn't have to worry about losing it at a sharp turn or stop. Hopefully, *I* wouldn't fly off, although the truck's cap had rails on the side, the kind used to secure luggage or tools or whatever. I fished a strap out of a side pocket of my pack and looped it around one of the rails, then held it loosely, an added support, just in case.

That done, I lay down and closed my eyes. The sun shone down hot on my face, too bright, but it heated the cap's metal construction and the warmth seeped into tired, stressed muscles.

Worry gnawed at my gut with sharp, jagged teeth. Was he still at HQ, looking for me?

No. Hell, no. It had been close to two hours by this point. He might have given it another fifteen minutes but once my scent started to fade, even a little, he'd know I wasn't there and he'd move on. Whether he'd just decide to look for me at the Lair tonight or keep hunting for me like he'd been doing this morning, I had no idea.

Doyle was out of the city, so his best tracker wasn't available.

Neither was I, for that matter.

At best, I figured I had maybe ten to twelve hours before he realized I hadn't headed out on a random job. Once he didn't track me down at the Lair later today, he'd really start looking for me and he'd only freak out more when he couldn't reach me on the phone.

Those gnawing, nagging worrying teeth grew sharper, razored in their intensity.

I wanted to call, tell somebody to let him know I was okay. But that wasn't going to happen. Somebody would be monitoring the GPS and tech tracking systems. Usually, Chang handled tech-related needs for Damon, but I wasn't entirely sure of Damon would ask Chang to help him with this. Something about the edgy aggression between them the last time we'd all talked made me wonder if Chang would simply refuse the order—although not out of loyalty to me. No, he'd never shift loyalties. But if he felt an action would bring Damon more harm later down the road, he'd abstain and deal with the fall-out now rather than risk Damon coming to harm later.

The patter of male voices, all speaking in rapid Spanish, stirred me out of my reverie and as the workers climbed into the truck, settling in the back, I adjusted my own position slightly, crossing my ankles and gauging how long I'd be up here before I had to leap off.

If I was lucky, they'd stay on the small country road heading north for the next thirty or forty minutes. That would put me within just a couple miles of the church, if I recalled correctly.

The truck started with a choking sort of rumble, belching out fumes that made it clear the truck still ran on fossil fuel.

One of the guys in the back grumbled and I heard *gasolina* as the truck took off out of the parking lot, leaving behind a plume of smoke and gravel dust clogging the air.

Sighing, I flung an arm over my eyes.

Now I just had to hang on and wait. Might as well try to enjoy the ride, although how I'd manage that while worrying just what in the hell Damon was up to, I didn't know. Plus, my mind was spinning up terrible options about what he'd been planning when he called his top men to Assembly HQ.

ROUGHLY THREE MILES from the turn-off I needed, the truck slowed and I saw dust, plaster, concrete, other construction materials. When the truck came to a complete stop while waiting for a couple of slow, oncoming semis to pass in the opposite lane, I caught my bag. Steadying it in one hand, I held onto my blade with the other and rolled off the top of the truck.

I mistimed it and made the vehicle rock a little too hard, but none of the men noticed, so I just melted away into the heavy overgrowth on the side of the road.

"It would have been easier to ride in the vehicle."

I hissed at the sound of her voice, spinning to glare at the spectral form of Lemera, just a few feet from me. A dull ache pulsed at the base of my skull, as if in response to her appearance. After checking the road to make sure no cars were coming, I dropped the veil of invisibility and stared at her down my nose.

"Do you like hitching a ride on my shoulder or what?"

She frowned, gaze moving to my shoulder for a moment. Then she shook her head. "I do not ride on your person."

With that, she turned and lifted a hand, letting it hover in mid-air. "I feel nothing here. Why did you come to this place?"

"I'm still trying to figure that out."

Lips pursed, she looked at me, her unsettling gaze cutting deep into me, seeing through layers of skin, tissue and all the mental shields I'd constructed to keep people out.

"If you don't know why you are here, then why *are* you here?"

Were all spirits so damn literal?

Instead of asking her, I just hitched my pack onto my shoulder and started walking. She joined me and the questions came again.

"I'm walking to a place where a friend left me a ride," I said, cutting her off without thinking it was probably not a good idea to interrupt the boogeyman.

The truth was, she didn't exactly scare me anymore.

She unsettled me and her presence confused me, and all the unanswered questions she caused? *Those* terrified me. But she, strangely, didn't.

"You have no reason to be afraid of me."

I came to a dead stop and turned to her. "How do you always seem to know what I'm thinking?"

"I do not always know." A faint smile curved her lips as she met my gaze. "But you accepted my blade and the bond settles easy with you. That gives me a glimpse into your thoughts, from time to time."

"Whoa..." I held up a hand and shook my head.

Her gaze strayed past me as a car drove past and I looked over my shoulder to see what held her attention.

It was a county sheriff and he gave me—not *us*—*me* a narrow-eyed look.

"You should walk, little sister. He thinks you talk to the air, as he cannot see me."

Great. I gave the officer a polite smile and tapped my ear, hoping he wouldn't decide to swing around and talk to me. I started walking again, moving my hands in an animated fashion in hopes he'd think I was talking on a cell phone. Once I heard the car's electric motor powering back up, I heaved out a breath.

"So, exactly who *can* see you?"

"Whoever I wish." From the corner of my eye, I saw her shrug. "Taking my fully corporeal form requires energy and I'm still weary. Appearing before you takes little effort, though, as you accepted the blade. We're bonded, little sister, you and I."

I resisted the urge to stop again as I demanded, *"Explain that."*

A husky chuckle escaped her. "Do you know that I had lain in the earth for several centuries, buried among bones, although I wasn't truly dead? She was the one who put me there, but she had need of me and couldn't remember just where she'd left me. Then she decided to come and pull me from the earth, committed untold horrors to force her will upon me. And you, child, I *give* you my bond and you are displeased by it. Such a puzzle you are."

"Yeah, well, you're the queen's pet killer! Excuse me for not being pleased that you've up and decided we're *bonded*."

"I've never been her *pet*!"

I froze, terror turning my blood to ice as she was suddenly in my face, once more the specter from my nightmares, scraps of mummified flesh over graying bone, dull wispy hair blowing back from her face as she bent down to snarl into my face with breath that reeked of death and decay.

"She ripped me from the resting quiet of dark peace where I'd lain, so long in the dirt that I'd almost forgotten that I wasn't truly dead, so long in the dark that I could almost pretend I'd found my rest, you child!" Lemera grabbed the front of my shirt, hauling me onto my toes. "She destroyed the only ones I ever loved, destroyed my line, all because *she* feared death, and now my promise to destroy her is the one thing that keeps me bound to the earth after all these centuries. I've *never* been her pet, Kitasa. I will *be* her death. I am vengeance. I am fury. But I am *nobody's* pet."

Reactively, I'd gripped her wrist. Now, my fingers freezing from the contact, I squeezed and stared into her death-glazed glare. "You killed at her command."

Her eyes narrowed, then abruptly, she let go, shoving me back.

"You are a child," she muttered again, like it was a curse. But her voice shook this time and she moved away, looking defeated. "You've carried such a burden for so long. It makes me forget you're but a child. And they taught you *nothing*."

I gripped the straps of my bag, staring at her, uncertain what to say. Since I came up empty, I started to walk. Soon, she rejoined me.

"You said for centuries."

"Yes."

Darting a look at her, I asked, "How is that possible? I know we live longer than humans, but that just doesn't seem possible. Rana's almost a century and I know Fanis is probably two or three hundred years old, she isn't...she can't..."

"The woman who hunts you has lived more than just one normal lifetime, little sister."

For the second time in as many minutes, I stopped.

Lemera walked a few more steps before doing the same. Turning back to me, she breathed out a long, slow sigh and lifted her head to the sky. "She has lived lifetimes, more than you can imagine." She said something, a word I *almost* understood, then frowned, shaking her head. "She walked the earth when people built monuments to greats kings in the land called Kemet, Kitasa. She ruled before Rome came to power. She is older than civilizations."

Kemet—

"*Kemet?* As in *ancient* Egypt?" My eyes all but bugged out of my skull. I could feel them, pulling hard against the restraint of muscle and skin that held the damn things in place as I stared at Lemera, certain I'd misheard her. When she simply stared back, I strode over to glare at her. "Are you fucking *kidding* me? Egypt? You're telling me *Egyptian Pharaohs* were still strutting around the sands of Memphis when my dear old grandmother was born?"

She gave me another hard look, brow furrowed as she processed my words and translated through whatever filter she used. The scowl cleared and she sighed, gaze drifting off to stare into the distance. "No. I'm telling you she *predates* those pharaohs, girl. And it is more complicated than that. She is...more than your grandmother, if your grandmother even exists anymore."

"I...what?"

The sound of another engine approaching had her gaze cutting sharply to the road. "We must walk or find a place where we are not so exposed to discuss this."

I wanted to argue but she was gone, leaving me staring at nothing but the old country road, flanked on one side by an overgrown pasture and a rich, lush tangle of vegetation and trees on the other.

"Son of a bitch." Seething, I spun in a circle. I was angry enough to scream my frustration to the sky but the car, now coming into view around a curve in the road had me biting my tongue. I went to turn back around so I continue on my way to the church where I was supposed to meet Justin and Colleen, but the car's vibrant blue paint job caught my eye and I squinted, waiting a few seconds as it drew closer.

"About fucking time," I muttered. But the comment wasn't directed at Justin or Colleen. I hadn't expected to see them show up here. No, I was just relieved that *one* thing had turned out in my favor today, which was rapidly turning out to be nothing but one clusterfuck after the other.

Dropping my bag on the ground, I grabbed my water bottle from a pocket on my thigh and took a long drag as I waited for the car to come to a stop, edging off the road a few feet. Justin climbed out, and Colleen followed, using his door since there wasn't much space left on the passenger side.

She came rushing to me and caught me in a hug, her thin, strong arms tight around my neck. I still wasn't used to the physical changes that had happened to her body since power-hungry bastards had used her magic against her months earlier.

Magic burned an incredible amount of energy and she had too much of it in her now, leaving her too lean, bordering on the verge of ropey, with Justin constantly pushing food on her.

But she still smelled like herbs and tea and honey and it was a soothing, familiar scent. Breathing it in, I let the comfort of her embrace and that scent settle my mind, pushing aside whatever freaky discovery I'd soon learn about Fanis.

"I'm going to kill him, Kit," Colleen said, breaking the embrace and nudging me back with her hands gripping my shoulders.

I caught her wrists, holding steady as I met her eyes, my mind already connecting the dots and coming to a conclusion that left me alternating between furious and heartbroken.

"He was going to request the Assembly take me into custody, wasn't he?" I asked, feeling a little dead inside.

"Protective custody, until he could remove the threat posed by your grandmother and her people," Justin said, stepping up and giving me a quick hug before curling a hand over Colleen's shoulder. "He's claiming she's an imminent threat to the Clan and with you out doing what you do, the threat is even worse, because his people will stop at nothing to protect you—which is true, but it's not like she's going to slink into East O and try to pull anything there."

Spinning away, I shoved my hands into my hair and yanked. It didn't do any good.

"*Son of a bitch*!" I shouted to the sky.

Birds took the skies in surprise, their chattering and cries making it clear they weren't happy with my outburst.

I was shaking, so angry, my hands *hurt* with the need to hit something, to *hurt* something.

How could he *do* this?

"He thinks locking me in a fucking *cage* is an answer," I whispered. My gut twisted and sweat broke across my brow and nape while ugly, bitter memories fought to swamp me. A cage. He'd try to lock me in...after what had happened to me before...panic tried to swim up, grab a hold of me and I battled it back through sheer will.

"Kit, he isn't thinking."

Bitter laughter tore out of me and I spun to glare at Colleen. She caught my hands before I could respond, squeezing tight.

"I'm not defending him," she said, her voice blunt. "He's got his head up his ass and I want to beat him senseless for even thinking what he's thinking."

"I hear a *but*." My hands hurt and I had to force myself to unclench them.

"*But*..." She blew out a breath and stroked her hands up the outside of my arms to grip my shoulders. "*But*...Kit, I ran into him at the Assembly a few minutes after you bugged out and he's running on pure fear and instinct. I've never felt anything like that from him. He won't tell me what the hell is going on. I mean, I didn't expect him to, but he's locked down tight in a way I've never seen. I wouldn't say he's an open book, but he's never been a hard read, either. But now...he's so closed down, I don't think I could get a good feel for what's going on with him unless I blasted through his shields in a way that caused permanent harm." Her eyes searched mine. "What's going on?"

"Beats the hell out of me," I muttered.

But my mind spun back to the other day, Chang squaring off with Damon, his voice quiet and steady as he told my lover, *"You're not doing her or you any favors."*

A niggling suspicion in the back of my mind grew larger, demanded attention. Grabbing my bag, I started for the car. "I've got an idea, though. I need to get closer to where you guys saw him earlier."

I heard leather scuffing against broken pavement and looked back, saw the clashing gazes between Justin and Colleen. Going still, I asked, "What?"

"It's nothing," Colleen said, shoving the heavy fall of her red hair over her shoulder.

Justin stared at her back as she started for me for several seconds before shifting his attention to me. "That's not exactly true."

"Justin! Shut up!" Colleen whirled around, the air around her wavering as her temper surged and her magic reacted accordingly.

He strode to her and caught her chin, slamming a hard kiss down on her mouth. "You think she'll appreciate us keeping secrets from her, the same way her dickhead boyfriend is?" Without giving Colleen a chance to respond, Justin shifted his attention to me. "He petitioned the Assembly to make a formal request that Green Road be barred from interfering."

My mind blanked out. For the span of a few heartbeats, I couldn't think of a single thing to say.

Then I laughed. Sagging against his car, one hand pressed to my belly, I laughed until my chest ached with it. "Did he...did...did he think that...would do jack shit?"

Justin's lips twitched.

Colleen wrapped her arms around herself, glaring at both of us.

"Green Road has been a power to contend with in Florida for decades, Coll. Even *before* the Clan was—and long before Damon showed up here," I said, laughter finally giving away to chuckles and a lingering, cynical sense of amusement. "Then there was what happened to you and now only a lunatic would take on the Road. Plus?" I jerked a thumb in Justin's direction. "Nobody is going to say it out loud but if it comes down to it, Justin will side with the Road in any conflict, because that's where your loyalties lie and he'll put his strength in the place where it best benefits you. The Assembly knows about my ties to you, Justin *and* the Road. They're going to stay neutral here. Even with Damon snarling like he's got a thorn in his paw, the Assembly will *not* dictate anything when it comes to the Road. Not on this."

They'd damn well better stay out of it, otherwise, that was one more thing Damon and I would be clashing over.

My heart, already so battered, tore apart a little more.

Shoving off the car, I went to climb inside. "Let's go. I'm going to get to the bottom of this if it's the last thing I do."

Chapter Twelve

We'd been driving less than twenty minutes when Damon called. The car's automated system announced the caller's name and Justin's eyes met mine in the rear view mirror. "I'm ignoring his calls right now, Kitty. He's pissed me off but good with this latest stunt."

I waited until the ringing stopped before I asked a question that had been in the back of my mind all day. "Why were you two at the Assembly this morning?"

"According to the Speaker for witches who called me in?" Justin snorted. "The Alpha of the Cat Clan had a favor to request of me."

"Same," Colleen said with a heavy sigh. "The call was routed through the Father of the local Green Road House, and he had a heavy dose of suspicion in his voice when he made the request, advising me that he wasn't certain any favors requested by the Cat Alpha would be above board, especially if you were involved."

"And your response to that?"

Colleen looked at me over her shoulder. "I told him I was more than likely going to tell Alpha Lee to fuck off. He looked surprised."

"You look so sweet, nobody expects you to cuss—or that you might be capable of telling dominant shifters to shove it where the sun doesn't shine," I said, turning to look out the window again.

The phone started ringing again.

"You might as well answer it," I told Justin as the car's AI-generated voice announced the caller's ID. "He'll keep calling. Tell him to fuck off—or let Colleen. She loves doing that."

"Can any of his tech people trace the call?" Colleen asked.

"Please." Justin sounded offended. He punched a few buttons on the console, then gave two terse commands to the car's onboard computer. "Give me some credit." After that, he initiated the call, with a verbal command for audio only.

Damon's voice filled the car a second later. "When's the last time you talked to her, Justin?"

"Good afternoon to you, too, sunshine," Justin said, his voice filled with false warmth and cheer. "How are you doing today, Alpha Lee?"

"Cut the shit, Justin. Have you talked to Kit recently?"

Justin winked at me in the rear view. "Sure have. I checked to see how the DOA went and made sure she was healing up after that buffoon you had trailing her caused her to get injured. What's the matter? You two have a lover's quarrel?"

A taut, pulsating silence followed.

"*When* did you see her?" Damon demanded.

Justin made a humming noise. "Hmmm. Been a minute. Colleen, when did we last see Kit?"

"I don't keep track, Justin. I'm not her social secretary." Colleen was staring out the window on her side. "She crashed at my place the night before she went on the DOA hunt. We talked earlier today when I checked to make sure she was healing up okay."

"Today," Damon said in a low, angry growl. "You talked to her *today*, after I specifically requested Green Road stay the fuck out of what's going on."

"With all due respect, Lee," Colleen said, her head whipping around, voice suddenly tight with anger. "*Very* little respect—and dropping by the second—you have no fucking place to make such requests of the Road and you damn well know it. Had you made such a request to my face, I might have deep-fried your balls—while they're still fucking attached to your body."

Justin grimaced and muttered, "Ouch."

Louder, he added, "Damon, you should probably know that Colleen is still walking a fine line with control when she gets pissed. You don't want to be the target of her ire, big guy. And this counts as a formal warning, so if you get burned, that's your own damned fault."

"Shove it up your ass, Greaves," Damon responded. "Colleen, your relationship with Kit aside, it's my responsibility as Alpha to address *all* threats to my Clan."

"Kit's your lover. She's not a shifter." Colleen chuckled, a sardonic sound. "Even though she shares blood with a high-ranking shifter in your Clan, neither of you have ever acknowledged that publicly and while some of your Clan mates accept that she's your mate, there's been no formal acknowledgement of that, either. So, as far as anything related to Kit is concerned, it's not a *Clan* threat. And...while you've yet to tell *me* what this threat is, let me assure you, I already know. It *might* be a threat to Kit, one you think you should handle for her. That will piss her off even on a good day."

"Stay out of it, Colleen," Damon warned.

"Is that what you're telling Kit?" Justin asked, flicking a look at me in the rear view. "I mean, whatever you've been doing north of Orlando has something to do with her people but she's in the dark about it."

The muscles at the base of my neck locked up. My lungs did the same, making breathing impossible as I waited for Damon to respond.

"I don't know what in the fuck you're talking about," Damon said, his voice coolly neutral—and so utterly full of bullshit, I wanted to *scream*.

"Yeah." Justin snorted. "I just bet. Maybe I'll ask Kit when I talk to her next."

"Keep your fuckin' mouth shut, Greaves." Damon's voice had dropped to a near-bass growl, only barely understandable. "None of that concerns you."

"Really? Seems you wanted to involve not just *me*, but Colleen and the Road when you hauled a couple of witches into HQ into today to ask a *favor*, Alpha Lee. Maybe think about that next time you try to abuse your authority as Alpha, okay? Call me when you get that big head of yours unstuck from your ass."

Justin disconnected the call and slowed to make a turn.

Up ahead, the small, abandoned church where we'd once worked a job waited.

"Kit?" Colleen asked softly.

I shook my head, staring hard out the window.

"You know what he's up to already, don't you?" Justin asked.

I ignored him, recalling what Lemera had told me just hours earlier, when she'd invaded my dreams.

A dream path, she'd told me.

"Didn't she return to the Hall when she left Florida?"

"She never left."

Damon had her. In the pit of my stomach, I knew it. After Reshi had been sent from East O, he'd sent his soldiers after her and taken her down.

But where the fuck was she and what was he doing with her?

My breath caught in my chest as a memory snapped into focus in the back of my mind, clear as a bell, the morning I'd gone to find Damon. He'd been in the dungeon, an unknown shifter showing up and trying to throw me out on my ear. Gary Snyder, doing some unknown job. Breathing hard, I said, "I need a phone. *Now.*"

Colleen silently passed hers over.

Plugging Gary Snyder into a search engine, I prayed, although I had no idea what I was praying for—maybe that he'd turn out to be in construction, a cab driver, something mundane.

But even before the search results loaded, I knew that wouldn't be the case.

The first few hits were death announcements, his passing connected to a dispute that arose while he was in Alpha Damon Lee's territory, finishing a job.

I found the first listing referencing his work and the dread creeping through me turned to pure ice.

Gary Snyder—aka the Spider—had been a freelance merc. I'd actually heard of him, under the professional name. The Spider took big dollar NH targets that others turned down, and he wasn't overly concerned with little things like ethics.

There were rumors he used to work out of East Orlando, but he'd left before I'd moved to the city years earlier.

I felt sick.

Had he gone after Reshi?

If so, where was the Royal Guard? Had they all been killed?

Where was Reshi now?

And what the hell had Lemera meant when she'd said that Reshi wasn't wholly Reshi?

"COME OUT AND TALK TO me, you dead hag!" I called out, turning in a circle.

Anger knotted the muscles of my neck and shoulders while twisting my innards until they felt like they'd been through a vice. Reshi was still here, somewhere in Florida, and my gut said she was close. Damon would be keeping her on a short leash.

Why?

"Lemera!" I shouted, my voice echoing around the four walls of the empty sanctuary and coming back to me. The windows, long since boarded up, only allowed mere slits of the fading sunlight to filter through the gaps. Those faint bits of light did little to penetrate the coming gloom of night. The creatures I'd heard scurrying, both in within these walls and without, had gone silent at my first shout.

So had my companions, although their thoughts were *loud*.

"Come out and talk to me, Lemera, *now*!" I said again.

"Um, Kit?"

I ignored Justin and focused on the blade that held the dead *aneira's* spirit, pulling the image into my mind. It didn't want to form. I pushed harder and slowly, like the sun melting away the fog, the image of the old blade became clear in my mind, and the blade's discordant song of endless whispers started to echo in the back of my mind.

The melody grew louder, hitting me in a rush of cold wind, tormented whispers and shattered screams. Shuddering, I flexed that part of me that let me call weapons.

"What are you doing, girl!" Lemera's angry snarl sounded from behind me just as my palm started to react, itching like it did only seconds before a weapon would appear.

Ending the call, I spun around to glare at her.

And Justin lashed out with silver.

"What the *fuck*!"

Lemera wheeled on him, her almost-normal appearance falling away to reveal a sepulchral monster. She shot out a hand toward him, the chains flying in her direction no impediment.

"No!"

I lunged toward, cutting between the specter and Justin, grabbing her by the arms.

The resulting icy chill sent a gasp through me, my hands numbing on impact.

"Kitasa..." Lemera's voice came again, softly this time, devoid of anger, although the irritation was there. "Foolish child. Brave, foolish child. Breathe, girl. Breathe."

She'd said that to me before.

A jolt hit me in the chest, painful as hell, and my heart lurched into a hard, quick rhythm.

"The grave is cold, little sister," Lemera said gently, brushing my hair back. "It is unwise to grab on with both fists. It might grab back and never let go. But I am not letting them take you. I am not letting *her* take you—she has stolen enough."

Teeth chattering, I stared up at her. When had she gotten so tall? It wasn't until I felt the sharp discomfort of glass cutting into my knee that I realized I'd collapsed on the floor of the church, with Lemera now gripping my arms instead of the other way around.

"There you are," she murmured, a faint smile flitting across her features.

Her face was once more whole—no, even more so, her lips full and plump, cheekbones high and sharp, while her eyes were the clear blue-green of the Mediterranean. And her hair fell over her shoulder in a braided rope of white-gold.

Hearing the scuffling behind me, I forced a hand up and croaked out, "Justin, don't do anything stupid. She won't hurt me."

"All is well." Lemera gave me an amused smile. "His witch is watching him, little sister. I am sorry. I did not realize these were...friends. I felt you call the blade and reacted."

Thoughts clearing, I pushed upright. The metallic, coppery scent of blood stung my nose and I looked at my knee, saw a shard of glass sticking out. I tugged it free and tossed it over to the wall, ignoring the resulting trickle of blood that began to flow. Straightening, I met the gaze of the other *aneira*. "I was calling your blade because I have questions and you have answers."

"I told you before—I am not to be summoned, girl." Lemera's eyes darkened. "Calling me comes with blood and death. You don't want that burden, Kitasa. *I* do not want that burden but I cannot stop it. I refuse to let you carry it as well."

Aware Justin and Colleen were watching with a mix of horror and acute interest, I decided to put that aside.

"I have questions," I said again, another chill wracking me. "About Reshi—and my...about Fanis. And Damon."

Colleen sucked in a breath. Justin's reaction was more subtle, but he'd gone from watchful to ready in a blink.

Lemera cocked her head, gold-tipped black lashes lowering in a lazy blink as she considered me. "Why do you ask me? Why not ask your protective lover?"

"Because he'll lie," I responded sourly. "You won't. So tell me...did Damon take Reshi?"

Lemera lifted her gaze upward, a soft sigh escaping her. Even though her form looked fully corporeal, the sigh sounded as though it came from something not fully of this world, and it came with the chill touch of death, and those eerie, dead whispers.

"I believe he has, little sister."

Chapter Thirteen

" *Shit!"*

Spinning away from Lemera, I shoved my hands through my hair and yanked.

My two best friends stood a few feet away, both still watching with stunned expressions. Justin's smooth, warm brown skin had gone slightly ashen, his green eyes darkening with something that whispered of fear as he stared at the lemera.

Guilt gripped me and I lowered my hands, moving over to touch his shoulder. "It's...hell." What did I say? I couldn't logically look at him and *lie*, tell him that Lemera was *okay*—in what world did a reanimated corpse or ghost or whatever she was pass for *okay*? "She was only going to hurt you because she thought you were a threat to me."

"Yeah." His voice came out in a low, tight rasp, pupils mere pinpricks lost in a sea of green. "I got that. But, fuck, Kit, when did you start courting revenants?"

The word had me going still.

"Revenant."

He glanced at me, but it was a slow, almost forced movement, like he feared looking away from her. "Yeah. That's a fucking *revenant*, Kit—an *old* one. Somebody reanimated that thing's corpse and brought it back—"

Lemera was standing next to me in a blink, that cold, graven wind rushing around us for a split second. "I am not a *thing*, witch."

Justin's words froze in his throat.

Colleen lifted a hand, her voice gentle. Not conciliatory, exactly. But something in it reached Lemera and she pulled back, the rage no longer pouring from her. "Alright. That was pretty rude, I guess. But he's right, isn't he? You *did* die, right? A *long* time ago. And somebody brought you back."

"In a matter of speaking. I *did* die, but never truly—not completely. A curse bound me here."

"A curse," Colleen murmured. "What sort of curse could hold you trapped here for..." She shook her head. "I can't even guess at how old you are? Do *you* know?"

"Centuries have passed since I was born. The Roman Empire was the dominant power when I still lived." She lifted her hand and there was the bronze blade, the one she said came with death. "When I had this forged, a gift to one I loved, it was considered a masterpiece. Now there are weapons that can kill from farther than any bow or spear—so far even a shifter couldn't see the assailant."

My brain was still stuck on the *Roman Empire* part.

"Who cast the curse?"

Justin's question jerked me out the reverie in time to hear Lemera's answer.

"*I* did, witch."

I started and focused on the specter's face.

"What?"

She canted her head to look at me, a haunting sad smile on her lips. "I worked the curse, me and another, using the blood of someone I loved—somebody who had been betrayed by the queen. We were to die as well and I decided if I would die, then I might as well do so in a way that sealed the queen's fate along with mine."

"It wasn't as simple as I'd hoped. She left me buried in the cold dark, alone for so long that I started to forget, alone for so long, I even started to find peace." A long, harsh breath escaped her, one that sounded like the rattling of a death sigh. "Then, she came back for me, pulled me from the earth to use as a weapon. It was not my choice."

She looked at Colleen and Justin as she spoke, voice turning hard and brittle as glass as she added, "Nor was it anything Kitasa did. We have both been made pawns."

Colleen's eyes softened. "You remember...before. What it was like, when you had forgotten...you'd found peace and now that's lost to you."

"I do not wish to think on that, Healer." Lemera's gaze shuttered. "It brings naught but pain. Until the bonds holding me here are broken, I am trapped, chained to this world."

Maybe she didn't want to think on it—and honestly, I couldn't blame her. But I didn't have the luxury of *not* thinking about it. Knowledge might not be the sort of weapon I could draw from a sheath at my back, but it was a weapon nonetheless and I needed as much of it as I could gather. "It was Fanis."

Lemera's breath escaped in a cold, shuddering sigh, like the wind blowing over an abandoned grave.

Justin and Colleen didn't seem to notice as they both shifted their gazes to me.

Slowly, Justin shook his head. "That doesn't track, Kit. This..." He stopped, gaze flicking to, then from Lemera before seeking me back out. "She's too old. I feel...*centuries* within her. Your grandmother can't be that old, even if your people live as long as some witches do."

"Yeah, well...I think that's where it gets complicated." Although I felt no hint of humor, I dredged up a smile for him. Turning to the ghost standing at my side, I gave her a hard, direct look. "It's time to stop beating around the bush. Tell me whatever it is you're hiding. Like what in the hell you meant when you said Reshi wasn't *wholly* Reshi."

Lemera's features wavered—her entire formed flickered out of view for the barest moment.

When she came back into view, she was on the far side of the room. She reached up and touched the boards covering the window. In the next second, the wooden boards lay in splinters at her feet. "How do you breathe in this world, Kitasa? Everything is so closed up. There is so little space, so many people."

Justin stirred behind me.

I held a hand out toward him, although I didn't think he was about to fly off the handle on her.

Wind blew in through the open rectangle, stirring loose tendrils of the ancient *aneira's* hair. In that moment, it might have been possible to forget she was from a time so long ago, it was lost to the sands of time, relegated to stories known only by the few scholars among my kind. Even her clothing wasn't that dissimilar from what the warriors back on the island still wore.

But Justin was right. She carried the ache of ages in her, and something else, a deeper ache that spoke of grief and rage.

"Lemera?"

She glanced to the side—not at me, but over her shoulder, as if she couldn't bear to look fully on me. "I wouldn't even know where to start, little sister."

"Maybe try the beginning," Colleen suggested.

At that, the specter smiled. "The beginning. I wonder if you are prepared for that."

The wind picked up again and it was rich, heavy with the scent of earth. Lemera's voice wrapped around me as she began to speak.

"That cold desolate island where the undeserving queen sits on a throne...that's not our true home, little sister. Did you know?"

"Yes. Well, I know it's not where the people originally came from." What little knowledge I had on our origins was haphazard at best, pieced together from bits I'd overheard when cleaning or doing whatever tasks had been flung at me when my cousins and the other children had been taking their lessons. I'd been greedy for knowledge, though, even then. "We'd once lived somewhere near the Mediterranean, I think."

Her lids lowered to half-mast, her head cocking.

In the back of my mind, I heard that rush of whispers, that now-familiar chill, like what I'd sensed the morning she'd healed me after Riordan bit me. I didn't let myself jerk away, even though everything in me was freaking out. Whatever weird connection had formed between us, I wanted no part of it. But I don't think she'd done it on purpose.

"The Mediterranean." Her voice was softer now, husky with memories. "Yes. The home of my heart. When I was a child, we roamed a land of mountains and green plains and beaches by a sea so blue, it hurt to look at it. The village where I'd lived as a young girl was high on a cliff but I could hear the water at night when I slept. We were still...we wandered, then. Our people. What is the word, little sister? When a people doesn't always stay in one place?"

"Nomadic?" I ventured. "A nomadic tribe?"

"Nomadic." She considered it, nodding slowly. "Yes. We were a larger people once, traveling out of the east in small tribes and gathering to winter together. But those times passed long before I was born. We'd been living in our winter home near the sea for centuries when I was born. The warriors would travel in the summer months while the rest stayed behind at the home camp. Children, the older warriors, teachers. The tribal leaders...and the queen."

The caustic edge in her voice held a vein of bitter anger.

It stirred something familiar inside me.

"The *queen*. She raised me after my mother's death." She laughed and it was a cold, wintry sound. "They told me I was *lucky*. My mother had been her sister—they were close, although separated by decades. My mother was years younger, and more beloved by the people...and her parents. There were rumors that rule was meant to go to her. But when their mother died without naming an heir, it was my aunt who stepped in to lead. And how very *lucky* I was to have an aunt who loved my sister enough to raise me when she died so unexpectedly, still in her prime."

Lemera lapsed into silence for long moments, the air around her bitterly cold.

I had the odd urge to say...something. But how did you comfort a ghost? Without thinking, I reached out. Touched her arm. She stilled, then slowly, covered my hand with hers. It was a brittle, frigid connection, but I couldn't pull away and she was talking again.

"She was beautiful. Even now, I remember my mother's face, how she smiled at me the morning she left, how strong her arms were when she hugged me. I never thought it would be the last time. She was Olympias...one of our greatest warriors. But she died, taken down by a coward's arrow when she stopped to water her horse."

The burn of Lemera's rage was an icy fire at the back of my tongue, a roar in my mind. I struggled to block it off, the push of it trying to consume me. And she kept *talking*, the words wrapping around me and pulling me into the eye of the storm.

"Since Olympias had been the queen's beloved sister, she would take me in, raise me, care for me like I was her own. But she was a cold creature. I knew the moment I looked into her eyes that my life would be the worse for knowing her."

Her voice had softened. My eyelids felt heavy.

Dimly, I was aware of Justin taking my arm.

But the spell of her words pulled at me and the rush of whispers, the cold chill of peaceful death in my mind, it all made it so much harder to focus on him.

"Weak, she told me," Lemera murmured.

Such a waste, Fanis purred into my nightmares. *Your mother should have strangled you with your cord.*

I heard the words again, like Fanis stood before me. But it wasn't the same voice.

"Were that it had been you who died, Lemeraties. You, and not Olympias. Had you been older, stronger..."

"I am sorry, Aunt."

A bruising, burning blow across my cheek sent me flying.

Images, faces, names, they rushed by in a blur and I had the impression of time passing, even though some part of me was still trapped on my hands and knees. Then she was over me again.

"Get up, Lemeraties. Wipe the blood from your face and be silent. Do not speak unless I tell you to do so, girl." She glared at me and she no longer towered over me. No, she had to tilt her head back slightly to meet my gaze and her lip curled in dismay. *"Get out of my sight. And pray you prove to be an adequate soldier. Otherwise, I'll throw you out into the dark beyond the campfires one night and the hell beasts can have you."*

"Kit!"

Justin's voice boomed around me and I flinched in reaction, jerking away from him as he went to shake me again.

"What the hell?" I snapped.

Or rather, I tried to. My throat was too dry. My lips were parched.

He was staring at me with wide, startled eyes and Colleen hunkered down next to me, holding my hand.

And behind them, looking incorporeal and like a monster from the grave once more, Lemera hovered.

"I'm sorry, Kitasa," she said softly. "I didn't mean to pull you into my memories."

"What the hell was that?" I asked, smacking Justin's hands away. My throat was still too dry.

Colleen offered me a bottle of water and I took it, draining half of it. A shiver raced through me and I frowned when I saw night had settled around us, all lingering signs of twilight erased. "What do you mean, you pulled me into your memories?"

Lemera's image pulsed in front of me. From one moment to the next, she went from her sepulchral form to the lovely, lean warrior.

"When I had healed you from the wound before," she said after a long moment of quiet. "It was by sharing some of the...essence that traps me here. The magic, you might call it. It's made of hundreds of trapped souls, Kitasa. Including mine. I did not think there would be so strong a connection between us, but it seems there is. That connection is how I can find you, how I was able to slip into your dreams...and how you can apparently slip into my memories."

"Why is there a connection at all?" I asked uneasily.

"It's because of the blade; you're now bonded to it, just as I am. And that isn't good. She can't know you have the blade, Kit. I've broken free of her hold, but once she realizes the blade isn't still with Fenele's body or Reshi's, she'll come seeking it." She looked away, her jawline tight. "She's pathological in her desire to keep what she sees as hers."

"Sounds like Fanis," I muttered.

"I see so much of myself in you," Lemera murmured, touching my cheek. "I chased freedom as much as you did. I fought for it. And even if it meant dying for it, I would. But I was very much my mother's child." She gave me a hint of a smile. "Our bloodline was strong with warriors. My mother was swifter, stronger, better than the queen. More beautiful, too, although that didn't matter, not to my μήτηρ."

The word bounced in my head, not quite connecting—but then it did. "Your mother."

"Yes." Lemera inclined her head. "Olympias was born second, many years after her first child was, long after the time when her mother would have thought she was past the age of conceiving again. Olympias was her beloved, her treasure. It's said there was love between my grandmother and the man who sired my mother. They didn't just meet to conceive a child and never see each other again as many of the women seeking lovers outside the people. It was common, even then. Few boy children were born to the people and we had to seek partners from elsewhere. I'm told my great-grandmother, the warrior for whom I'm named, was courted by a man who she favored, even after her daughter's birth. He wanted a second child from her, but it never happened. They remained devoted to each other, though. He was a powerful fighter, too. There were even whispers that he was descended from one of the most legendary warriors of all time." Her eyes glinted when she looked at me. "I do not know if he is still remembered. In my time, he was still spoken of with reverence: Ἀλέξανδρος. He claimed territory from blue-green seas where I lived as a girl south down to Egypt where they worshipped him as a god and far into the east."

Her words clicked.

"Are you..." I had to swallow. "You're talking about Alexander the Great. One of your ancestors was *Alexander the Great*."

"So he *is* remembered." She looked pleased. Then her smile widened as her gaze came to mine. "He's your ancestor, too, little sister. You come from my bloodline, child. It's why I feel you so strongly."

Something else clicked as I stared into her eyes, recognition. Some part of me had known this already, and not just because she insisted on calling me *little sister.*

"Great," I murmured. "So I have a famous ancestor."

A famous ancestor, and a homicidal ghost who liked to hover in my vicinity and a batshit crazy grandmother.

And that trait seemed to run in the family.

Lemera's features softened, even as her eyes turned somber.

"Yes. The evil in the bloodline runs deep," she said, coming closer, until just a few inches separated. "It took me ages to understand just how deep, and how old the evil was."

"I don't know if I want to hear this," I said warily.

"You do not have a choice." She caught my face in her hands.

They were icy, cold enough to steal the breath from my lungs.

I felt Justin grab me, but that cold sank into him, too and he stumbled back, crashing into Colleen. They both fell against the nearby wall before Justin managed to steady himself, but his teeth were chattering, so loud I heard it even through the dull roar of blood crashing in my ears.

"Kit," Colleen said, her voice sharp with anger and the air cracked in warning as her power fluctuated.

Staring into Lemera's eyes, I forced the question out through lips gone numb with cold, "What are you doing?"

"You have to see," she told me.

And everything around me blurred, then went dark and cold like I was falling into a deep, deep pool of black ice.

Chapter Fourteen

Lemeraties
Approx 250 A.D.
Greece, Roman Empire

"Zabbai will accompany you."

I stared at the woman on the elevated platform before me, wanting nothing so much as to walk out of her elegant home into the night. Alone.

I had my horse and I had my spear, my knives, my bow. I did not need her pretty, fawning son at my heels.

None of this was his doing. I would mind my tone and treat him with respect as he had always treated me.

Zabbai, somehow, had been raised with the morals of a decent man, unlike his mother, the queen of our people. My monstrous aunt who craved power like a dying man thirsted for water. It was likely because he had spent his formative years in the lands of his father, only coming to us in recent years.

If he had been raised by the queen, he would have been as soulless as she.

But if he had been raised by her, I would not have the problem of ridding myself of his incessant attempts to woo me to his side.

I had refused his suit for a number of reasons and not just because I had not wanted another tie to my aunt. There were some suggesting she would name him her successor. In all our history, a *man* had never led us. That was not my quarrel with her, or him. He was far more fit to lead our people, any people, than her. But a drunken goat would be more fit to lead us than the woman sitting before me. It was not even that our mothers had been half-sisters, although, that, in my mind, did make me shy away from such a pairing. Many thought it was silly, but I made my decisions based on my thoughts, not the thoughts of others.

"Have you nothing to say, Lemeraties?"

"Zabbai has never undertaken such a hunt," I said coolly. But she had already made up her mind. I would be taking her son with me. Not caring for the disrespect the gesture conveyed, I looked away from her to meet her son's gaze. His eyes were a rich, deep brown, an oddity among the people, and his skin was a deeper shade of gold, a trait he had inherited from his father, a warrior from one of the lands farther southeast.

I had heard that he had been a commander in Rome's armies, and that he was the descendant of a warrior queen.

Had she been as mad as the one who led our people? Biting back the amused smirk, I inclined my head at the tall, powerful male. "You are a skilled warrior. But you did not grow up hunting the monsters of the night, prince."

"No." He did not look insulted. "But it is a skill I must learn if I am to take my place here, warrior. My men will accompany us. They are highly skilled—"

"No," I said, cutting him off.

His eyes narrowed slightly, a hint of arrogance creeping. "You do not issue commands, Lemeraties."

"I lead the scouting parties and I take down more feral night creatures than any other in camp," I countered. "When it comes to leading such a hunt, *yes*, I do issue commands. Otherwise, people die."

He went to respond. But one of the men at his back stepped in, spoke quietly. I knew him. I disliked Marius—his arrogance and way of treating my people bordered on cruel. However, he had more wisdom than many of the people in camp, possessed more cunning.

And when I heard him murmur that the others were not as swift as Zabbai, or as skilled as Marius, and certainly not as skilled as myself, I had to bite back grudging appreciation. Perhaps I would be forced to take the prince. But not those who followed at his heels like shadows.

Turning to the queen, I said, "Aunt Madae, it is one thing to lead a party of two, perhaps three. But another to lead four, or five, or six, especially when most of those you would have me lead have little knowledge of those we hunt, and even less of the land we must travel."

A grumble from the men at Zabbai's back and he silenced them.

"Marius and I alone will go." Zabbai moved to stand with me.

I did not look at him. If she wanted me to take him, she needed to be aware that the more cumbersome the hunting party, the more likely it would be to get him killed.

Her lips curved. "Will this suffice, Lemeraties? Since you do seem to think you can give the orders, I want to be certain this...meets your approval."

IT WAS A HARD, BRUTAL ride to get to the small village. It was not yet dusk and while my eyes were gritty with dirt from the road and my stomach an empty knot, I ignored Marius when he asked Zabbai if he would like to find a place to wash and get a meal.

This was no town on a merchant route. These were farmers and all of them were terrified. I could hear their panicked breathing as I strode to the home of the witch I had been told to ask for.

"Lemeraties, where are you going?"

I did not spare Marius a look. "A local woman has information we need. I am going to her home."

"Will she have food and beds?"

That did make me pause. With a grunt of amusement, I stopped and looked at him, then gestured at the hovel at the far end of the packed earth that made up a path. "She lives there. What do you think?"

Marius looked at me in horror. "You think to take the prince *there*?"

"I care little if you bring him or not. But she has answers I need and I am going to fetch them."

I turned and started for the small, humble home. After two steps, I slowed, watching as a woman emerged.

She held a basket in one hand and across the distance that separated us, our eyes connected. Her mouth firmed into a tight, unyielding line as she looked past me. Whether it was Marius or Zabbai who made the frown deepen, I did not know. But I had no time for squabbling, even less for personal, petty dislikes.

Still gripping the worn leather reins of my mount in one hand, I lifted a hand in cautious greeting.

"Theophila. I come as requested."

She gestured for us to follow and I looked back at Marius. He scowled in disapproval. "She is the village wise woman and knew how to reach the queen. I suggest you show respect," I advised him.

Zabbai strode by him and clapped him on the shoulder. "Care for the horses, my friend. Lemeraties and I will talk to the woman and see what we can discover."

THEOPHILA WELCOMED us into her home and prepared a simple meal. Zabbai showed courtesy by accepting the bread, olives and a few strips of meat with a bow of his head, and Marius was left with no choice to do anything else.

"Let us step outside," she said to me in a softer voice. "The men may eat and we will talk of the troubles within the village."

"Discuss them here," Zabbai ordered, waving a hand at the hearth. He caught sight of the look on Theophila's face and smiled. "Please. If time is short and these...night creatures will attack soon, then should we not make haste?"

I touched Theophila's hand. "My people are mostly women, *gerona*."

The word came to my lips easily, one that meant *wise one* in my language. I did not stop to think of Theophila would understand it but she gave me a considering look, then nodded slowly. "You do not take meals separately from men among the blood?"

"No." Shaking my head, I gestured for her to lead to the way. "The elders dine first in formal gatherings. On feast days, the warriors who have had the most victorious hunts will lead the celebrations...after the queen has given her blessing." She always selected her favored warriors. I had never been selected but I had no issue with it. Her favor came with costs. I did not know those costs, but I had seen the weight of it in the dulling of eyes among others. I preferred my freedom.

Once we were even with the men, I sat, recognizing Theophila's lingering reluctance.

Zabbai gave a charming smile. "The meal is most pleasing, *gerona*. My thanks."

"I can claim no credit," she said. "I help with those in the village. They pay me with food or grain."

Her eyes moved to the door of the small home, a shadow falling across her gaze. "You must help us, warrior."

Zabbai stirred but when Theophila turned her head, her gaze connected with mine, not his.

"The beast is a mad thing. She has already killed..." Her words faded and she closed her eyes.

I took her hand and squeezed. "I will help you. You have my word."

THE WOLF CAME IN THE quietest hours of the night.

I had laid traps at the vulnerable points of entry and slyly maneuvered Zabbai until *he* suggested he take the position I'd felt was the most unlikely point of attack. That had been the easier part. The harder part had been convincing him I had not needed his man Marius with me. Only goading and pointed remarks that fighting with an unfamiliar male at my back was likely to get me killed finally made him see reason.

My skin was tight, mind so clear and thoughts racing fast as I stood in the pale light of a half moon, pacing as I waited.

She was out there, the murderous night beast of a wolf who had gone half-mad after being attacked by another of the sort. Not all of them killed. I had met more than a few who only wanted to be left in peace. But some made no attempt to control the blood lust.

This wolf was one of them.

I could feel her hunger for blood, just as I had felt her eyes on me earlier as she had crept closer during the night.

She would attack soon.

A prickling on the back of my neck had me tensing.

Of all the foolish...

Spinning, I lifted my hand and pressed it to Zabbai's chest, holding him at arm's length.

His teeth flashed white against his deep, golden-brown skin, his dark brown hair pulled back to reveal the clean angular lines of his face.

"Did I startle you, Lemeraties?"

"Go back to your post," I told him. "She is close."

"I know. I sense her as well. That is why I am here. You do not have to fight these beasts alone. I am at your side."

The urge to curl my lip and sneer rose inside, but his offended wounded pride would do nothing. "Marius needs your aid more than I. I have been on night hunts for years. This is his—"

A low, ugly snarl came to us.

I spun away and crouched, lifting my bow. "Stay clear."

Off in the night, I heard a scream.

"Marius," Zabbai whispered. Then he did the worst thing imaginable. He turned away from the monster that lay in front of us, stalking us in the darkness...and ran.

Stupid man.

Yes, he ran because he wanted to help his friend.

But one never *ran* from monsters—it only made the monsters want to give *chase*.

And the wolf most certainly wanted to do just that.

I stayed where I was, crouched low with my arrow at the ready as the monstrous thing leaped out of the darkness and sailed over my head. Her shadow seemed to blot out the night, she was so massive.

I loosed one arrow, grabbed another. Loosed it.

Both hit and I felt the hot spray of blood on my face, tasted it on my lips.

She crashed down hard but I was already moving, dropping my bow and calling the spear that all but leaped to my hand, his jubilant music and death song a pulsebeat on the back of my tongue.

The wolf spun toward me in a desperate attack to kill before I could kill her.

But the arrows were lodged in her heart, the silver working to slow her. I just had to buy enough time for them to *end* her. Throwing myself to the side, I tucked into a roll. The wolf let out an enraged howl. At the end of it, I heard a wet, pained noise and knew she did not have much time.

I heard something else, as well.

Screaming.

"Die, bitch," I told her.

She came for me again. But she was even slower and when I feinted to the side, she stumbled, then went down hard. Her pained yelp told me that she had managed to drive the arrows deeper into her heart as she hit the earth. Poor, miserable beast. I darted to the side, then around, to her back. She was shuddering, her breath rattling in and out of her lungs.

When I drove the spear in through her ribs, finding the massive heart, she went rigid, then...slowly, her body went lax.

I wrenched my spear side to side, destroying the heart before yanking the weapon back.

"Is she..."

"Yes," I bit off to the foolish villager who had come out to watch me kill a monster. "Get inside unless you want to join them."

Then I turned and ran toward the sound of sobbing.

The screams had already stopped.

I was too late.

"RETURN TO YOUR MOTHER, Zabbai," I told him two mornings later. "Take the body with you and do your mourning."

Zabbai moved in on me until I had to tilt my head back to hold his gaze.

I did not back up or look away.

With him so close, it was impossible to miss the changes in him. His eyes were too wide, the whites showing around the warm rich brown of his irises and fine red veins streaked through, the evidence of tears shed and sleep lost.

Marius's death had hit him hard.

He was close to his men, but there had been something deeper between him and his second in command. It had not bothered me that they were lovers. One of my many cousins had asked if that was why I had turned his suit down. It was not. I simply had no interest in marrying the son of the queen, in becoming more entangled in her life. I wanted to be *away* from her, not tied to her through marriage, and eventually children.

"Return to my *mother*," he said, all but spitting the words into my face.

The heat of his anger beat at me. But even when he grabbed me by the arms, I did not flinch away.

"That thing that killed my..." He stopped. "Marius is dead. Some of those beasts still live, are free to kill others, to make more of their ilk. The queen sent us out to fulfil a task. I will not return until it is done. And neither will you." His hands gripped me with bruising force, his gaze locked on mine with obsessive intent. "Do you understand?"

"You will get yourself killed," I told him gently.

"Do you understand?" he demanded a second time, shaking me as he spoke.

Madness glimmered in his eyes as he stared at me and I wondered if he had any hint at just how well I understood.

"Let me go."

His hands fell away. Hollow-eyed, he shook his head. "I will not return until the task is done. It is all I have left to me."

"So be it."

Chapter Fifteen

Victory

The cave along the shoreline was a tight fit once we had our horses settled in. There was no choice, though. A storm had blown in. I was not going to leave them outside, exposed to the wind and rain...and the wolves still hunting us.

At this point, it would be hard to say who hunted who.

Over the past three weeks, I had killed three large beasts and Zabbai had killed one.

There were two more yet to be taken down. One was the alpha beast, the other one of the females we had been hunting from the start. Neither would be an easy kill.

Zabbai had lost weight, refusing to eat unless I threatened to shove it down his throat, sticking to wine and water only because thirst drove him to drink. Typically, he preferred wine. His body was pared down to muscle stretched over bone and if he did not start eating soon, it would affect his strength.

Eying him over the fire as I finished the fish I had caught in a net earlier, I said, "We cannot hope to continue on tomorrow if you do not eat something. You will weaken. You are a warrior, Zabbai. You know you need to fuel your body if you want to fight."

"Lemeraties." He took a sip from the wineskin. "You hover like a mother goat with her kid. I tire of hearing it."

"Act like a grown man—a soldier, and I will not have to act like a mother."

Through the smoky haze, he looked at me and his eyes glinted, hard and bright. "Marius told me you were a hard, demanding woman who would be impossible to please." He took another sip of wine. "I knew he was right."

"If that is your belief, I do not know why you insisted on trying to court me." Bored with the topic, but glad he was no longer trying to lose himself inside the wineskin, I passed him some of the fish. "Put some food in your belly and rest."

"I insisted because, I, like Marius, knew I would get strong sons off you." He stared at me with a near fanatical look in his eyes. "It was the reason we accepted my mother's request to come stay with the lot of you, half-mad, warring women who fight as men do. Why else would I have left my people?"

"The women in our line almost always breed true—girl babes, hardly a boy among them." Amused, I leaned my back against the rock wall, the surface worn smooth by storms and rain and time.

"The men in my line almost always breed sons." His lids drooped. "If it took several tries to get a boy off you, so be it. A child from your people, and one of Alexandros's line...he would be a fine leader. Marius..."

He trailed off and looked away.

"You do his memory no honor by getting yourself killed," I told him. "Eat."

"You are incessant," he muttered. But a faint smile curved his lips and he tore a flaky piece of fish off and shoved it into his mouth. "And wise."

He ate half the fish before putting the rest aside. "Why do you dislike your queen?"

I wondered why he did not call her his mother, although I was not surprised he did not consider her his queen. He had been raised in the land of his father, far from our lands and his loyalties were not with my people...but he had honor and he would not wage war against his mother's people even if he did not give her fealty. At least, not without cause.

As to his question...

I met his gaze, considered him. "Do you like her?"

His brow arched but he did not answer.

And that was answer enough.

MY SLEEP WAS RESTLESS.

I lay down with the intention of sleeping lightly, too aware the heavy rain would limit the ability to hunt and track, but it would also muffle the sound of anything approaching.

The prickle of awareness that raced over my skin had me rolling to a crouch with a blade in hand, the grip so familiar it was like an extension of my arm. The rain had lessened. That was not what had woken me.

No, there was an odd tension in the air, a heaviness.

A *waiting*.

The wolves were out there.

Both of them.

Until now, they had stayed spread out. The humans-changed did not hunt together like natural wolves. These beasts possessed so much of their old way of thinking, both more, and less, sly than their true-born counterparts, operating with a cruel cunning that was unnatural to animals, while still possessing the speed and instinct of the predator whose shape they took.

Putting the blade down, I called my bow.

The smooth wood settled in my hand as movement rustled quietly behind me. *Please,* I thought, praying to whatever god might listen. *Let him be still.*

Even one whisper could alert them.

The horses were awake and alert, but they were beasts bred by the people, knew better than to betray me. If they panicked, we would be in trouble. For now, their training held true.

Zabbai eased closer, not stopping until he was side by side with me in the darkened mouth of the cave.

The clouds had not cleared enough for the moonlight to pierce through but my night sight was keen. He held up a hand to get my attention. Reluctant to break my focus, I glanced at him quickly. He showed me his fist, then lifted one finger, then a second. *One? Or two?*

I showed him two fingers.

Both wolves are out there.

His face was grim, but thankfully, I caught no sign of the grief-induced madness that had driven him since we had left Marius's body behind while a messenger sent word back to the people.

He crept silently to the other side of the cave entrance and I saw that he had brought his bow and arrow with him.

A soft brush of sound in the darkness had my attention back on the nightscape before me.

Zabbai would have to look after himself now.

Otherwise, neither of us would live through the night and these monsters would continue to ravage the people in this territory.

There was another sound, the barest hint. Claws clicking on rough stone. And it was close. So close.

Next to me, I sensed Zabbai tightening his muscles in preparation to act.

The hairs on the back of my neck stood on end and it was like I felt the brush of death...but it came from the other direction. I lunged and grabbed the back of his tunic just before he would have moved. He hesitated, but was not yet deterred from his course so I shifted my hold to his neck and wrenched both of us backward into the cave.

"Trap," I rasped into his ear as we hit the worn smooth stone of the cave floor.

He rolled off me and grabbed his bow, moving into a crouch. He was ready before I was and over my head, I heard the arrow.

A pained yelp echoed around the cave.

But the beast was still coming.

My spear was in my hand. I had no conscious thought of calling it but once more I was on the stony ground, rolling to get out of the wolf's way, and then, on my knees as I plunged the spear's silver head into the thing's heart. It snarled and threw itself harder onto the length of it in an attempt to get at me.

Zabbai was at my side in a heartbeat, his sword joining my spear.

We both went down under the monster's weight.

An enraged howl shattered the night and I jerked away as the second beast, the biggest one, the alpha, rushed in.

I called my bow, mind a blur.

One arrow. Two. Three.

The beast crashed onto me, massive jaws snapping.

A brawny forearm came around the thing's neck and wrenched it back and an inhuman sound came from Zabbai's throat as he squared off with the injured alpha.

The arrows hadn't pierced his heart.

I'd missed.

Each shot had missed.

Rolling to my neck, everything in me hurting, I pulled my blade. "He is hurt," I told Zabbai. "Let us finish him."

But the wolf turned in a burst of speed and lunged out of the cave.

He was gone. Curse my luck. We were not done.

THE BEAST'S MASSIVE head sat by the mouth of the cave. The rest of the body was farther down the beach, already being picked over by carrion.

We had survived and one more wolf was dead. The dead female was the one who had killed Marius. Zabbai had his revenge.

The alpha still had to be tracked and killed but I could do that alone.

Zabbai sat in front of me, wrapping a length of linen around the bite on my arm. "You are protected from their curse?"

I looked at him, surprised by the question, but then I shook my head at my own foolishness. He had only spent the past five years among us. Of course, he would have questions. "Yes. As you would be had you been bitten. Our blood protects us from the curse of all night creatures. We would be no good at our quest if we were so easily felled, Zabbai."

A grim look entered his gaze. "No wonder you were so determined my men not accompany us. I thought you arrogant, even though I have heard of your skills. Now that I have seen it...I should have left Marius behind. He would be alive now."

"Would your friend have so easily stayed behind while you left on a dangerous task?"

Zabbai's mouth tightened and grief darkened his eyes but he did not answer.

A headache pulsed at the base of my neck, my skin heating as the fever edged closer.

Zabbai eyed me narrowly. "We have fresh water thanks to the rain. How bad will the fever be?"

"Not bad," I told him, glad he understood that much of the process. "But I will not be ready to travel for a day or so. You should return. You have completed your quest—"

"I go nowhere." He grasped my face in his hand, glaring down at me. "You saved my life, Lemeraties. As much as grief chokes me, I cannot abandon my men, my people. I will not leave you here injured and alone. I have more honor than that."

He released me and rose. "You will rest and heal, then we will hunt the alpha and kill him. Once that is done, we both return."

THE FEVER HIT FASTER than it ever had before.

Zabbai passed a damp cloth over my brow and it was like ice on my skin. Swatting out at the offending thing, I bared my teeth at him. "Stop it. Leave me alone."

"We need to bring your fever down before it boils your brain."

But when he tried to approach again, I swung out. The fever might indeed be boiling my brain because I missed him. He caught my fist and eased my hand to my side as he sat, bringing the cloth to my brow. "The fever has risen sharply, Lemeraties. It will ease soon and you will feel better."

"You used to be quieter, Zabbai. Might you go back to the times when you were quieter?" I squeezed my eyes shut and moaned. "Curse the lights around us. Why do you have so many lamps ablaze?"

There was a brief silence and then he moved away.

Darkness returned, then, so did he. "Forgive me, Lemeraties. I needed the light to check your wound, but they are all out now, save for one. Take some wine for me now...that is the way. Would you like more?"

His voice faded in and out, endlessly, until I fell back into sleep.

THE EMPTY EYE SOCKETS of a dead wolf greeted me when I woke.

The air had cooled since my last clear thoughts and I shivered, instinctively retreating back against the warmth behind me as I stared at the wolf's skull. How many days had it been?

A hand drifted down my side.

I stilled.

When a mouth nuzzled my shoulder, I sat upright so fast my head spun in dizzying circles and it took precious moments before the world stopped wheeling around before me. Slowly, I looked over at the man lying next to me.

It was Zabbai.

He was just starting to stir from his slumber, a thick, heavy fringe of lashes lifting over his eyes before drifting back down. That happened three times before he finally opened his eyes fully and looked around, focusing on me after what seemed like an eternity.

"You're awake," he murmured, a half-smile on his face. "The fever broke?"

"Why are you lying so close?"

Instead of making excuses, he sat up and touched the back of his hand to my brow. "Still rather warm but not frighteningly so." Then he looked into my eyes. "The temperature dropped during the night. There was another storm. You were shivering and I was cold myself. We had not come out expecting a journey that would last almost a month or one that would take us into the northern climates. I will not have you take ill because you aided me, Lemeraties."

"You will not *have* me," I echoed, amusement and irritation warring inside me.

Zabbai's lids drooped. Heat flared in his gaze.

And be it the fever or something else I could not name, I felt an echo of it inside.

He rose, leaving nothing but his lingering warmth on the blanket where we had slept and I watched him walk away. "Are you strong enough to travel if we move at a slow pace?"

"Yes." I rose, taking care not to push myself, but my head was steady, my balance secure, even if my limbs did feel weaker than I liked. That was the way of these fevers. Some food and another few days of moderate pace and I would be back to normal. We could not risk lingering. Lives depended on us tracking the alpha.

Zabbai had moved from his place and I hesitated, eying him by the dying embers of the campfire, acutely aware of his eyes on me. When he lifted a hand to touch me, I did not pull away as I should have. When he moved in closer, I stayed there, waiting.

And when he kissed me, I held still for long, long moments...until need overtook me and I was kissing him back.

Chapter Sixteen

Betrayal

"I will not return to my mother's home."

Zabbai and I sat in the quiet around the fire.

Another wolf's head had joined the first. The alpha had been a giant of a man, large, brutish and fast. But Zabbai had learned from his mistakes and we had taken the beast down easily, despite the fact that this one had been one of the stranger ones, who could take on a form between man and beast and walk on two legs. He had been in that strange, half-form when he had died and his skull was more monstrous than anything I had ever seen.

Looking at it gave me nightmare thoughts but I forced my attention from the rotting meat to the man next to me.

"So you mean to return home?"

He nodded, still gazing at the skull. "My men already have. I sent word back weeks ago. They were to collect Marius and take him back to the land of my father. I will return there."

It was strange that his words left an odd, empty space inside.

"I will give your regards to your mother," I told him.

"No." He rolled to his knees and came to me. "That is not why I am telling you, Lemeraties."

"Oh?" He took my hand and I studied him, trying not to let my thoughts linger on the odd, heavy ache in my chest. I should not *have* odd, heavy aches in my chest—not over *this* man. Our task was done, the goal accomplished. He should be able to collect his men and return home if he no longer wanted to spend time among his mother's people.

"Why are you telling me?"

He rubbed his calloused thumb over the back of my hand and his gaze was intent. "Do you know..." His words trailed off and after a moment, he tried again. "Marius and I knew each other from the time we were boys. We trained together. Fought together. We were more than just friends."

Tugging my hand free of his, I reached up and cupped his cheek. "My people are mostly women, Zabbai. If you think I have not guessed that the bond between you and Marius went deeper than mere friendship, then I am insulted you think I am a naïve fool. You mourn a lover as well as a friend."

"Yes." He met my gaze then, held it. "My mother would not understand this, for all that there are those among your people who take lovers of the same sex, as Marius and I were. I had already tired of listening to her disparaging prattle, Lemeraties. If I have to listen to her insults against him now...I might resort to violence."

I could not say I blamed him. "Madae thinks she alone knows what is right, Zabbai. You are far from the only one she has cast judgment on. I know that does not help, but it is who she is."

"And she is a terrible queen, an even worse parent. I am done with her." He traced a finger over the back of my hand. "But...I do not wish to be done with you. I want you to come with me, Lemeraties."

I stared at him. "What?"

"You heard me. I am not fit to help lead my father's people, not as I am. I will never be a governor in the Roman empire as he is, as my brothers aspire to be—I have older brothers and I am glad of it, but I still expect to be entrusted with my former duties once I return home. Marius provided the wisdom I lacked. And over the past months, you have done the same. *Come with me*," he urged. "I can offer you far better than Madae ever would—and you would have more freedom at my side than she allows you."

Stunned, I shook my head. "My people do not simply *leave*, Zabbai."

"The boy children do." He crooked a grin at me. "Am I not proof of that? The boy children are all but cast out among your kind. And it is not as if she has ever made you welcome. She will treat no child of yours any better."

"I had no plans to become a mother."

He reached down and placed a hand on my belly. "We have not taken care to prevent such an occurrence, Lemeraties. What will you do if you are with child now? Let her take your daughters and turn them into her puppets?"

His eyes held mine as I realized he was right.

Slowly, I reached down and covered the hand on my belly. "She would not take well to losing me, Zabbai. I am one of her best."

"You will be my wife, my partner and whatever duty I am assigned when I return home, you will share it with me—my father is a man who respects intelligence in a woman." Sliding his hand down to grip my thigh, he leaned in. "I cannot promise any piece of my heart because it is already gone. But you would have all the might of my father's leadership at your side if you accept me, Lemeraties. And she cannot stand against that."

WORD WAS SENT ALONG with the wolf skulls once they had been completely stripped of all flesh and fur.

The task is complete. Payment for the task accompanies the skulls of the killer and her alpha, Queen Madae.

Please accept also the gift of twenty-five thousand denarii from Zabbai...

The cost was given in exchange for the loss of income I would have provided, Zabbai told me, because he was well aware of my aunt's greed. The money was coded as a gift from his father, by way of Zabbai.

The missive went on to praise Madae and bless her beauty and strength as a warrior, thank her for bestowing such a powerful mate upon Zabbai. But it ended in a short, clipped fashion, leaving it clear that neither Zabbai nor I would return.

During my pithier moments, I let myself imagine how irate she would be, knowing her son had *dismissed* her, and that I just walked away.

I expected reprisal, because she never let anybody simply *leave*—she dismissed those she found lacking, but people did not just *leave*.

But as one year drifted into two, then three, I simply forgot about her.

The world was trapped in a time of unrest. Rome continued its unending march, expand the empire. Zabbai's father had survived two assassination attempts and two of his three older brothers had died in war.

The past several years in the Roman empire had been chaos, the emperor Valerian ruling from afar as he continued waging his war distant lands. I was no stranger to battle, but it seemed to loom ever closer with each passing day.

Now, as winter edged closer, Zabbai came to me after we had eaten and told me what had darkened his mood the past two days. "My father had told me that you and I are to travel to Athens."

I stared at him. "Athens. Now?"

Uneasy, I touched my belly and he covered my hand.

I had lost a babe the summer before last, a boy. We had both grieved and when I told him my suspicions that I was with child a few days earlier, he had swept me into his arms and taken me to bed before we had eaten supper. He had spent long hours marking me, kissing and touching. He did not love me with the ferocity that had bonded him and Marius. But we had a bond and it was one I had come to treasure.

Now, as he relayed this news from his father, I understood his fierce protectiveness over the past few days.

"Yes." He pulled me close and touched his brow to mine. "It is your aunt, Lemeraties. There are rumors she threatens to join forces with those who make war against Rome. My father hopes I can dissuade her. If I do not..."

His eyes took on a grim cast.

"If you do not, will Rome march against my people, Zabbai?"

"I think you and I both know the answer, dear wife."

IT HAD BEEN ALMOST five years since I had seen my aunt.

Travel to Athens took almost a month. If I had not been carrying the child, it would have been easier, but while I was healthy and strong, I still needed rest. And Zabbai worried.

So did I.

I did not argue when he decided we should make camp early that final night instead of pushing on into the city.

Some of the men in our entourage grumbled, but fell silent at one look from him and he joined me at the fire, sitting behind me and rubbing the tension from my shoulders.

"You are quiet," he murmured into my ear.

"Just tired," I told him. Tired. Cold. The past few years had softened me, but I was reluctant to mention it. I had come to like having a comfortable bed to sleep on, and on the nights when he was not out following his father's dictates, having Zabbai with me was...nice.

Perhaps I loved him.

It had been a long time since I had loved anybody, although the driving protectiveness I felt for my unborn baby was rooted in a mother's instinctive love. Yet it was not anything like what I felt for Zabbai. Strange, having it come on like it had. Just a few short years ago, I had simply wanted him out of my life and now...

A cold chill raced up my spine. Darkness edged in from the corners of my mind.

A whisper of foreboding creeped along my senses.

Turn back.

"Lemeraties?"

Slowly, I rose, one hand braced on Zabbai's shoulder. I was only halfway through the pregnancy and the babe did not seem to be particularly large but I was not yet accustomed to the balance of my ever-changing body.

"Have the men douse the fires," I said quietly.

Zabbai hesitated only a moment before giving the order. I closed my lids in rapid-fire bursts, forcing them to adjust to darkness beyond the camp. Some of the men were resistant to the idea of being on this windswept plane in near darkness and a few small campfires lingered in the distance. Not having the patience, I bit off, "The moon is half-full. Are they so soft they fear the light of the moon?"

The rest of the fires were doused within a few breaths.

Flexing my hand, I listened to the whispered warnings in the back of my mind, heard the frenzied murmurs and in response, I called my bow.

"Lemeraties?"

His whisper was all but soundless.

It was still too loud.

"They are coming," I told him, because the things in the night had already heard him—heard us. The hair on the back of my neck stood on end and just as the air above me whistled, I jerked my bow up.

"Attack!" I shouted.

The warning came too late for some.

Screams rose around me as our men were hauled into the air by night monsters that fed on blood. Why were they *here*? These monsters—

I shoved the questions aside. There was no time for them.

"Take off their heads!" I called to Zabbai. "It is the best way to kill them—"

Pain ripped into me as fangs sank into my shoulder, one of the things grabbing me from behind.

"Not that one!"

The thing behind me froze. I summoned two blades, banishing the bow. With a fluid move, I drove one dagger into the thing's gut, then spun and took its head. It toppled, the body going to one side while the head went another.

Zabbai placed himself at my back. "Lemeraties, what are these things?"

"Blood drinkers. Destroying the heart completely or taking the head is the only way to kill them. Fight, Zabbai, or we will all die."

Another scream punctuated my statement, sending a shiver down my spine. A prickling awareness ran down my down, a warning that there was another threat drawing closer.

But a pale, thin woman flung herself at me, her fangs exposed, eyes pools of an endless, empty hunger devoid of all humanity.

We will all die regardless, I thought, despairing.

The child in my womb kicked, sensing my grief and I swung my sword once more. I would not quit. I could not give into despair.

Chapter Seventeen

Blooded

I woke to darkness.

A weak groan came from somewhere beyond me and I froze, knowing who it was on a deep, instinctive level.

Closer, there was a low, husky laugh and it held a malevolent pleasure that made my skin crawl.

"Darling child, are you *awake*?"

The words came out in a voice more akin to a sibilant hiss than anything human, and yet, I knew who it was. Carefully, I sat, flexing my muscles and trying to isolate any injuries. I felt none, not even the bite on my shoulder.

"What is this, Madae?" I asked softly. "Instigating an attack on your own son? Have you gone mad?"

"He is disloyal, Lemeraties," the queen said.

Light flared and I flinched away, lifting a hand to shield my eyes. As I adjusted to the lamp she had lit, I took in more of my surroundings. Every sight, every sound, every scent made my skin crawl.

We were underground in a tomb.

The scent of death, new and old, lay on the back of my tongue. I swallowed my gorge as it rose up my throat.

In the darkness, beyond the lamp, skittering things waited.

Another pained groan came from the far edges of the lamp's flickering light and I looked, even as everything in me told me I should not.

On a stone slab, my husband lay, a bloodied broken mess. Zabbai's warm, golden skin had gone sallow and he was streaked with blood, most of it old. The scents that came to my nose told me blood was not the only thing staining him. Edging closer, my eyes more acclimated to the darkness, I took in his injuries and a scream of rage threatened to tear out of me.

She had cut him open.

The foul *bitch* had cut him open.

Rushing to his side, I touched his brow, then immediately yanked my hand back.

He burned with fever. So far, the healing from our bloodline had kept him alive, but he would not survive these injuries—not down here in the dirt, without water, food, care.

She had wanted me to see him suffer.

"I see you are well-recovered from your own injuries," she said, sounding pleased.

Lifting my head, I stared at the woman my mother had called sister—the woman my mother had *loved*.

She had moved out of the darkness and stood before me

"What bit him?" I asked.

"Many things, child." Her eyes flashed in the darkness.

They went *black*. A strange, sinking sensation wrapped around me and I swallowed, fear filling me, a fear unlike anything I'd ever know.

She reached for me.

Adrenaline filled me and I leaped, putting the stone altar that held Zabbai between Madae and me...and the babe in my belly. I brought my arm up, pointing the dagger's sharp tip toward the queen.

"What bit him?" I asked again.

"Such an unimportant question." She clicked her tongue. "He no longer matters, girl. He will die soon, his blood on your hands."

"If he dies, it is because of you, you foul bitch." I would not have her laying that guilt at my feet. "You never change. When you sent my mother out on a mission *alone* through a land rife with marauders and monsters, it was *her* fault that she died, not yours. When our warriors leave and choose to never return, it is because *they* are disloyal, not because their queen is a monster. You are the problem, Madae—you are our greatest monster, our biggest nightmare."

Her eyes gleamed in their madness, the black swallowing up what little light came from the lamps.

"You should take care to not taunt monsters, Lemeraties. They may not care for it."

I laughed. "You think to terrify me? I lost my fear of you as a child, you old hag."

"Perhaps. But you have so much more to lose now."

I blinked and it was like she loomed larger in my sight, filling my vision until she blotted out all else.

My heart leaped into my throat and in that moment, I *did* feel fear.

Do not give in, a small, deep knowing murmured in the back of my mind. *She feeds on it. Do not give in.*

"Such as?" I forced myself to give Zabbai a dispassionate look. "It would seem as though my husband will die so the one thing in this life you might have used against me has already been taken from me, Madae. Stupid, that."

Her burgeoning image flickered and for a moment, she appeared normal again.

Zabbai's chest stuttered on a breath and he gasped out my name, his eyes opening.

No...

I did not look at him. Not then.

But Madae did. And she raced forward.

"Since he is to die, then, let us hasten it along. Why let him suffer?"

She shoved a hand into his chest.

I heard the bone crunch, *shatter*.

He screamed.

I lashed out, swinging out with my blade but she caught my hand in her free one, staring at me as she yanked Zabbai's heart out.

How...

Between us, Zabbai lay, lifeless and as I gaped at her, she crushed his heart in her hand.

"What..." The word squeezed out of me, but no others came. They echoed in my mind instead as a strange, eerie light, white and shining, rose from the bloody, ruined heart Madae clutched. *What are you?*

The light wound in a spiraling mist and I reached for it, uncertain why. I just did not want it to *touch* her.

She opened her mouth and as I tried again to grab for that pretty light, she inhaled.

"No!"

"Yes," she said, releasing my hand.

I stumbled back away from her, horror rising within as I realized what had happened.

She had somehow stolen Zabbai—not just his *life*, but *him*.

I stared at the man who had been my husband, my lover, her *son* for a long moment, the gaping hole in his chest a brutal, stark display of her madness.

"You are a monster," I said softly. "He was your son."

"He was a tool and he failed in his purpose," she said, flicking a dismissive hand. Then her gaze went to my swollen belly. "Although not *entirely*."

Cold terror tried to rise inside me. I banished it. I could not lose myself to fear because if I did, both the child and I were *truly* lost—Zabbai's child. It would not happen.

I would not let her have that victory.

She reached out a hand.

I backed up.

A low, amused laugh escaped her.

"You cannot run from me, Lemeraties. You are well and truly trapped." She smiled, displaying teeth that looked too white, too sharp in a face no longer familiar to me. "Enjoy these final hours with your husband. I will leave you alone with him. Bid your farewells. You have until morning before I have his body removed."

IN THE QUIET DARKNESS that followed her departure, Zabbai's body turned hard and cold in a way not normal for the dead. It should have taken far longer. He was already like a man dead several days yet I could still scent the faint trace of the herbs his murderer had used in her bathing water lingering in the air.

I prayed to whatever gods listened that I would find a way to free him.

But if that could not happen, then I would protect our child from such a fate.

Eventually, she would turn her maniacal appetites to our babe. I knew it in my bones.

How many times, I wondered. How often had she turned and grabbed one of our kind out of the dark?

Zabbai was not the first. In my gut, I knew it. *That* was the truth of our declining numbers. Oh, I was sure many of our warriors had left to find a mate in the outside world, promising to return and yet, they had chosen not to—but it was not only because they had found a better life far from the people. It was because they had fled a monster.

These were the whispers I had long ignored, not out of any loyalty to the queen, but because I had always planned a solitary life.

Now I wish I had listened, wished I had more knowledge.

The fear my people had shown, but hidden behind a veil of submission, the terror that would leak out when one of the younger women was found to be with child.

"A girl! A girl child to raise in the ways of the warrior!"

Because the boy children were sacrificed?

My mind shied away from the possibility. Madae, after all, had birthed a boy. But his father had been a powerful leader in the Roman Empire, had publicly approached Madae. He had returned to her several times over, as well. Perhaps Madae had sacrificed that one boy in hopes of having her own daughter.

"Zabbai, my love." Standing by his side, I stroked his cheek, the flickering light of the lamp highlighting his face. Pain and fear had left his handsome features disfigured in death, another insult. I smoothed his lids down until they closed, fished out a few coins from the purse at his belt and placed them on his eyes. "I am so sorry."

A deep, cold fury settled inside me once the task was done. She would not win. I would not *allow* it. Taking his wineskin, I drained half and went about my task, grisly as it was. I knew he would understand.

"Forgive me," I murmured once I was finished, tucking the wineskin in at my waist before fisting my hands in his tunic, making a show of smearing the blood on him, as if I had clung to him in grief. I brought the lamp closer, checked to see if she might be able to ascertain what I had done and decided not. As long as luck was on my side, and it must be—it *had* to be—she would never know. Not until it was too late.

"I will not let her defeat us, Zabbai. Even if it takes eternity."

Then I slid a hand down to the knife he wore strapped to his calf, the bronze dagger I'd gifted him a few months earlier.

Retreating into the shadows, I began to plan.

WHEN SHE CAME TO TAKE him, I stayed in the shadows, the dagger hidden by a few carefully placed rocks.

She eyed me narrowly, taking in the cavern with care as if searching for a trap.

There was no trap. Not yet.

I would take my time.

"I am parched. His wineskin is nearly empty and I had no chance to grab mine," I said coolly, holding his wineskin up, letting her see my bloodstained hands, the bloody drips along the wineskin itself—the weapon I would use to end her hidden inside that very wineskin—not yet forged. If the gods were kind, she would not see the attack coming until it was too late, until I destroyed her. "Am I to be left here to die of hunger and thirst or will there be food and water?"

Her lip curled. "You have blood all over you. I thought you did not mourn him."

"Did I say that?" I considered the blood on my hands, the wineskin before looking back at her. "He would have helped me raise a child. He warmed my bed. He was a decent man. I did not love him—you beat that emotion out of me as a child, Madae. I do not have to love to mourn. But that does not mean I shall gnash my teeth and tear at my clothes now that he is gone."

"And the babe?" She bared her teeth at me in a mockery of a smile.

"I cannot live my life as I would have without Zabbai. Not with a child." I started to heft the wineskin, then stopped. "You did not answer me about the water, or food."

"You do not *want* the child?"

Now I curled my lip at her. "I did not say that, either, dearest aunt. But above all else, I understand how life works. I understand how hard it is. This babe..." Laying a hand on my belly, I pretended to consider my options, knew she would never understand the deep, unending love I already felt for the baby Zabbai and I had created. Madae could not, because if she had, she would not have been able to kill her own child. "This babe belongs to a life I no longer have. I do not know what options lay before me, whether the baby will be a part of those choices or not. But I am no fool blinded by emotions, Madae. I learned that lesson at your knee."

That strange darkness swelled, swallowing the pale blue of her eyes and I found myself staring into the unrelenting blackness once more.

"I knew, that out of all of the blood, you were the one most like me." She smiled, cold and malicious, then flicked a hand at the wineskin. "Drink your fill. I will have food and water brought. I cannot have you wasting away on me. You may not yet know the options before you, but I do."

Shadows swelled into the cavern and I tensed, flowing into a crouch as robed figures came in to collect Zabbai's body.

I bit my tongue to keep from screaming out in fury.

She watched from the entrance.

I held her gaze and lifted the wineskin to my lips, forcing myself to take a small sip of the blood-tinged wine and kept my face blank as they took him away.

We will have vengeance, Zabbai. I swear it.

Chapter Eighteen

Unending Death

She returned with food, water...and a witch.

The witch was all but thrown in, only seconds before the entrance to the cavern was sealed, and the dusky-skinned woman turned and flung herself at the heavy rock, beating on it with her fists until they had to be bruised, and then more, until the iron-wet scent of her blood filled the air.

"You waste your time, and your strength," I finally said.

Tiny, natural crevices in the cavern allowed some sunlight to filter in and over the past few days, my eyes had adjusted until I could see as easily now as if it were fully daylight.

When the woman spun around to stare into the darkness, I could make out her features, a blade-straight nose and hair as black as onyx, eyes a liquid, dark brown. She was dirty and her clothes torn, streaked with blood, but under the dirt and blood, the material was finely made. The beaded band around her brow meant to hold her hair back from her face had slipped, but it was brightly colored and glinted with what I thought might be gold under the filth.

Madae had gone and stolen away a witch, I realized. A well-trained and respected one, judging by her garments. My aunt had truly gone mad.

This stranger...she would not disappear in silence. A woman of her rank would be missed—would be hunted.

Her eyes narrowed when she finally located me in the shadows. After a moment of consternation, she spat out words in the same language I had, but they were heavily accented and some were...awkwardly used. I frowned, trying to place the accent.

She spoke again, but in another tongue. I could place a few of the words but I shook my head, curious as to how many languages she spoke.

She said something else and those words, I *did* recognize—the language of Zabbai's homeland. I responded and watched her eyes widen.

She darted a look to the door, then slowly came closer.

"You are one of hers," she said slowly, using the same language. "Why not speak in her tongue?"

"I am not hers." I curled my lip. "We might share the same blood, but I am *not* one of hers."

She narrowed her eyes. "Where did you learn this tongue?" she demanded.

"My husband," I replied. "We lived in Tyre."

She raked me up and down with a look. "Golden hair. Blue eyes. You do not come from Tyre."

"No. I moved there to be with him. His father was from Tyre." I did not know if it would hurt me or help to tell her who Zabbai's mother was yet, so I remained quiet. But lying, I decided, would *not* help. "I moved there with him to be away from her. I despise her, and always have."

"Who is she to you?" the woman demanded.

Power crackled from her as she flung the question out and I knew if I lied, she would know.

"My mother's sister," I admitted with a weary sigh.

That made her frown and she gave her an aborted shake of her head. "That..." She pressed her full lips together. "Her..."

She stopped and looked at the door again, her reluctance becoming clear. When she looked back at me, she asked, "She knew where to find me. Even though I have lived in hiding for years. She...hunts. She *senses*. Can *you* hunt like that?"

"Yes." I inclined my head and pushed upright, hiding a grimace as my lower back protested the movement.

She sensed the pain nonetheless and a hiss escaped her. "You are with child!"

"I know." Giving her a dry look, I moved across the uneven stone floor, avoiding the raised stone platform where Zabbai had lain, where he had died, where she had killed him. The blood was starting to stink, even down here in the earth where the heat was blessedly less. Lifting my face to one of the narrow crevices where the sunlight filtered down, I let my senses stretch out. "She is close. But she is not close enough to hear."

"And the others?"

"They cannot hear us, either."

"How do you know?" she demanded.

I gave her a narrow look. "Because I cannot hear them, witch."

After a huff of irritation, she paced around the tight confines of the cavern, then returned to me, stopping only a few feet away.

"Why are you here?" she demanded, glaring at me with her near-black eyes.

"Because I angered her. Because she..." I stopped and looked down, laying my hands on my swollen belly.

Slowly, the witch raised her gaze to mine. Knowledge burned deep in the darkness of her eyes and she flicked a look at the thin beam of sunlight streaming in on us.

"You do not know what she is," she said to me in a low voice. "You cannot know, otherwise you would have run far from her, and never stopped. Not while there is a child in your belly—one who shares her blood."

Those words did what even Madae had not been able to do. They made chill terror flood through my veins.

"What do you mean?"

She spun away and paced for long moments, so long the sun slid farther down in the sky and I could no longer sense Madae or the people she had dragged from the village to do her bidding.

We were alone.

Was that why the woman waited?

"She is gone," I told her softly.

"She is never *really* gone," she muttered, shaking her head so that the beads woven into the tangled strands clicked together. "She lurks in the shadows, she waits, she...*pounces*. She is..."

She lapsed into silence and when she did not continue, I tried to push. But the witch shook her head, staring at me with grim determination. "You say she is your *aunt*, your mother's sister, but she is not. That cannot be. Because when she came to find *me, my* grandmother *knew* her. And my grandmother was *ancient*. Her father was one of Auletes's priests."

"I do not know this...Auletes." I frowned and added, "For that matter, I do not know *you*—what is your name?"

"I do not know *yours*—only that you are related to *her*, or so you say." She gave me an austere look, and despite the dirt and blood that stained her clothing and face, she had an air of authority about her that told me she was used to being heeded—and obeyed.

I rarely obeyed anybody. But trust had to begin somewhere and her distrust and hatred of my aunt was palpable. Going with my gut, I said, "I am Lemeraties."

Something flickered in her eyes.

"I have heard of you," she said quietly. "Even in Alexandria, we have heard of you. They say on one hunt alone, you killed four of the turned wolves."

"I was not alone." Zabbai had been with me. He would never be with me again. I covered my belly with my hand again, the grief gripping tight, squeezing.

Her gaze followed the movement and this time, I recognized the look in her eyes.

Sadness. Pity. Understanding.

"She killed my grandmother," the woman said. Then, with a deep breath, she squared her shoulders. "I am Charmian. As to who Auletes was...he was the father of the last queen of my homeland, Cleopatra. My great-grandfather was one of Auletes's most trusted priests. My mother...she died in childbirth, having me and I was raised by my grandmother. She named me after one of the queen's most devoted servants." Her lips curved with the hint of a smile and she looked upward. "I wonder how much destiny is at play here, Lemeraties."

She did not explain what she meant and I did not ask. My mind was full of too many questions. "Why do you worry so if your grandmother knew my aunt?"

Charmian's gaze went hard. "Because my grandmother knew her when she was my age, Lemeraties. Hundreds of years ago—and her *father* warned her about the monster who had come knocking at their door. She was old even then, to him, and he lived almost as many years as my grandmother. Is your aunt truly so ancient?" She arched a brow and continued without waiting for an answer. "I can tell you that she *is* old, but she should not be. Her life is...unnatural. She feeds and whatever she feeds on, it is not blood or flesh the way some of the night creatures are. She is not one of the turned ones. She is something else. My grandmother told me that she..." She lapsed into silence and looked away.

Uneasy, I moved to the stone surface where Zabbai had been.

Feeds.

She had *fed* on him...his essence.

"His name was Zabbai. He was her son," I said, reaching out and tracing the tips of my fingers over the bloodstains. "When she gave birth and he was not a girl, she let his father take him back to

Tyre. Twice more, the man returned to her, and once she went to him—she wanted a girl child, and he hoped for another boy. But this one child...she had only him." I looked at Charmian, swallowing around the knot of grief and rage that had settled in my throat, nearly choking me. "He came to stay with my people—she called him to us. He tried to court me. I told him no, because I had no intention of staying there, raising a child under her aegis. But...it was the hunt. One of his men was killed. We hunted the turned-wolves together and things between us...changed. I went with him to Tyre instead of returning. We married. Then she began to talk of making war again Rome."

Charmian snorted. "She lies likes she breathes and you believed her?"

"My husband's father is a governor. At the time, it seemed we had little choice." Tears burned my eyes. "My gut told me things were not as they seemed. But I could not let him go alone—and he knew I would not have stayed behind."

"And she killed her own son." Charmian moved to stand across from me, her eyes boring into mine.

"She did not just kill him." I told her the rest, watched her flinch as she absorbed what I had told her.

"Then my grandmother was right. She feeds on souls."

"On the very essence of what makes us."

She lifted a brow. "Yes. Do you think she intends to let you and this child leave here in peace?"

I met her gaze, my hand protectively covering the child in my womb. "No."

"What do you think she has planned for this babe?"

"I do not know." Tears burned my eyes but I shook my head. "What she has planned is worse than death, is it not?"

"I am sorry."

Instead of responding to the softly spoken words, I went to the small crevice where I had stowed the bronze blade and my own wineskin, emptied now of wine and carrying the blooded wine I'd stolen from Zabbai before Madae had taken his body.

"There is one weapon that weakens us," I said to her. "Silver weakens the turned-wolves and if you destroy their heart with it, you can kill them. For us, it is a weapon of copper. It poisons us, slows us down, impairs our senses and ability to heal, hunt. This blade? It is bronze, made with the best copper in the empire. I designed it myself, watched as it was forged. It was a gift to..." I had to clear my throat twice before I could finish. "My husband. I thought in case we ever had to face her again, he would need a fine weapon and I wanted him to have the very best."

She lifted it and held it to the dying light, then moved away, walking to the lamp by the door. "What are these markings you carve into it?"

I joined her, taking the blood-wine with me. "They are the words for a curse."

Charmian went still. Slowly, she looked up.

"A curse?"

Inclining my head, I nodded. "She killed my husband, the father of my child—and as I feared, she took more than his life—she stole his very essence. I do not know if she plans the same with me, but I know if I resist her, she will kill me and steal my child, steal his or her soul, go on to steal the souls of others. If I have to chain myself to the earth until the moon falls from the sky, I will find a way to stop her."

Chapter Nineteen

If I have to chain myself to the earth until the moon falls from the sky, I will find a way to stop her.

I fell back into myself and stumbled away, one hand gripping the ancient blade, the other searching for purchase, for something to ground myself.

Lemera stood in front of me, her eyes the milky white of death once more, her hair fanning back from her face in an unseen wind.

Justin caught me, his strong hands steadying me when I found nothing else to hold on to. Colleen moved to stand several inches in front of me, off to the side, but the message in her stance was obvious: *Stay back.*

But Lemera only had eyes for me.

"What did you do?" I demanded, my voice scratchy.

"I showed you who she is," the specter said simply.

That wasn't what I'd meant. I'd understood, almost from the second I'd looked at the woman through the eyes of Lemera—*Lemeraties.* The features were different, altered somehow. But the gaze, the cruelty...the *malice*, it was the same.

"You said..." I swallowed, then coughed, my throat dry and tight, as if I'd been without water for days. "You said if you had to chain yourself to the earth, you'd do it. But that's not what you did, is it?"

Lemera cocked her head. "No. Charmian and I bound my soul to *hers*—I cannot *truly* die until she does." A look of bitter, unending hatred came into her eyes and she added, "Not that she hasn't *tried.* Once she realized what I'd done, what I'd become, she collapsed the earth around me, claimed that I had been cursed by a witch and there was no hope but to give me over to the earth. I was there so long, I forgot myself, forgot the color of the sun. I forgot Zabbai, even our child. When she pulled me from the earth, I knew only vengeance and rage. Each time, just as my mind started to clear, I found myself trapped again. But then came you."

She canted a queer smile at me, one hand lifted to display the blade she was bound to. "She put this blade in Fenele's hand and sent that weak-minded fool after you. Fenele couldn't hold me and there's no room for two in this bond. The farther she was from the queen, the weaker *her* hold became and within days of arriving in this land, the hold began to splinter. Each time Fenele used me, it shattered more. Then the day came when she tried to turn the blade over to the one you said had dishonored you. The one you killed the day I first spoke to you. He was *nothing* to me. A gnat. A bug. And he thought to use *me* to kill you. The bond shattered then and before the queen could find the blade and reforge it, you bonded with the blade—and with me. Now her grip on me is broken and all that is left between us is the curse...and my promise."

"I'm so confused right now," Colleen muttered, echoing my thoughts.

Yeah, me, too.

I had a million questions and I tried to formulate them.

But Lemera was still talking.

"Perhaps I should have left after I killed the vampire who harmed you." She shook her head, her features drawn and tired. "My thoughts weren't clear when I first woke—they never are. I was still focused on vengeance and blood, but something wouldn't let me leave here. So I lingered, and watched..." Her gaze came to me, eyes sharpening. "I watched *you*, Kitasa. Once my thoughts were clear, I looked at you and I *knew*; I knew she planned to use you just as she has used others."

A chill ran down my spine and I wanted to demand answers on that.

But so many questions spun through my mind. "I need to rewind a little bit. Like...I don't know. A few hundred years. Ten, maybe fifteen, sixteen centuries...*more*. You were talking about the Roman Empire—and the emperor *Valerian*. He ruled..." I racked my brain and realized it was closer to *two thousand* years ago. "How is that possible? She can't be *that* old."

"No?" Lemera's eyes bore into mine. "You feel it in her, the rot. The wrongness. And the dreams of late, Kitasa...you've seen her in those nightmares that are more than simple nightmares. Haven't you?"

I didn't answer, too dumbstruck to do anything but wonder how she knew that.

"You sense that she isn't as she seems." Lemera came closer, eyes compelling to look at her, to listen.

"How do you know that?" But even as I asked, I knew. "Right. The fucking bond. How is she doing it? This *soul-feeding*? Is that it? What, does she just gobble up a soul a day to keep the Grim Reaper away or something?"

"Nothing quite so simple."

The answer came, not from Lemera, but from the doorway.

I whirled, knife in hand, and at the glimpse of a man moving into the doorway, I reacted.

Chang caught the blade, swinging his torso to the side in a fluid, *impossible* movement that told me I'd never be able to take him by surprise—not with the way he'd just crept up on me. On *all* of us, judging by the way Justin and Colleen were practically vibrating. Even Lemera looked uneasy at the sight of him.

But the ages-old shapeshifter didn't look at them. He looked at the blade he held, wiped it on his sleeve. "My apologies, Kit. I did not mean to startle you."

Panting, I stood there as he crossed to me. The magic-sharp scent of his blood danced in the air and realized he'd caught the knife by the sharp edge. I swiped it from him and glared.

"Damn it, Chang."

"Again, my apologies." He looked around, gaze flashing gold, then, eerily to complete black.

Terror chittered in my brain, my memory feeding up an image of the woman Lemera had called Madae looking at her with ink-black eyes. But her eyes had been...soulless. Void of life, warmth, anything of heart and kindness.

Chang's came to mine, and even though his eyes were pure black, I saw...*him.*

"I have never seen you so terrified, Kit," he said quietly. "In all the time I've known you, you have never held this much blind fear."

The acrid taste of it was crawling up my throat, all but choking me, so I was pretty damn sure it was pumping out of my pores, too. I wasn't surprised he could pick up on it.

"Sorry," I said, shooting for a bitchy tone and failing. "If I had known a shifter sniff test was coming, I would have picked a stronger deodorant."

His lids flickered, then he blinked and just like that, the dark brown of his eyes was back and he chuckled. "It isn't in your scent, my friend." He leaned in and pressed a kiss to my forehead.

Unsettled, I held still as he pulled back, his eyes still studying me carefully.

"I guess if you tracked me here, then Damon isn't far behind," I finally said.

"I didn't track *you.*" Chang looked away from me then, turning his head to look at Lemera. "I tracked her."

Her visage flickered and when it reformed, she was as she'd been in life, beautiful, tall, strong and golden. Her sea-blue eyes rested on Chang's with an odd sort of recognition.

"I know you," she said finally.

Well, yeah. The two of you tried to kill each other.

But the thought had only barely formed when Lemera shook her head. "No. I know *of* you. She has sent me to kill you before. I failed. You're the great hunter. The one she's always feared. You and your cub..." Her eyes widened and she looked at me. "Your stubborn male."

Chang blew out a tired, heavy breath and walked past us to look out the window. It was opposite the one Lemera had used earlier. With the ease I might use to rip off a bandage, he pulled the boards from the window, not stopping under all of them were gone. Once his view was unencumbered, he leaned forward.

"There was a time when I would have ended you the moment I saw you," he murmured.

Justin tensed. Colleen's breath caught in her throat.

Lemera's visage faded back to the spectral form of the grave.

And I think my heart stopped.

I had no idea who he was talking to, not until he turned around. His gaze skated past me to land on the revenant.

"Do you think it so easy?" she asked, the screams of untold dead echoing in her voice.

"Now that I know what you are?" One corner of his mouth quirked up in a smile that spoke of faint amusement. "Yes. You're of the grave, revenant. The largest part of you yearns to return to it."

Silence rippled through the desolate church and through the strange bond I shared with Lemera, I felt her surprise...and her *longing*. I touched her arm, afraid she might rush toward him, *beg* him for what he'd just offered.

The contact was viciously cold but I didn't pull away.

She brushed her fingers over mine and in that instant, she warmed and her body was once more fully human, as she'd been in life.

225

"I cannot go to my rest yet, little sister," she said, meeting my gaze. "No matter how much I wish to. You know the promise I made. And the hunter, powerful and old as he is, cannot undo the curse binding me to her."

Tugging my hand away, I curled my fingers into a tight fist and watched as she moved to stand before Chang.

"Why would you end me?" She studied the slim shifter, head canted to the side and eyes curious. "Because she pulled me out of the grave? Because she sent me to hunt you?"

"Because I smell the magic that was part of your remaking." His lip curled and the black spiraled in his gaze once more, giving way to an old, ancient anger. "I smell it...and I *know* it. I spent years hunting the persons who stole her from her family. It was one of the few quests I ever failed, one of the few promises I was unable to keep."

"You talk of Charmian."

His mouth tightened and rage flashed in his eyes. "You might not wish to speak her name, revenant. I am not who I once was, but that doesn't mean I've forgotten my vows."

"I did not kill her." Lemera flicked her hand, the gesture not quite dismissive...but close. "She and I made a pact, and yes, she died trapped down in a hole with me, but it wasn't my hand that ended her life."

A growl escaped him. "Don't toy with me."

"Why would I bother?"

He shot out a hand.

It went through Lemera—the first time. But when he went to yank it back, brilliant gold flashed—and it flared around them both, blinding all of us. It burned with power, light and tasted of the wild, of the earth and the deep, dark green forest.

I flung up an arm.

Justin spun and flung himself against me and Colleen, silver flashing all around us.

Then the golden light dissipated.

Tears blinded me from the sheer brilliance of it and I swiped my forearm over my eyes to see, ragged breaths chopping out of my lungs as I shoved Justin out of my way.

Chang had Lemera pinned to the wall.

And there were two thin slits in the back of his suit coat, framed by charred marks, as if a burning blade had sliced through the material.

The afterimage of what I'd glimpsed before the light grew too bright danced across the inside of my lids when I closed them but my mind shied away, not quite ready to process what I *thought* I'd seen.

"Do not toy with me," Chang said again. "I can put you so deep in the earth, you won't emerge until the end of time."

"Don't threaten me with such promises, hunter." Lemera's eyes held nothing of fear, even though he had her pinned to the wall, her feet dangling inches of the ground, his hand around her throat steady and unyielding. "The thought of endless peace and quiet after so many lifetimes...do you really think such a thing would *scare* me? You, who have lived even longer than I? Even longer than *her*?"

My chest constricted.

"Perhaps I'll bury the two of you in the earth *together*," Chang said.

"Oh, that would be *lovely*." Lemera smiled then and it was beautiful death, her eyes luminescent. "Perhaps I could summon up a lie, even a few tears and feign terror if it would bring such a boon. To have her trapped and at my mercy until the skin rotted from her corpse? I wonder how long it would take for her to truly die, if she couldn't steal lives to replenish herself."

Disgusted, Chang dropped her.

She landed lightly on her feet and moved closer to him when he would have backed away.

"You're one of them," she murmured. "No wonder she fears you so. You could crush her easily. No wonder she had me hunt you...and no wonder I failed so miserably."

"What is she talking about?" I demanded, knocking Justin's hand aside when he tried to grab me.

Chang rubbed his neck, a look of weary annoyance on his face, but the rage I'd glimpsed earlier was gone. He looked at Lemera like she was an annoying bug he'd like to squash, and considering the supreme confidence I'd heard in his voice when he mention ed burying her in the earth, I thought maybe that was all she was to him.

A memory danced at the edges of my mind, mere weeks earlier, when Lemera had first torn into East Orlando and assassinated entire vampire houses. We'd tracked her to one of them and during the fight to stop her and Fenele, Chang had shifted. I'd seen his animal form for the first time and it was nothing I'd recognized.

When I asked Damon what he was, Damon had only said, *"A force of nature."*

Blood roared in my ears as I realized just how close to the truth Damon might have been, if my instincts were accurate—and damn it, they usually were.

Soft, liquid brown eyes met mine, Chang's gaze assessing.

"It's a long story, Kit, not one I want to discuss here, or with an audience," he said, glancing at Justin and Colleen.

Odd that he didn't look at Lemera.

Not so odd that Justin and Colleen noticed.

"But the ghost girl can hear?" Justin demanded. "That's just fine?"

"She's part of the story," Chang said with an elegant shrug. He adjusted the cuffs of his shirt. "Just as much..."

He stopped, head cocking.

I started to ask what was wrong.

But Lemera had taken a step forward.

She was back to her spectral form, hair stringy and thin, her face pale and discolored, while there were parts of body where bone showed through. In her left hand, she held her blade. In stark comparison to her desiccated body, the blade looked as if it come fresh from the forge.

As I watched, she lifted it, her head cocking to the side.

Her eyes glowed white in the darkness and in that eerie light, I glimpsed something I hadn't.

Script on the blade.

"Soon," she whispered, her gaze following mine. "This blade holds the name of every soul she's forced me to take, every life she's forced me to end...it remembered when I could not. And it senses when she's near..."

"Fanis," I whispered.

"Yes. Her time is all but gone, her strength waning. She must claim another or she will be too weak to fight."

Chang's lip curled.

"Kit is too strong for the magic...*fuck*!" He turned on Lemera, grabbed her arm. "Can she take only take of her own? Can she—"

"Reshi." My tongue felt too thick as Chang clamped his mouth shut on the question, refusing to finish it. He didn't need to. I'd already figured it out, after all, hadn't I? "Damon's holding her here, in Florida. Somewhere close."

Justin snarled behind us and I saw a flash of silver as he let out a burst of his magic, but I didn't dare look away from Lemera and Chang.

"She can take one of her own, but it will not be an easy—or lasting fit," Lemera said. "It's one reason why the blood started to looked outside the people to breed—she had a harder time taking those fully of her blood. But she needs somebody...broken, too."

Useless waste. Dirty pig.

Did you really think I'd let you run in the Dominari?

Ugly, hated memories from years ago.

"What you all talking about?" Justin demanded.

Colleen caught his arm. "I think I know, but it's...not good." Her face was pale and taut as she looked at Lemera. "Your...Fanis. She steals souls somehow?"

"No. She possesses bodies." Chang's bones cut tight against his cheekbones, fury giving a kiss of color to the soft golden skin. "Taking souls would be cleaner and she'd last longer, but she hasn't done that in centuries." He shot Lemera a look. "I suspect you had something to do with that."

She inclined her head in answer to his query. Nice that *he* was getting questions answered—I just had more of them, but I shoved them aside. There was no time for them now.

"Where's Reshi?" I asked Chang.

He gave me a wary look. "It's not wise for you to go anywhere near her. Madae—" He frowned, as if the name surprised him, even though he'd been the one to say it. "Your grandmother is already coming. I can feel her."

I didn't. Not yet.

But the way Lemera stood, primed and ready, told me she sensed it, too.

"Then maybe we shouldn't stand around here waiting." I hitched up a shoulder. "And I think maybe we could dispense with calling her my *grandmother*, too. I'm not sure exactly what she is, but it's definitely not so simple as that, is it?"

Chang opened his mouth, then closed it on a sigh. "This isn't wise."

"Neither is standing around arguing," Lemera said. "And if Madae comes, there is nowhere on this side of the world where Kitasa *would* be safe. But if we kill the one host open to Madae, then it leaves her weak, with limited options. She'll have to retreat."

"Can she reclaim you?" Chang asked, his dark eyes pinning Lemera in place.

"No." Lemera's hair blew back from her face, unearthly power wrapping around her. "I'm bound to her, as she is to me, but now that I am awake, and now that I have my blade, her control over me is shattered. The blade has bonded to Kit as well and it cannot be taken by force."

Chang considered a moment, then with a short nod, he said, "We'll go."

He looked at Justin and Colleen. "You, as well, because I'm not going to waste time arguing with either of you when you're as stubborn as Kit."

"Fuckin' straight," Justin muttered.

Chang headed for the door and I fell instep next to Justin. His gaze landed on the back of Chang's jacket, but all I saw was speculation there.

It was Colleen who caught my hand on the way out and her gaze slid to Chang in an expression of utter, explicit terror.

I squeezed her hand.

"You can stay." Once everything slowed down, I'd probably find the room to be terrified, too.

"No." She squeezed tighter. "I just...no."

"I'd understand."

Justin paused to look back at us.

She dredged up a smile and pulled me into a walk next to her. "I know you'd understand," she said in a low voice. "But...regardless of...everything..." Her eyes darted to Chang once more. "He's always been on your side. That has to count, right?"

Chapter Twenty

"You spoke to Kit of a curse," Chang said as we all sped along through the night, Justin and Colleen following us behind on his bike. Chang was at the wheel of Justin's flashy blue sportscar, taking the small, winding road at a pace that had me gripping the door in one hand, the console in the other.

His calm persona had vanished behind a veil of cool, icy death.

He's always been on your side, Kit. I tried to hold onto Colleen's words, told myself to trust my instincts—they said Chang, no matter what, was still to be trusted. But fuck, he was scary tonight.

"Yes. Madae, when she was my queen, trapped me in an earthen tomb along with Charmian. I was pregnant—the baby would have been her grandchild. She'd killed her own son because he dared defy her—he was already dying and as I watched, she ripped out his heart and crushed it, then drank in his essence, right there in front of me," Lemera said. She sat in the seat behind me, telling me she would stay with us until it—whatever *it* was—was done, conserving her strength.

I held her blade in my lap. She'd pushed it into my hands before climbing into the car maybe thirty minutes earlier.

"It is strange to ride in this metal beast," she murmured. "I think I prefer horses."

"Horses are slower. Cars are more convenient," Chang said. "The curse."

"The curse." She sighed. "She brought Charmian a few days after she killed Zabbai. I knew she had plans for me, and for the baby. If I had agreed to go along with what she wanted, she might have let me live, allowed me to care for the babe, even raise it. But in the end, she would steal the babe away, either take the girl and get more babes off her, or feed from it if it was a boy child."

"She wouldn't have needed a host back then. She fed from souls. Things didn't change until you came into the picture—I didn't make the connection between you and Charmian. After Charmian disappeared, she had to change how she fed. She needed host bodies," Chang said shortly. He shot a look at me from the corner of his eye. "That was always her plan for you, Kit. That's why she wanted you back so desperately. It's why she treated you so cruelly. She can't take somebody who's emotionally and mentally strong—they have to be broken."

"There are plenty of broken ones left back there among the people," I muttered, turning to look out into the night. "Why chase after me?"

"The bodies aren't strong enough," Lemera said simply. "For some reason, she needs a body that isn't wholly of the blood."

"Why?" I asked, flabbergasted—and completely dismayed. "And how could she even *tolerate* the idea? My grandmother *hates* the other races."

"Perhaps this is why she hates them—they have the strength to hold what she herself cannot," Chang offered. He slowed a fraction and whipped the car around a turn that seemed to come out of nowhere. "And to *why*...I imagine it has something to do with...inbreeding."

I felt that weird tug on my mind, knew Lemera was filtering the word through me, then she laughed, the sound coldly amused. "Yes. Inbreeding. That explains much of the weakness in the blood I sensed the last few times I've woken. So many have lost their way, know nothing of honor, know nothing of *who we are*."

"They follow a broken leader," Chang said. "They know no other way."

"They could leave." Lemera's voice, her words, held no pity. "I did. I never should have returned. None of this—"

"There's no turning back the clock," I said. "What's done is done. And you still haven't finished explaining this curse."

"You are incessant, the both of you." She leaned forward and jabbed her index finger toward the blade. Her bone showed through at the tip. I kind of wished she'd do the shift thing and wear the other form, but I wasn't sure how to ask. "Hold the blade up, Kit. Look...see the words?"

Her eyes were glowing again.

And...yes. Words formed even as I stared, the script appearing to glow red in the dim light of the car.

"What language is..." I squinted, my eyes attempting to focus on the script, but it seemed to...change. "Why are the words changing? I see...it's Greek, maybe. And are those...hieroglyphics?"

"Charmian and I forged the curse together. It's a living thing, written in her blood, my blood, Zabbai's...and the blood of my baby."

Her voice caught. The pain in her voice tore through me and I turned to look at her, while Chang's gaze flew to the rearview mirror.

"Your baby," he said softly. There was no accusation in the world, although I knew he'd come to the same conclusion I had.

"I was only halfway through my pregnancy when she threw me in the hole." Lemera said, looking outside the window now. "She would leave all three of us there to weaken, threaten Charmian with attacks on her family, her own daughters and her son, would wait until I was weak from labor and attack me then if she thought I meant to betray her—somehow she would get my child. I wouldn't let her do it. And I couldn't just take my life. Somehow, I had to find a way to stop her. I never imagined it would take so long."

If I have to chain myself to the earth until the moon falls from the sky, I will find a way to stop her.

"You didn't chain yourself to the earth," I murmured. "You chained yourself to her, using the blood of her son, sacrificing your own child and your life, with this witch Charmian sealing the deal with her blood, her life."

"Yes." Lemera stroked a finger over the blade. It flared in response, as if it recognized her. "It took weeks to craft the curse. We were weak by the time it was complete, tired and the babe in my belly was growing cumbersome. And Madae was talking about moving us. She wanted me closer to the village. We decided our time was up."

"You worried she'd discover what you'd done."

"Her blood was Zabbai's," Lemera said simply, not looking at Chang. The blade glowed anew, flashing red. "When the curse was cast, Charmian plunged the knife into her heart, then gave it to me, and I..." She touched her belly once more, then placed her hand on her chest. "I'd written the curse using blood I'd stolen from Zabbai's body after she killed him. I'd learned of curse tablets in the years after I left the people to be with him. With Charmian's magic and Zabbai's blood, we bound ourselves to the blade, and Madae, too. But..." Lemera sighed heavily. "We bound ourselves too well. I cannot be the one to hold the blade that ends her life. I've tried. Each time, I'm forced to stop. She cannot truly kill me, but I cannot kill her."

Chang swore under his breath. "That won't be a problem," he said a moment later. "If she shows up, I'll tear her head off, just as I should have the first time I met her."

"You've met my grandmother." I looked at him.

He pulled the car to a stop in front of a small, dark building, almost completely surrounded by trees. It was completely desolate.

And I could feel Reshi, her presence a prickle on my skin.

"As she is now?" Chang looked at me. "No. But in the other skins she's worn? Yes. But that's another story. Come. We don't have much time and Madae isn't the only one on her way."

He climbed out before I could ask but when I looked at him over the car, his eyes met mine.

And I knew. I couldn't feel him yet, but he had deeper, older bonds to Damon, through clan, through family, through whatever bonds clan members give an Alpha.

235

Although Chang was the stronger of the two, he'd pledged loyalty to Damon long ago.

"Damon," I murmured.

"Yes." We started inside before Justin and Colleen had a chance to park the bike, Chang's hand on my arm. "Get inside, the inner room and open the door. You'll see her. Kill her. Do it fast, before either of them get here. Damon will try to stop you and Madae will try to take her over. We can't risk either."

There was a flicker in his eyes as he said Damon's name and I recognized the guilt, knew he wasn't easy with the choice. But I didn't stop to argue.

Holding the knife in my hand, I met Lemera's gaze, then headed inside, heart lurching inside my chest, pounding so hard, so fast, it made it hard to breathe. *She was coming, she was coming—*

"Breathe, little sister," Lemera said. "I will not let her harm you."

The revenant's hand was icy on my shoulder, but I didn't immediately shrug it off. Crazy that I let myself find such comfort from a ghost, but...out of everybody I'd ever known, she was the only person who'd experienced a similar hell—and worse.

"I can do this," I said stiffly, putting one foot in front of the other, spying the only door in the building. It was a new door, too, set into a wall that looked equally new, which was...strange? This building was decrepit, or it seemed that way on the outside. The interior smelled of fresh lumber and plaster and wet cement.

The latter scent intensified as I opened the interior door as Chang had ordered.

Bile rushed up my throat as a rancid stink poured out—waste matter and unwashed bodies, mingled with the smell of cement...and something else.

The scent of the forest and the wild and thunderstorms...

Damon.

I reached out and felt a light switch, hit it.

A single bare bulb came on overhead and I squinted in reaction, staring at the woman in the space across from me. She was behind a set of bars that kept her locked in, a set of bars with no door. I was confused for a moment, but closer inspection told me the bars had been welded shut—a door *had* been there, but no longer. Damon had put her in here with no intention of ever releasing her.

But he wasn't content with just caging her in.

The lower half of the bars was covered with solid cement bricks easily four inches thick.

He was walling her in.

Chains rattled and I flinched at the sound, watched as the woman on the wall rolled her head my way. A plastic water bottle fell out of her hand but she didn't pay it much attention as it hit the floor and rolled.

Her eyes were locked on me.

"Hello, niece. Did he bring you here so you could enjoy the sight of my suffering?"

My stomach rebelled. At the sight of her, at the knowledge of what he planned to do, at the stench of waste and unwashed flesh...at the *cruelty*.

"No," I said, swallowing the gorge and taking a step forward. "He doesn't know I'm here."

Her lids flickered, then, a rusty laugh escaped and Reshi let her head fall back. "Oh, dear child...you pathetic *miserable* child."

"Kit!" Chang said in a warning growl. "Get it done."

My hand was shaking, gripping the knife Lemera in put in my hand. I tossed it once, trying to get a grip for the feel of it.

"Ooohhhh...he sounds worried." Reshi pushed upright, using the wall at her back to support her, grinning all the while. Her face was thinner, her lips cracked, but madness and malice shown in her eyes. "Does your feral beast want the killing of me all to himself?"

It wasn't her death he wanted, and that was the problem. He wanted her alive and suffering. *I* wanted Reshi dead. If she'd died already, we wouldn't have hell breathing down our necks.

I lifted the knife even as I felt the heat rolling across my skin in warning.

A roar tore through the air, followed by a crash.

I threw the knife—magic shattering the tension around us in the very same second and it disrupted the air currents *just* enough, spoiling my throw. *Fuck*, it would never hit the heart!

Reshi fell backward, her hand going to grab the blade as it buried itself in her chest.

I went to call it.

Lemera appeared in the cell before I could. She shot me a dark look over her shoulder. "No! I have told you. Do *not* summon this blade."

She wrenched it from Reshi's chest and disappeared, forming in the space next to me.

"Madae comes," she whispered.

The wall next to me disintegrated and Justin smashed into the concrete at my feet, his face a bloody mask, his teeth bared as he flung his hands out, silver forming thick, heavy cables.

There was another bellow and the blood vessels in Justin's neck bulged. "Fuck, Kit...I can't..."

A massive *pop* echoed, like a sonic boom, magic shattering.

Justin's eyes rolled in the back of his head and the thick silver chains fell to the earth, then dissolved into the small, almost delicate ribbons that made up the fine filigree on his sleeves.

"Justin!" Colleen screamed his name.

He didn't stir.

Damon filled the gaping hole in the wall, naked, his muscles swelling and eyes green-gold as the cat inside him pushed close to the surface.

"Get back," he told me, voice nearly unintelligible.

Flexing my hand, I called my bow.

"You're not doing this," I told him softly, my heart shattering as I stared at him.

"You don't get to make that call!"

Chang stepped between us, giving me an unreadable look.

"End it, Kit, while you can," he told me. Then he turned to Damon. "I told you not to go down this road, that it was courting more trouble than you could imagine. Why can't you ever listen, son?"

Damon stepped forward.

Tears burned my eyes as the man I loved shoved his face into Chang's and bellowed. "Get her out of here!"

"You've put her in more danger, Damon. She has to end it."

Their voices grew distant.

Lemera's grew loud.

"Now, little sister..."

Shadows seemed to swell around me, blotting out the world.

Lifting my bow, I looked at Reshi.

She was smiling, but as our gazes locked, that smile faltered. It wasn't because of me. A cold wind blew in through the missing wall. It stank of putrid death and foul things that didn't belong in this world.

Colleen's voice rose, but I couldn't make out the words—just my name. It was a warning, a plea. Hurry, maybe. *Hurry, Kit.*

Looking at Reshi, I lifted the bow.

There was a crash as Damon slammed into Chang, but Chang was the one who took Damon to the floor.

They were yelling.

Their voices made no sense, couldn't pierce the roar of blood in my ears.

Useless waste.

239

Dirty pig.

I come to claim what's mine.

I felt her now, a cold wind on the back of my neck, death drawing near.

Nocking an arrow, one tipped with a copper-bronze alloy I'd had specially made as a gift for my family, I stared at Reshi. "We were never anything but pawns to her," I said. "Pawns for a mad queen."

I loosed the arrow, nocked another even as the first buried itself in my aunt's heart. The second made its way home in her left socket, slamming her back into the wall, pinning her there.

"Granddaughter."

Chapter Twenty-One

S pinning, I lifted the bow.

There she was, every nightmare I'd ever had made flesh, only feet from me.

Inside, I quaked.

She tilted her head to the side, brows arching but she said nothing.

Time slowed to a crawl as we stared at each other. Her eyes were no longer the brilliant blue I remembered. No, they were dull and filmy. Her skin was waxy and sallow—but not like she was sick. A fetid smell clung to her.

It was like staring at a two day old corpse left to rot in the sun.

"You don't look well, grandmother," I said.

Damon howled and lurched upward under Chang.

Chang sprang up, releasing the other man and moving fluidly to plant himself between me and the woman who had haunted my nightmares for years on end.

Damon lunged for Fanis.

She sidestepped, swinging out with her sword, striking him in the head with the butt.

Well, her strength wasn't affected—at all.

He stumbled, but didn't go down, crashing into the wall. He shook his head, then pushed upright, tensing for another attack.

"Don't waste your energy, boy," she said in a voice that dripped ice. "I'm not here for her...not now."

Her gaze slammed into mine and I felt the crush of thousands of years boring into me.

"And you know I didn't come for you, don't you?" she asked, her eyes slitted, burning with fury. "You…"

Her nostrils flared and she dragged in air through her nose. The cartilage took longer to return to its shape, giving the impression the nasal passages were clinging together. Her body was wasting away before my eyes.

"Just what else do you know, dearest granddaughter?"

A cold breath whispered along my neck and I lowered my bow. The bronze blade came to my hand—I didn't call it. It was just there. I lowered my gaze to the ground for the barest instant. When I looked up, Lemera was behind my grandmother.

Madae, I told myself.

She was *Madae*.

If she'd ever been Fanis, that woman was long gone, had possibly been gone before I'd even known her.

The bands of fear around my chest eased and I found the breath to speak.

"More than enough…Madae."

I took a step forward, blade in hand.

Her eyes widened.

"No…"

With a startling force and speed, she tore from Lemera, but when she went to grab me, Chang was there, his hand wrapped around her neck. That brilliant gold began to form, inside his skin at first, spreading out until it shone through his clothes, spilling through the slits in his jacket—

"*No!*" It was a garbled, strangled noise that came from the female I'd hated, feared for so long. A sound of terror. Fanis—no, *Madae*…she was terrified of Chang.

Madae lifted her head and something black, thick and viscous came spilling out of her mouth, shot to the ceiling. It formed a humanoid shape, clinging there a moment as it turned its face to me.

"I'll just..." A coughing sound, before the thing spoke again in Fanis's—*Madae's*—voice. "Take the boy. His body is strong enough to hold me, yes? And it will hurt you all *so* much..."

The thing melted into a greasy-looking ball, then into nothing...fading away.

Chang threw the body he held to the ground.

Dazed, I stared as the head turned to the side, facing me.

The eyes were lifeless.

Going to my knees, I reached out and touched the hand nearest me, jerking back when I touched flesh icy with death.

"What boy?" Damon growled behind me.

I squeezed my eyes shut.

"Who is she talking about?" Damon demanded.

I lurched upright as Chang answered, desperate to block out the response, although I already knew.

I heard a snarled response from Damon, low at first, then rising in denial.

"No...what the fu...*No!*" The roar nearly shook the trees, it was so loud.

And it changed nothing. His fury, his strength...none of that could stop anything.

Rushing to the door, I puked, emptying my stomach of everything I'd eaten in the past day.

Doyle...

Lemera came to me.

I pulled away, shoving upright, staring out into the night.

"We will find him," she said.

"But can we save him?"

When she didn't answer, I spun around and grabbed her arms, not caring that it was like taking death by the hands.

"That's her body!" I half-shouted, shooting a desperate look at the corpse on the floor. It looked even worse now, shriveling in and collapsing on itself, a macabre, sickening sight. "Is she going to just fly that diseased ball of magic we saw right into my cousin? Is she?"

Lemera reached up and touched my cheek. "She cannot take the strong-willed, Kitasa. That's why she failed with you, time and again. The boy has your strength. We *have* time."

She shimmered and then she was whole, as she'd been in life.

"I failed my husband. I failed my child. I will *not* fail you and the boy," she said, pulling me in tight for a hug. "I swear it on the blade that binds me here, Kitasa. I will *not* fail you."

Chapter Twenty-Two

Damon

"Why didn't you tell me what she could do?" I stared at Kit from the end of the hall, watching as she went through the gear she had packed in a room so thick with magic, it made my teeth hurt.

"Some old magics are so heinous, it's better they are left forgotten in the sands of time."

Guilt hung around my neck, a stone that threatened to drag me under and drown me. When this was over, it just might. But...not yet.

Turning to Chang, I said, "You should have told me."

His eyes bled black. "I told you, time and again, you were taking the wrong path. You wouldn't listen. Why should I have expected you to listen if I told you that using one of that thing's pawns as bait to lure her here would only endanger Kit and Doyle?"

I went to snarl, only to stop.

Because he *had* told me.

"Fuck," I muttered, turning away from him, and Kit. From the guilt that was eating me alive.

"Can we stop this?" I asked, not turning back to look at him as I asked, because I couldn't handle seeing my own guilt reflected back at me, not yet.

"I don't know." He was quiet a moment. "I have to stay here. If all three of us go, it leaves the city vulnerable and gives her other weapons to use against us."

I wanted to tell him I didn't care. But I couldn't. This was why I hadn't wanted the responsibility of being any kind of leader. Unless you were a fucking psycho, ties came with commitments, and sooner or later, that meant caring. I'd stopped wanting to care about anybody a long time ago. I knew what happened when you cared about people. You lost them.

I heard a soft feminine mutter behind me, then a curse, and when Kit's voice broke, I squeezed my eyes closed.

"This is my fault," I whispered.

Chang sighed. "You can let guilt choke you, cloud your choices—*just* like you've let rage and fear do for the past couple of months. Or you can step up and be the fucking leader I raised you to be. Which one are you going to do?"

I looked at him.

"I never wanted to be a leader."

"I never wanted to raise another child," he said softly. "But I found you lost and alone. Should I have left you?"

"Maybe you should have." I went to turn away.

Chang caught my arm, his grip making it clear that unless I chose violence, I wasn't getting away. I really, *really* wanted to choose violence—craved it, craved the punishment and pain I knew I deserved.

"People are alive because I saved you. And at the end of this, people may well be alive because of you." His eyes burned, the black bleeding to the gold he rarely allowed to show—not the gold of his cat, but the other being that lived side by side with his beast, a being so rare, only a few of them still walked in the world. "Are you going to make wise choices, or stupid ones? I think you've made more than enough stupid ones myself, so maybe it's time you start *thinking* instead of *feeling*."

He let me go and resumed his watch on the hall.

"Unlike Kit, you let your rage guide you, son. She follows her gut and her heart, but you...you listen to something else and it's not serving you well."

Another soft curse from the room where Kit kept her weapons cached, a ragged breath that told me she was trying not to scream, or cry, or both.

"Fuck you for being right."

To Be Continued

The Pretern Wars

New Paranormal Romance Series

Over a century ago, a war broke out between humans would kill every non-human on earth and the shapeshifting Therians, Atargarians, Nightdwelling Fae and their human allies.

Millions died.

Cities destroyed.

Children left orphaned.

But in the end, bigotry and hate lost.

A reformed world was built, run under the Aegis of the Council of Primes and the United Reformed Nations.

A Prime's Passion

Excerpt

2159

The Mermaid's Tale

Provincetown, Massachusetts

" ••• this place is a hole in the wall and the servers can be ruder than all get-out if you're not local, but oh, my goodness, if you want some eye candy, you have to check this place out. Apparently, almost all the employees are actual Atargarian merfolk!"

-online review, anonymous user.

"You're the sweetest damn thing I've ever seen in my life."

Zennia Day, known to most people as Zee, looked up from her reading pad to study the tall, sexy piece of work who'd sidled his way up to the bar. He gave her a slow smile that flashed white against brown skin and made his eyes, an even deeper shade of brown, crinkle up at the corners.

Inside, her seductive, base nature flexed and stretched, trying to slip away from the leash that always tried to keep it in place.

Amused by the man's comment, and captivated by the warmth and appreciation in his smile, she braced her elbow on the scarred surface of the bar. "Have you had your eyes checked recently?"

"Actually, yeah." His face lit up with a smile. Dimples appeared in his cheeks, deepening his already strong appeal. "It's a requirement for the day job. I'm a pilot for Air Command. I assure you, ma'am. My vision is perfect. You're definitely the most beautiful woman I've seen in... well, a long time."

The way he watched her told her he meant every word, and while she *did* have to throttle that inner, base seductress, that wasn't all of who she was. She was also part wolf and her wolf scented no lies on the man.

He thought *she* was the most beautiful woman in The Mermaid's Tale, an Atargarian pub in Provincetown.

Atargarians were notoriously beautiful, and the merfolk even more so.

Oh, wow. Sexier and sexier. The hungry thing inside her whispered even as her more cautious, pragmatic aspect advised her to send him on his way. There wasn't really even any *point* in this, something she'd learned over the past ten years.

But that hungry thing had already gone from *hungry* to *starved, desperate*, and *ready to devour*.

It didn't take much for that voice to overrule caution and pragmatism.

"Day trip from the base?" she asked, gesturing casually to the seat next to hers, appreciating that he hadn't immediately taken it.

Air Command had permanent bases located along the coasts of every country allied with the United Reform Nations. It was a requirement of membership, not to induce fear of martial law, but so that the various races could act together in a quick, cohesive unit during times of natural disaster or in response to the occasional—and often violent—revolt against the parameters set out to protect the fragile peace put in place after the Slaughters.

Mortals called the Slaughters the Preternatural Wars. Depending on which side of the line one fell on, those same mortals might attempt to lay the blame solely at the feet of those *Preternaturals*, or Preterns for short, the moniker given to any person who didn't identify as human, despite the fact that Preterns were made up of several wholly unique and different races.

This man was clearly mortal, but if he was with Air Command, then he had to know he was dealing with a Pretern. And he still liked what he saw.

"Yeah." He held out a hand. "I'm Dumond Haines—AC Lieutenant First Class. My friends call me Duke."

Slowly, Zee slipped her hand into Duke's much larger one and the hungry creatures within her yowled in demand. "Zee," she said softly and braced herself.

But Duke only cocked his head. "As in the letter?"

"Sort of." She laughed, a nervous giddiness spreading through her belly. *He doesn't know.* "The name is Zennia, but I've been Zee all my life."

"Well, Zee. Would you let me buy you a drink?"

The giddy nerves went from vibrating nervously to jumping. He *really* didn't know. "I'd love a drink."

As he turned to look for the bartender, she chanced a look around the bar. The place looked like a dive—on purpose—Meridia preferred it to look inhospitable. Her hope was that it would keep the "tourists" out. It didn't work, but still, she persisted.

Zee saw a number of familiar faces, but these were friends. Some had come to be family and it was almost enough to ease the ache inside her sometimes.

As one of the few Therians in this region dominated by the water-based Atargarians, Zee had applied for a job teaching Therian history and culture to a middle school located in this small town. To her surprise, she hadn't just been called in for an interview, she'd been hired on the spot.

That had been eight years ago and over time, the Atargarians had come to consider her as one of them.

None of them would look at her sideways if she left this place with a man. A few male Atargarians had even attempted to court her, but all of them had been brutally dominant. Their dominance hadn't been the problem. She knew if push came to shove and outside forces interfered, blood would be spilled.

She didn't want that on her conscience.

Too many of the human males in the region had heard about her *issues* through the grapevine and they, like the few Therians she'd met over the years, avoided her. For them, it might have been more out of fear, or at least a healthy respect for Therian male dominance and possessiveness.

This man, though, had *no* clue who she was.

"Heya, Zee." The man who came to stand in front of them was tall and heavily muscled, his eyes a warm, velvety brown unless he was angry or hyped up on other strong emotions. Now, those eyes smiled at her.

Donner Hawthorne, big and brutal and as deadly as the orca he shifted into, also had a decidedly mischievous bent to him, especially when it came to those he considered part of his family.

She could practically *hear* him encouraging her. *Go for it, Zee. Now.*

Hell, if there was a private room in the bar other than Meridia's office or the supply room with the busted door, he'd probably lean in and tell her to drag the man with her and get it over with already.

Zee blushed, a part of her hating how easy some of her friends could read her. At the same time, their love and support meant everything.

Donner turned his attention to the man at her side. Duke could meet him eye to eye easily. He smiled, although he averted his gaze in a telling manner, alerting both Zee and Donner to the fact Duke was well aware of certain aspects about Atargarians.

Donner took his measure in one quick glance. "You stationed at the AC outside Boston?"

"I am." A rueful grin curved his lips. "I think it must be written on my forehead. Does it say anywhere up there *Midwesterner, born and bred*, up there too?"

"Nah." Donner shrugged. "But the accent gives you away. What's your pleasure, AC?"

"I'll buy the lady whatever she wants," he said, looking over at Zee with a warm smile. Then he named a beer from a local brewery.

"You want your usual, Zee?" Donner looked at her and gave her a quick wink.

Her cheeks flushed and while Duke was facing the other way, she mouthed, *Stop it*.

Instead, Donner put a hand to his chest and mimicked a throbbing heart.

From the corner of her eye, she saw Duke looking back toward them. Quick as a wish, Donner had turned away, whistling innocently like he wasn't already looking forward to teasing her like mad later on.

"Here you go... " Two minutes later, Donner was back in front of them, putting a beer in front of Duke before placing an electric blue cocktail in front of Zee.

Her cheeks flamed even hotter, a groan rising in her throat.

"And for you, honey, a Mermaid's Orgasm."

"That's *not* my usual," she said in a choked voice.

Donner gave her another look of pure innocence.

She fought the urge to pound her head—or his—against the surface of the bar. "It's not? You and Meridia binged on them the last time you two were in here. Here. I'll take it—"

"It's fine," she said, taking it before giving him a dark look that promised revenge. Turning to Duke and effectively dismissing Donner, she said, "So, why P-town?"

He hadn't noticed Donner's antics, or he'd chosen to ignore them, keeping his attention on her.

The clawing, tugging hunger inside her stretched even more. *Stop, we don't even know if we like him yet.*

We don't need to! The twin urges inside her were one on this. *We need skin. We need touch. We need—*

She slammed the door shut on the voices so she could focus on Duke.

After a few seconds, he looked up from her drink—the *Mermaid's Orgasm.* "It's very... blue."

"The owner of the bar likes to play around with the recipes." She took a sip of the fruity cocktail, acutely aware that almost everybody in the bar was sending glances her way, and more than a few were grinning, just like Donner. "So, the Midwest, huh? How long have you been stationed out here near the Cape?"

"Only a few weeks." He gave her a boyishly charming grin. "My people lived in St. Louis. I got sick a lot when I was a kid. It was so bad one year, they thought I might not survive to see Christmas and since I'd always wanted to see the ocean, they took me to Virginia and we stayed at a hotel right on the coast. I got better eventually." A bemused look entered his eyes and he shrugged. "Like a lot better. My folks were well off so my mom rented a house right on the beach while my father traveled back and forth for the next two years. I kept getting better. Then my dad died when I was nineteen. Mom slipped away less than a month later. Since I didn't have anybody else, I decided to join AC. I've been at almost every base along the Atlantic Coast." He paused to give a teasing smile. "Once I hit Fort Lauderdale, I get a special souvenir, I hear."

Charmed by the playful joke, she smiled at him. "And after that special souvenir, are you done or are you staying in for another six years?"

"As long as they keep stationing me in coastal bases? I'm in." He shrugged. "I love the sea. It's not because of whatever crazy stuff made me sick as a kid. I grew out of that—doctors theorized it was some allergen local to that part of the country that caused a severe reaction in me, although others disagreed. I just..." He sighed, a far-off look in his eyes and a faint smile on his lips. "I love the sea."

"Let me guess. You saw one of the mermaids on that first trip." She couldn't help but return his engaging, charming smile.

"No." He grinned. It was infectious, that smile, bright and humorous against his dark-as-coffee skin. "At least, if I did, they weren't in their water form. I'm sure I saw a few while I was there but I was too young to know human from Atargarian at that age. Plus, again, the Midwest. Not a lot of mermaids roaming there. There are plenty of Therians, although the largest populations in Missouri are the fox."

That's why he doesn't know. Glee and hope now mixed with the hunger inside and she breathed a little easier, relaxed. She let him pull her into a conversation unlike any she'd had in recent memory.

"I've only met a couple of Therian foxes," she said, smiling a little. She'd liked the mated pair she'd met just a few months after settling down here. They'd come on vacation to see the Cape and Zee had connected with the woman immediately, although it had hurt her heart to hear them talk about their den. None had asked about her own pack. It was considered rude to ask about what wasn't freely offered. "Do you miss home?"

"Not so much." His smile faded. "To me, home was my mom and dad and with them gone, there's nothing left to go back to."

Reaching out, she touched his hand. "I'm sorry."

"Thanks. Let's talk about something else, like that sexy-as-sin voice of yours. I think I'll hear it in my dreams."

Years of practice let her keep a straight face, even as she flinched inside. She had a handy lie, one she told to keep people from dwelling on it, because it *did* hurt to think about the soft, mellifluous voice she'd once had. Years ago, it had once been as bright and clear as a bell, she'd once been told.

"Actually... " She gave him a pained smile that wasn't entirely feigned. "I was injured when I was younger—my throat never healed well. I don't like to talk about it."

"Fuck, I'm sorry." Duke winced.

"It's okay. You didn't know." She touched his hand again, and this time, he turned his over and laced their fingers.

The contact made her breathless. Looking up into those dark, velvety eyes, she thought, *Maybe... Please...*

She was so tired of being alone, so tired of the aches inside that came from a complete lack of touch.

ZEE ACTUALLY FLIRTED.

And giggled.

And smiled so hard her face hurt.

Through it all, the hungry things within her demanded freedom.

She smashed them down time and again with the ease that came from years and years of containing those aspects of her nature.

Because she was part wolf, she understood in some ways. Therian wolves, like their animal counterparts, were pack creatures and they thrived best when with their pack.

Zee had no pack. She had nobody to offer the casual touches Therians grew accustomed to, and needed, almost from the beginning.

That other part of her, she understood little of it, but she felt the hunger, and the pain.

This *hurt* went deep, and it wasn't an emotional pain, but a physical one. Lately, it was worse than normal too.

Tonight, that pain was edged with something sweeter.

Finally, she *might* be able to have sex and do something about the physical needs she'd had to stifle for so long.

A wolf wasn't meant to be alone.

And the other aspect of her nature... she didn't understand it, but the little she'd been able to learn had told her that touch wasn't just wanted, but *necessary*. Those who were full-blooded would wither and die without touch. If she didn't have Therian blood within, she would have wasted away a long time ago. She had nobody around to teach her more about that other eerie part of herself; her mother had died when she was a baby and Zee hadn't even learned about this aspect of her nature until she was already a young woman, growing into a person who needed physical contact like it was her sustenance.

That need raged within her now.

More than an hour after he'd first arrived, Duke moved in so close, she felt the warmth of his breath brush over her lips and she had to choke back the whimper that almost escaped, thrash the other part into submission—and it didn't want to listen.

"I've got this crazy need to kiss you, Zee. Am I risking life and a limb if I try?" Duke's eyes, so dark brown they appeared black, held hers.

"No." She licked her lips and *hoped* he'd kiss her, *hoped* he'd touch her, even as she hoped he'd never notice how foreign all of this was to her.

He reached up and cradled her cheek in his hand and then his mouth was on hers. Soft at first, his tongue tracing the curve of her lower lip before seeking entrance to her mouth.

This... kissing... *this*, she remembered. A hungry noise escaped and she eased closer—or tried to. Duke stood next to the stool where she was perched, making her position awkward. But then he moved closer, and in what felt like a completely natural response, she parted her jean-clad thighs and he stepped between them, deepening the kiss.

She pulled away to gasp for breath—and maybe ask if he'd come upstairs to the apartment where she lived.

But he was already kissing her again, with more focus and determination this time.

She moaned and reached up, cupping the back of his head, the short, raspy feel of his hair abrading her palm.

"Son of a—*fuck*, Donner!"

A scent hit her—holly, cedar, birch... and fur and wildness and sweet mountain air.

Pack... except, no. It wasn't pack. Not anymore—pain spliced through her heart, tearing and clawing. It all happened in microseconds while she clung to Duke and then she wasn't even touching him.

The big, strong military man was stumbling back into a wooden table, but he moved fluidly with the movement, eyes going sharp as he instinctively recognized a threat. He drew a knife from his boot—as an officer with one of the military branches, he'd be authorized to carry any number of weapons, and he moved *fast*.

But not fast enough. Panic clawed at her and she swiped out, emptying the drink and smashing the glass. She wasn't military trained, nor a part of a lethal pack, but she was no pushover either. No meek thing to be thrown around and abused—not again. Not anymore.

Then it didn't matter, because Donner was there, slamming a fist into the Therian wolf who'd entered the bar and seen her being kissed by a man who *wasn't* the Prime who had laid claim on her years before.

It didn't matter that he'd never actually followed through.

Therians understood and respected their own customs and laws before anything else. And to them, Zennia Day belonged to Nikolai Whelan, the Prime of Appalachia, a man who lived hundreds of miles and several states away, the man who'd once promised he'd love and care for her always, and then told her to get the fuck out of Appalachia.

BLOODED BLADE

And stay out, Zennia. You're not welcome here.
Visit Website[1] For More Info and Buy Links

---

1. https://www.shilohwalker.com/website/the-pretern-wars/

About

J.C. Daniels is the pen name of author Shiloh Walker.

Shiloh Walker has been writing since she was a kid. She fell in love with vampires with the book Bunnicula and has worked her way up to the more...ah...serious works of fiction. Once upon a time she worked as a nurse, but now she writes full time and lives with her family in the Midwest.

She writes romantic suspense and contemporary romance, and urban fantasy under her penname, J.C. Daniels.

Follow her:

Twitter (@shilohwalker)

BookBub (https://www.bookbub.com/authors/shiloh-walker)

Facebook (http://www.facebook.com/AuthorShilohWalker)

Read more about her work at her website (shilohwalker.com) and learn more about her latest paranormal series, The Pretern Wars.

Lightning Source UK Ltd.
Milton Keynes UK
UKHW012001120123
415233UK00001B/120

9 798215 474389